FOLLOW MY LEAD

LOUISA MASTERS

READERS LOVE LOUISA MASTERS

Charming Him (previously published as The Bunny and the Billionaire)

"Looking for a story that's the very definition of sweet romance? Here it is."
—Scattered Thoughts and Rogue Words

"I really really loved this one and very much recommend it."
—Diverse Reader

"The bottom line is that this book was incredibly entertaining."
—Just Love: Queer Book Reviews

Offside Rules (previously published as The Athlete and the Aristocrat)

"…a good book. Laughter, a few tears, and happy ones too. A good read."
—Love Bytes

"Would definitely recommend to readers who enjoy billionaire romance, or sports/athlete heroes."
—Joyfully Jay

FOLLOW MY LEAD

LOUISA MASTERS

A Joy Universe Novel

Follow My Lead

Copyright © 2020 by Louisa Masters

Cover Designer: Reese Dante
Interior Design: RMGraphX

1st edition February 2020

All rights reserved.

No part of this book may be reproduced in any form or by any means without the prior written consent of the author, excepting brief quotes used in reviews.

Please do not participate in or encourage piracy of copyrighted materials in violation of the author's rights. Purchase only authorized editions.

This is a work of fiction. Names, characters, places, events and incidents either are the product of the author's imagination or are used fictitiously, and any resemblance to persons, living or dead, business establishments, events or locales is entirely coincidental.

To the extent that the image or images on the cover of this book depict a person or persons, such person or persons are merely models and are not intended to portray any character or characters featured in the book.

Paperback ISBN 978-0-6483374-6-1

ACKNOWLEDGEMENTS

Ginormous thanks to Sara Jo Montgomery for naming Rick and to Becca L'Amour for naming *Walk of Life*.

ABOUT FOLLOW MY LEAD

Dimi Weston has always loved the theater—just not as much as loves managing things. His job at Joy Universe lets him coordinate to his heart's content, and he fills his free time with community theater. Now, though, he's being offered a promotion to his dream job: managing Joy Universe's brand-new theater production company. JU really does make dreams come true—or so he thinks until he meets the ex-Broadway director he'll have to work with.

Jason Philips is shocked to discover the hot younger guy he was trying to impress at a community theater is going to be managing the production company that just hired him. Scarred by the bad breakup of a long-term relationship, Jase is already nervous about getting back into dating… and now he's accidentally offended the first guy he tried to flirt with and now has to work with.

As Dimi and Jason get stuck into the craziness of the theater, they have to contend with family, exes, and the nosiness of their colleagues, but nothing will stop them from making this venture a success.

FOLLOW
MY LEAD

CHAPTER ONE

Dimi

I'M NERVOUS. I SHOULDN'T be, because I've done this before. Lots of times. But that doesn't stop the nerves. Especially because I'll soon be doing this professionally, and isn't that freaking weird?

"Dimi!"

I turn and smile at the teenager who's been assistant producer for this season's community theater production. Emma's smart, capable, and wants to eventually go into movie production. She's been a part of Joyville Amateur Theater since she was thirteen, first as a gofer, then working her way through every other back-of-house job and occasionally taking a small performance role as well. She's in her senior year of high school now, so we won't have her around much longer.

"What's up?" I ask, glancing quickly at my watch.

The curtain is due to go up in five minutes, and everything seems to be under control, but Emma doesn't get all worked up for nothing.

"Did you know? Did you know he'd be here?" She grabs my arm, practically shaking it with excitement.

Butterflies erupt in my gut, because I know exactly who she means. "Uh, I wasn't sure. Trav invited him, but he was driving down from New York yesterday and today, so he didn't know if he'd make it." But clearly he did. Which means he's going to watch the show. The show I'm producing.

I shouldn't be nervous about this, because starting Monday I'm actually going to be working with the guy. He's going to be the director to my producer for the new theater company at Joy Universe. Technically speaking, I'll be his boss, but I don't think of it that way. It's going to be a collaboration more than anything else. Because he's a freaking decorated Broadway director and my experience in theater consists of a few elective courses at college and amateur theater. I'm a good businessman, and I know I can run this company well, but the creative side is mostly going to come from him and Trav, who's the only performer permanently attached to the company.

But none of that changes the fact that Jason Philips is about to watch one of my shows for the first time.

It's a good show. Every year we do a three-performance run for a holiday show over Thanksgiving weekend. This year it's a traditional pantomime, and we've already done the Friday night and Saturday matinee shows to appreciative audiences. This last show, Saturday night, usually gets the biggest turnout, though, and we have a small party afterward in the foyer.

"Ohmigod," Emma breathes. "Do you think I can talk to him after? Can I ask Trav to introduce me?" Her eyes are shining, and I grin.

"I don't see why not."

She kisses me on the cheek. "You're the best. Are we ready to go?"

I look at my watch again and nod. "Let's get everyone in place."

***

I wander through the crowd with a grin on my face and a plastic champagne flute in hand. It's filled with a cheapish sparkling wine we got from a discount wine distributor, but the taste isn't bad and the alcohol goes to my head just like the expensive stuff. Not that I've had the expensive stuff that often.

People stop me to say hello and congratulate me on the show, and I make sure I talk to each for a few minutes. A community theater is dependent entirely on community goodwill—local businesses sponsor us, and we get free labor from volunteers. Not to mention all our amateur performers and crew. It's important to keep interest and engagement high. We won't begin work on the winter/spring season until next year, so it's especially vital to leave a strong impression tonight.

I thank the elderly couple I've been talking to again for their generous contribution, and they drift away with smiles on their faces. I'm about to go looking for my friends from JU who were in the audience tonight when a hand touches my arm and a smooth, deep voice says, "Hi."

I turn, and oh my God, Jason Philips is talking to me. He's smiling at me. His sherry-brown eyes are warm, the corners crinkling attractively. The silver at his temples and scattered amongst his thick chestnut hair gives him that air of distinction some older men get.

"Hi," I breathe, then mentally slap myself and offer a hand for him to shake. I am a respected professional, damn it. "Hello."

He takes my hand and shakes it but doesn't immediately let go. "I'm Jason."

Would it be totally unprofessional to say "Yeah, I know" and make heart eyes at him? I mean, I've seen his picture, so I knew he was attractive, but nobody warned me that in person his attractiveness becomes devastating.

"Dimi," I manage, pulling back my hand before it gets weird. "Nice to meet you. Did you enjoy the show?" I try not to sound too eager to hear his opinion.

He shrugs. "It was charming. Nothing like what I'm

used to in New York, of course."

Uhhhhh.

Did he really just say that?

Like… really?

Does he not know how rude it was? The words were… fine, not great but not overtly offensive, but his tone…. That dismissive shrug. I'm the producer of the show he just flippantly blew off, so how can his comment be considered anything but rude?

Don't get me wrong, I know the show doesn't compare to anything he's used to in New York. Or even to anything we'll be doing with the new production company. This is community theater, and while we have some talented amateurs on cast, none of them has had formal acting training. Nobody's a professional actor. Nobody's even worked on a professional show before. But they worked hard and did a great job—*I* did a great job. Our performances are always entertaining and sold out.

I still don't know what to say. I have to work with this guy, so calling him a dick and storming off is probably a bad idea, as much as I want to. But I can't just let him think his behavior is okay. Joyville is the only town anywhere near Joy Universe, which means he'll be living here and a part of the community.

"I don't think anyone involved aspired to reach the lofty standard set by New York. They did, however, work hard to provide entertainment in a community space that's accessible to everyone. Enjoy the rest of your evening." I shoot him a cool smile to match my cool tone, then turn and stroll away as though I've already forgotten all about him. Inside, I'm leaping in the air and high-fiving myself.

"Hey, Dim!"

I look in the direction of the shout and see my boss—*ex*-boss—Derek waving at me. Grinning, I head in his direction.

"Great show," he declares. "Those kids at the end were super cute."

"Thanks." He's right about the kids, but oh my God, it was absolute murder getting them to cooperate. Five-year-olds are way too distractible.

"I saw you talking to Jason. He's a nice guy, yeah?"

I hesitate, because if I say Jason was a huge douchemonkey and that working with him is going to be a nightmare, is that too much like complaining to my boss that my job's too hard? But Derek's my colleague now, not my boss, and lately we've been becoming friends, too.

In the end, I settle on, "We might have rubbed each other the wrong way, but I think he'll be great at the job."

Derek raises an eyebrow and looks over my shoulder in the direction I've just come from. I look too, and see Jason talking to Trav, Derek's boyfriend and the person who put us in contact with Jason in the first place. They've worked together before, are friendly, and Trav heard a rumor that Jason was looking to get away from the city for personal reasons, so it wasn't a huge leap.

Trav sees us watching and waves, then says something to Jason and gestures in our direction. Jason turns, scanning the crowd, and I know when he sees Derek because he smiles and waves. Then his gaze moves to me, and his jaw drops.

Ah.

Suddenly I get it. He didn't know who I was. I thought he'd come over to introduce himself because Derek and Trav had told him we'd be working together, but the expression of horror on his face as Trav talks is pretty indicative that he had no idea.

I lift my hand and give him a little finger wiggle, smirking. It's a dick move, but he called my production "charming" in that smug voice. I'm entitled to a little petty revenge.

"Why do I get this feeling I need to install spy cameras in your office?" Derek asks, a thread of laughter in his voice.

I give him my best innocent look. "I have no idea what you mean."

***

By the time I get home, it's into the wee hours and I'm utterly exhausted. The benefit of the holiday shows is that they only take up one weekend. But the downside is that it's a really intense, packed-in weekend. And then after we kicked out all the theatergoers, most of the cast and crew and the professionals from JU who consult with us on a volunteer basis all went out for a celebratory drink. We won't be back together again until late January, and that always feels weird after spending so much time together. There's no break between the end of the summer season and preparation for the holiday weekend, and only a two-week break between the end of the winter/spring season and prep for the summer one, so most of us have been seeing each other a minimum of twice a week for ten months.

In about a week, I'm really going to start missing everyone. Right now, though, I'm kind of glad for the break.

I leave a trail of clothes from the front door to the bed, purely because I can. When you grow up as a middle child in a brood of eight, you've got no choice but to put your stuff away or have it get lost—or be appropriated by a sibling. College wasn't that much different—people everywhere, all the time, and shared facilities. When I got my first job, I made sure I lived in a place with only one roommate, and I loved it. He was a flight attendant who was hardly ever home, which made me realize I could happily live on my own as long I worked in a busy office and maintained a good social life. So when I came back to Joyville to work at Joy Universe, it was a no-brainer to find a place I could afford on my own. And I'm generally pretty tidy, but sometimes I like to take advantage of the privacy and scatter things around.

What's that? Oh, you caught it when I said I came *back* to Joyville. Yeah, I'm a local boy. My dad worked at JU while I was growing up—still does. Mom has her own clothing boutique here in Joyville. She started out working there part-time when she was a teenager, switched to full-time when she came back after college, worked her way up to manager, then eventually bought the owner out when I was a kid. She's a local too—her parents were among the first employees JU had. They moved to Joyville when it was brand-spanking-new and were working on the day JU opened. Joyville, Georgia, has always been home, and while I loved being away for college and then the first few years of work, it was great to come back.

Even if being in the middle of nowhere with a mostly transient population plays havoc with my dating life. I'm only twenty-nine. I have time to find someone.

Have I been going too fast? What's JU? Whoops, sorry—I didn't realize you've been living under a rock (just kidding). Joy Universe is the second-largest entertainment complex in the world. We have four theme parks, about twenty hotels, some campgrounds, and a shopping-restaurant-entertainment village called Joy Village—I know, seriously lacking in creativity there. JU is divided into five administrative districts, each one headed by an assistant director—like Derek. Until recently, I worked as Derek's right hand, but starting Monday, I will officially step into my new job as producer for the newly formed Joy Village Theater Company. Derek went to bat for me when the role was being created, and as a result the company won't be a subsidiary of the district that contains the Village, or part of the events or entertainment departments. Instead it's considered a department of its own, and I'll be reporting to the director of JU—who's a dick, but as long as things go well, he mostly ignores you.

This is a great career move for me, and it means I get to incorporate my theater hobby with my job, which is awesome. I've been super excited ever since the concept was floated, and back then, I had no idea Derek was planning to nominate me to run it. He basically sold the higher-ups on that idea before I heard anything about it, and then offered me the job on a silver platter. I'm technically on probation, since I've never had a job like this before and the big bosses might trust Derek's judgment, but they're not stupid. It doesn't matter. Nothing is going to stop me from succeeding in this job. I already have detailed plans and forecasts and reams of research. My plans are ambitious, but they need to be—I have to prove to everyone that I am the perfect choice for this position. I can't let Derek down.

I'm really going to miss working with him. He's a brilliant boss, but more, he's just brilliant at his job. I've learned so much over the last three years.

Still, I'm sure I'll see him all the time anyway, since I'll be working with Trav. And now I've got this dream-come-true of a job.

Working with a douche who thinks he's better than me.

Every silver lining has a cloud, though, and I'm not going to let this one rain on my parade. Or something.

I snuggle into my bed and close my eyes. I'll worry about how to deal with Jason Philips on Monday.

CHAPTER TWO

Jason

I PARK MY CAR at the head office building and exhale a long breath. I'm supposed to meet Dimitri Weston, the producer I'll be working with, here this morning. There are some last-minute forms for me to sign, key cards to be issued and crap like that, and then Dimitri will show me where our office is in Joy Village.

Dimitri.

Or, as he introduced himself to me on Saturday night, Dimi.

Because of course shit couldn't be simple.

I'm such a moron. If my ex could have seen me, trying to hit on a hot younger guy, he would have pissed himself laughing. The truth is, even if Dimi had been my age, I wouldn't have been successful. Did you hear my line? What possessed me?

What I was trying to do was impress the hottie

with my suave New York charm and hint that I was a bigshot in the Broadway scene—which I am. Instead, I managed to insult the show and everyone involved, which would have been bad enough if he'd just been an audience member, but is a thousand times worse because *he's the producer.*

At least he's a good producer. I was worried when they told me I'd be working with someone who has a business background but no theater experience. The show I saw, although definitely amateur and clearly on a limited budget, was produced with great attention to detail. The whole event ran like clockwork. So I can put that concern aside and just hope he's willing to accept my apology. He might not, since I'm not willing to explain why I made such a dumb comment to begin with. I've humiliated myself enough already.

No point hiding in my car and adding tardiness to my list of sins, right? I'm going to have to face Dimi—can I call him that? Maybe he'll prefer Dimitri now that I've insulted him—sooner or later, and it may as well be sooner.

I get out of the car and head into the building. It's only about three stories but sprawling. I guess it needs to be big to hold all the administrative functions needed to run a place like JU, and keeping the profile low means guests won't see it. But that doesn't make it more attractive. The inside is a bit better, the lobby redone within the last decade to be open and airy. There's a coffee cart with a short line of people waiting, and a few "conversation circles" of chairs and sofas scattered around. In other words, it's like most corporate lobbies in the world.

I approach the reception desk and smile at the young man ensconced there. He's wearing a suit and a headset and a name tag that says Chris.

"Good morning, and welcome to Joy Universe," he says. "What can I do for you?"

"Hi, Chris. My name's Jason Philips, and I'm here to see—"

"Oh, Mr. Philips! We're so excited to have you here. This new venture has been all anyone's talked about for months. Let me get Dimi for you." He taps his headset to activate it and types something into his keyboard while I become very aware of all the eyes suddenly on me. Chris didn't exactly keep his voice down. I make sure my smile is pleasant and even and hope to hell that Dimi didn't spread any gossip. If he did, at least Chris hasn't heard it yet.

He murmurs something, listens, then says, "Okay, sure," and taps his headset again. "Dimi's getting your tablet and company phone from IT. He says to meet him in the executive reception—take that elevator there up to three and turn left. Someone is coming to get you from there." He opens a drawer and pulls out a white key card. "This will get you up there. Don't forget to give it back when you leave—Dimi will have yours."

"Thanks, Chris." I take the key card. "I guess I'll

see you in a bit."

He winks at me and taps his headset again, which either means he's getting a call or wants to make one, so I leave him to it and head for the elevator he pointed to.

Gotta admit, this is not the welcome I hoped for. Turn left and hope someone meets me before I wander through too many miles of corridor is not that positive—and since Trav Jones and his boyfriend were both so effusive about Dimi, I can only assume this means he's still pissed.

Fortunately, when the elevator doors open on the third floor, there's a familiar face waiting for me.

"Hey, Jason!"

I've only met Derek Bryer a few times, the first when he came up to New York with Trav for my initial interview about the job, but he's easy to like. In fact, you could say he's hard to not like. I'm grinning at him before I even realize it.

"Hi, Derek. Fancy seeing you here."

"Dimi asked me to meet you. Come on, this way."

We stride along the hallway, people smiling and nodding as we pass. At first I think they're smiling at Derek, but then I realize that a lot of them are making eye contact with me.

"Do... do these people know who I am?" I ask Derek in a low tone, and he chuckles.

"Sure. We've been expecting you. This is the most exciting thing to happen at JU since the water park opened six years ago."

Great. No pressure, then.

We finally stroll into an area set up with four desks facing each other, one of them set almost in front of an office door. The women at three of the desks look up and smile and call greetings. The fourth desk, the one right next to the door, is empty. Derek grins and says hi to the women, then leads me into the office.

"Have a seat," he offers. "Dimi shouldn't be long. He's just battling IT for you."

I've never worked anywhere that has an actual IT department, but the way Derek makes it sound, I guess I should be grateful. I take a seat in one of the visitor chairs. "Please don't let me keep you from work," I say politely, even though I'm dying to ask him questions about Dimi. From what I understand, they worked together before Dimi took this new job.

Derek laughs. "You're doing me a favor. I was going to promote Gina into Dimi's job, but an opening came up in marketing that she decided to take, and nobody else on my team is really ready for it. So I told HR to advertise the role—both of them, actually—and now I have a pile of applications to go through. Dimi used to do that for me and narrow it down to manageable levels. I always knew he was irreplaceable, but I actually underestimated him. You have no idea how lucky you are."

Oh, fuck. I mean, yay, so glad my producer is going to be great at his job, but *oh fuck*, I pissed him off.

I smile weakly.

"I'm looking forward to working with him."

Could I have said anything less enthusiastic? Probably not, because Derek gives me an odd look.

Luckily—or unluckily?—the office door opens right then. I turn my head and there he is, the man himself, and oh, I forgot that I'm really attracted to him. Like, really. He's so good-looking: dark-haired and eyed, pale-skinned, tall, fit but not bulky. And he carries himself with a kind of quiet confidence that's so fucking sexy, especially because he's relatively young. Most people take time to grow into themselves, don't reach that level of self-possession until their thirties or even forties—or they have the kind of brash confidence that borders on arrogance and is off-putting. Dimi's self-esteem is obviously just a natural part of him, but he doesn't shove it in everyone's face. It makes me want to rub up all over him.

This is not good.

Especially because he smiled at Derek but is now looking at me with the kind of cool politeness reserved for strangers you know you're not going to like.

"Hi, Mr. Philips," he says, and holy crap, could he make me feel any worse? I'm a dirty old man for wanting this guy. Even Derek looks startled.

"Please call me Jason," I manage, and it doesn't even sound like I'm begging. Much. I stand and extend a hand. To his credit, he doesn't hesitate to shake it.

"We didn't meet properly the other night," he continues. "I'm Dimitri Weston."

That's it. No "call me Dimi," or even, "but everyone calls me Dimi." Am I supposed to call him Dimitri? Or, hell, *Mr. Weston*? Is this going to be like a period drama, where everyone on our team addresses each other formally?

Take it down a notch, Jase. You're getting hysterical.

"These are yours," he adds, and hands me a tablet, a smartphone, and a manila envelope. "The envelope has all the initial passwords and your key card to access employee areas. We need to duck into HR on our way out to get your photo ID done."

I take the items and swallow past the huge lump in my throat. "No problem. Thanks."

"Are you ready now?"

I glance at Derek, who looks utterly bewildered. Part of me wants to settle this right now, before we leave this office, but I don't know anyone here except Trav and Derek, and I don't want them to know what a complete dickwad I was on Saturday. I need friends. One day I'll tell them, but after I've sorted it with Dimi and we can all have a laugh about it. Maybe over a long, friendly couples' dinner. Because what's life without dreams, right?

No, I'll wait to apologize until Dimi and I are alone.

So I smile and say, "Sure," and then thank Derek and follow Dimi out of the office. He says not one word to me until we reach the HR department, where he introduces me and I have my photo taken and ID issued. We then proceed—still in silence—down to reception, where I hand over my temporary key card and thank Chris. By the time we make it to the parking lot, I'm wondering if he's going to say anything to me, ever, if there aren't other people around. That would be a neat trick, considering how much time we're going to spend together.

But he surprises me.

"I'm parked over there," he says. "I'll wait by the entrance to the road. Follow me, and I'll show you the quickest way to the Village and how to get into the staff parking."

"Okay," I agree dumbly, and then, "Wait!" This is probably not the best place for it, but who knows what the rest of the day might hold? I may not get him alone again. Plus, my courage is perilously close to failing. "I… I owe you an apology. I was a complete asshat on Saturday night, and I'm so, so sorry."

Silence.

He stares at me, clearly waiting for an explanation, but I can't give one. I'm fully aware that the apology is hollow without a reason for my asswipishness, but how can I tell this vibrant, amazing young man that I was trying to impress him? That will only make our working relationship even more awkward.

So I force a smile, trying to look sincere, and add, "I was impressed by the production. It can be really hard in an amateur theater to achieve any sort of quality, but you all did a fantastic job."

Could I sound any more condescending? Why didn't I leave it at the apology and shut my fucking mouth?

"Thank you," Dimi says coolly, and I know he's not feeling inspired to forgive me but is too polite to say so.

"It's deserved." This is starting to feel awkward. Well, more awkward. Okay, I want to set this moment on fire and never have to remember it again.

Fortunately, Dimi seems to feel the same way. "I'll be waiting at the entrance," he repeats, and turns and walks away in the direction of his car.

I let out a huge sigh and go to my own car.

This is not the best first day ever.

CHAPTER THREE

$\mathcal{D}imi$

IS HE FOR FUCKING real?

He's *sorry*? That's it? No explanation? Just "I shat all over your hard work, but I'm sorry, and hey, you guys did a good job for amateurs, have a pat on the head."

Well, fuck him. He may be a brilliant director, but clearly he's a turd of a human being.

I get into my car and slam the door, then bang my head against the steering wheel. The problem—aside from the fact that I have to work with this guy—is that he's not a turd. Trav speaks really highly of him, and Trav's a great guy. He wouldn't think well of a turd. They've worked together before, several times. Plus, Derek was the one who did his initial interview, and Derek's got an awesome bullshit meter. If this guy was a turd, he would have picked it.

So… that's not it. Whatever reason he had for shitting all over the show, it's not a natural inclination toward being a fuckwit.

Which raises doubt in my mind about the show. I thought it went really well, but maybe it didn't? Maybe everyone is just being super nice and not telling me how bad it was?

Nah. There's no point in that. It may not have been professional quality, but it was a damn good show. Besides, even if it was bad, him pointing it out just takes him back to asshole status.

So why—

I don't have time for this.

Yeah. Whoops. On the clock.

I start the car and head toward the lot entrance. Jason falls in behind me, and we drive over to the Village. I know these roads like the back of my hand—a lot of people find them confusing at first, but not me. Still, I take it slow so Jason can get a good look at all the signs and turnoffs. There's a map in the envelope I gave him, plus GPS works really well here, but there's nothing like seeing it and driving it.

In the staff parking lot at the village, I pull into the spot that's newly reserved for me. Gotta say, it feels pretty damn awesome. The spot beside me is for Jason, and the one next to him is Trav's. I wave Jason in, then get out of my car and wait as he parks.

"This way," I say when he joins me on the pavement. I'm starting to feel kind of like a dick myself, but

I'm not ready to let it go just yet, so I speak only the minimum words necessary as I show him the entrance behind the theater that's been allocated to us. We walk silently along the hallway, past the performer dressing rooms and the storage areas, and finally come to the office suite where we'll be based. There's a shared area for assistants—which neither of us has yet, although HR advertised and we've got a stack of applications—an office each, and a conference room. The whole suite is very new. The original plan was for us to be based out of the administrative building, but we'll be spending so much time at the theater for rehearsals and casting and whatnot that it wasn't really logical, so in the end, I wrangled some extra budget, "bought" one of the shops next to the theater, and banged out this space. The shop wasn't doing very well and was glad to be let out of their lease early.

"I've been working from that office," I say, pointing, "but if you prefer it, I don't mind moving." I haven't even unpacked my stuff yet, and the offices are identical, so I don't give a shit which one I use.

"The other one is fine," he says quickly, going to the door and looking in. It's not a huge space, but it fits a desk, a couple of chairs, and a filing cabinet, as well as a very small sofa and coffee table. When I showed Trav the plans, he said it was miles better than some of the "offices" in the Broadway theaters.

"When you log into the JU employee app, you'll find that HR have sent you some applications for your assistant that you'll need to go through ASAP so they can set up interviews. But Trav should be here any minute so we can finalize the choice of show for the first run." I'm nervous as hell about this. I have a definite preference, but I'm sure he does too, and he's the creative half of our management team. If we don't agree, it'll probably come down to Trav to be the tiebreaker, and I honestly don't know how that will go.

"I've been thinking about that," he says. "I've put together a list of options that will work well for an inexperienced cast." He winces almost before he's finished talking, probably because he thinks he's offended me.

He has, a little bit, but not really. Our performers, with the exception of Trav, aren't used to doing full-length shows. Their jobs currently consist of thirty-minute to one-hour abridged versions of feature-length children's films, or scenelets featuring characters from popular movies. And usually, the hammier it is, the better. There's a lot of excitement about Joy Village Theater Company, because this will give them experience they can really leverage to move on to bigger things—especially working under a director of the caliber of Jason Philips.

That's not to say we don't have some really talented performers on staff. They just need seasoning. Which means he's right.

"Trav will be here soon" is all I say, and I can see that it's the straw that breaks the camel's back.

"Okay, I was a dick. I've apologized. I am genuinely sorry, and I never meant to imply that the show wasn't great, because it was. But clearly I'm an idiot because I said the wrong thing, and you have every right to be pissed, but I've apologized and I don't know what else I can do. I'm sorry. We need to work together, and I don't think it's going to go well if you can barely bring yourself to speak to me." He takes a deep breath. "What can I do to make this right?"

A tiny niggle of guilt nudges me. He *has* apologized. We do need to work together. I probably need to let this go. A tiny voice in the back of my head suggests that I'm holding a grudge because I've had a professional crush on him for ages and he smashed it. Plus, there was that attraction….

I sigh. "You're right. You did apologize, and we're going to need to work closely together. I'm sorry I'm being so uncommunicative."

"But…?" he says, and I can't help smiling.

"No buts. I wish I understood why you said what you did, but it's none of my business and I'm not going to let it interfere with our working relationship." I hold out a hand, and he shakes it but doesn't let go.

"I really am sorry," he tells me.

"I appreciate that." Why is he still holding my hand? Should I pull back? Or is that going to undo the truce we've just achieved?

There's the sound of footsteps in the hallway, and Jason lets go as we turn to the doorway. I'm relieved and agitated at the same time. It was weird that he held on so long, but his hand was warm and dry, the skin lightly callused, though I can't imagine what he does to make it that way. It reminded me again that before he was a dick, I was attracted to him.

Trav comes into the suite, smiling. "Hey! How exciting is this?" He and Jason hug, exchanging pleasantries. I know that Jason asked Trav to help him find someplace to live, and they talk briefly about the apartment and what Jason needs before his stuff arrives from New York. I take the opportunity to check my email, only half listening.

Okay, that's a lie. I'm shamelessly eavesdropping while pretending to be absorbed in my tablet. I don't know why.

"You ready, Dimi?"

I look up when Trav says my name as though I haven't heard every word. "Ready?" I ask.

"To look at options for the first show."

I smile. "Sure, yeah. Let's go to the conference room." It's set up with a screen I can cast to with my tablet, so they'll be able to see all the info I have. And we can look up anything they need to support their suggestions, I guess.

We settle around the table and then just look at each other for a second. It's very clear that we've never worked together before, because none of us wants to go first, even though none of us is known for being reticent or shy.

"I was just telling Dimi," Jason says to Trav, "I have a list of shows that would work well for an inexperienced cast." He pulls a phone from his pocket—his personal phone, not the JU one I gave him earlier. "Do you want to take notes or something and then look them up?"

Trav laughs, because over the last few months he's seen what a tech geek I am. Jason looks confused, and I say, "If you unlock your phone, I can fix it so we see what you see on that screen." I don't want to be a douche, but I feel like he won't know what I mean if I say I'm going to cast it. He still looks a little abashed as he hands over his phone. It takes me about thirty seconds to do what's needed, and then we see his home screen on the big TV.

"Oh. Wow. I guess I need to get used to working with this kind of tech."

I make a mental note to make sure he's shown how to use the company app properly. It's pretty amazing, and I could probably run half the world from it if I needed to, but if you're not used to using technology on a regular basis, I guess it could be daunting at first. I hand him back his phone and he goes into the notes app and brings up a list.

My stomach sinks as I scan it. There's nothing wrong with the shows on the list. Some of them are excellent. Some of them we'll definitely want to do at some point. But none of them are inspired. None of them are fresh and exciting. They've all been done to death by a million companies the world over and feature heavily on the drama schedules of high schools around the country.

They're all so *safe*.

I look at Trav. He's considering the list with a thoughtful expression on his face, really thinking about the options, and I know he's taking into account the relative inexperience of our performers, our crew..., and me. Because the truth is, while I could organize any event in the known universe with my eyes closed and one hand tied behind my back, my experience producing theater is limited to local amateur productions. I *know* I can do this. But I guess I might have to prove myself.

"This is a great list." I seize the initiative. If I speak first, retain control of this meeting, I might be able to get what I want. "I wonder, though, if for our first production, we should look at making a splash. Grab some attention with something a little less well-known. Three of the shows on this list have been through the Village with other companies in the past few years." That, at least, is true, and cuts his list almost in half.

"Which ones? We'll take them off," Jason says immediately, and I'm glad he's at least listening to me. I tell him, and sure enough, he deletes them. I try not to be impatient about the fact that it takes him about five times longer than it would have taken me. We study the remaining titles on the screen, and then he asks, "What did you have in mind?"

I want to take a deep breath, but I don't. It would

show my nerves. I don't need to look nervous right now. I need to be in control. Confident. Calm. I project assurance and say, "I thought *Walk of Life* might be a good idea."

"Oh." The word seems to burst out of Trav unbidden, he looks so surprised. Jason's face is carefully blank, and I know I'm losing him. I forge on.

"It's new enough to be exciting—a lot of visitors won't have seen it. It has a lot of action and some really great musical numbers. And the combination of drama and humor means it appeals to a wide audience. I really don't think we can go wrong. It will premiere the Joy Village Theater Company with a bang."

"A loud, terrible bang if it flops," Jason points out. "It's a great show, and I agree with everything you said, but it's not an easy show. Is it really something we can pull off at the same time as dealing with teething issues?"

I hate him because he's not wrong. It would be a stretch. It would be a challenge. And there's a strong possibility that we would open with a flop. But I won't let that happen. This is a dream job for me, an amazing new career path, and I am determined that it's going to be a success. JVTC has been allocated a healthy budget for its first year, but it could be better. We have one theater, one production to begin with. Ultimately, I want six of the seven theaters in the Village to be running JVTC shows. We should only need to bring in touring shows if they're really special—crowd magnets.

And I want it to happen sooner rather than later. Which means we need to have a strong first season, a better budget next year, and the higher-ups willing to allocate me a second theater and show at the end of our first season.

A debut show that's been done a million times before and that people will only go to see because it's on and they couldn't get last-minute tickets to anything else isn't going to get me that.

"I think it's worth a try," I counter. "There's no point beginning this with a defeatist attitude."

Was that too aggressive? From the look on Trav's face, I think it might have been.

Jason's face is still carefully blank. I want to smack it just so it'll show a reaction.

"Dimi, as much as I'd love to play Cameron," Trav says carefully, "I think it might be pushing our luck to start with *Walk of Life*. It's a really complex and energetic show. There are a lot of details and complicated dance numbers."

Fuck.

"That's not too big a deal," Jason interjects, surprising the ever-loving crap out of me. "We can choreograph to suit the performers. I guess it depends on whether you want a watered-down version of *Walk of Life* or a really strong version of something more classic."

Oho.

Was that a challenge?

It sounded like a challenge to me.

I smile. It feels more like a smirk on my face. "Why don't you watch some of our performers in action before you pass judgment on how much we'd need to 'water down' the choreography?"

We stare each other down across the table. Silence reigns, neither of us willing to give in.

Finally, Trav clears his throat. "That's a great idea, Dimi. Why don't we head over to the parks? I know which of the performers are most experienced and best equipped to handle a full show, and we can track them down and see what Jason thinks."

I break our stare-down, deliberately looking away from Jason to Trav. "Sounds good to me."

CHAPTER FOUR

Jason

I CAN'T BELIEVE I'M walking through a theme park in a shirt and tie. Isn't there a rule that you have to wear shorts in these places? To be honest, it's been so long since I've been—twenty, maybe twenty-five years—that I'm not sure. Dimi and Trav don't seem to care that we stick out like sore thumbs, although Trav less so than Dimi and me, since he's wearing jeans. I guess they're used to visiting theme parks in a business capacity.

We've already been to one park, where we watched two cheesy stage shows and a few of those "spontaneous" encounters that happen "randomly" in the public part of the park. Trav quietly pointed out to us which performers he thought would be ready for something a little more involved. We won't be selecting them this way—the guidelines established for the company require the performers to audition, the same as they'd have to if this was any other show—but it's good to see them perform in their "natural habitat," so to speak. Actors who are inexperienced with the audition process often freeze up, so this gives me a better idea of their capabilities.

And they are capable. The shows they're performing in really don't stretch some of them at all. I can see a lot of promise. Dimi's idea for our opening show isn't a bad one—for a couple of years from now, when the company's found its feet and the performers are more seasoned.

I mention this quietly to Trav when Dimi's distracted by a call, and he bites his lip.

"Yeah, but the thing is, we may not keep these performers for years," he points out. "As soon as they get a little more stage experience, they're likely to move on to a city with more options for them."

Fuck. I knew that, of course, but I hadn't thought of it in context of what it would mean for us. If we're constantly working with inexperienced performers, the quality of our shows is never going to mature. Trav's brilliant, but he can't carry every show on his own.

"What about bringing in guest performers?" I could probably convince a couple of people to come down to sunny Georgia for a season, and if we start receiving some recognition, subsequent seasons won't be a problem.

Trav shakes his head. "All casting comes from the

existing pool of performers," he reminds me. "JU has to hire some more people to cover the number we'll need, so we can probably wrangle some input there, but we can't hire specifically for the company—they have to be willing to take a turn in the parks too."

"You being the only exception." I sigh. "Trav, you gotta help me out here. Some of these people are good. There's a lot of raw talent here. But if we're only ever using raw talent, I don't know that we'll be able to pull off a show like *Walk of Life*. Not without turning it into a high school drama club version."

Dimi comes back to join us before Trav can reply. I don't want to piss him off more than I have already, especially since it seemed like we might be getting close to being able to work amicably together, if nothing else, but I really, really think *Walk of Life* is not a viable option.

The fact is, right now I'm thinking with my dick. I'm not known for being a friendly, touchy-feely director. There are a lot of people who've worked with me who've called me a dictator. Autocratic. Inflexible and demanding. And those are the nicer things. I've never had a problem with telling it like it is, and I've never been hesitant to impose my will at work. I've been in this business for a long time. I'm a Tony award-winning director. Where a lot of directors bow to pressure from their backers, I haven't done that in twenty years—I just tell them where to go and find a new backer. Because *I can*. So me dithering about how to tell Dimi that *Walk of Life* is not going to happen is not because I'm worried about friction in the workplace. He might technically be head of the production company and my boss, but the company needs me more than it needs him—I'm the one with experience. Plus, my contract has a lot of stipulations in it that would make it easier for JU to move him to a different job than to get rid of me. Even if that wasn't the case, I expected that he and I would butt heads occasionally, even before I met him. That's what directors and producers do. I've worked with producers that I absolutely couldn't stand, and we managed just fine—that's where one of my Tonys came from.

There's really no reason for me to be hesitating—except that I'm insanely attracted to Dimi and I don't want him to hate me. Part of me is still hoping that maybe one day we can get something going. Sure, I'm probably nearly thirty years older than him, I have minimal flirting skills, and I insulted him before we were even introduced. But those might be things we can overcome, right? So my dick is voting to be nice to Dimi and let him have anything he wants so he'll like us.

Which is not just unprofessional, it's insulting to Dimi. And to me. And to everyone we're going to work with.

I sigh again. "Dimi, there are a lot of talented performers working here, but I don't think they have the experience to put on *Walk of Life* at a good standard."

There.

I said it.

Fuck, I really wish I hadn't.

No. No, I don't. I did the right thing.

Dimi's face is expressionless, his eyes fixed on my face. Trav is standing motionless beside me, seemingly anxious to hear what Dimi has to say. Not as anxious as me, I'll bet.

Finally, he turns to Trav. "Is that your opinion too?"

Trav hesitates, then blows out a breath. "I really want to say no, but yeah. It is. As much as I'd love to do *Walk of Life*, and as great as I think some of these guys could be in it, I just don't think we can pull it off across the board. Not yet."

Dimi's silent for another long minute. I'm sweating—and not just because the sun is warm today.

"Okay."

What?

"I'm not happy about it," he continues with blunt honesty, "but you two have a lot of experience, and I'd be an idiot if I didn't listen."

Wow.

Okay.

Maybe he won't hate me after all.

"But," he continues, and I brace myself, "I'm sorry, Jason, I didn't like anything on your list. They were all really safe choices, and some of them will definitely be in the plans for the future, when we're running more than one show at a time, but I feel strongly that we need to begin with something a little more unique rather than a show that's been interpreted a million times before."

Okay. This, I can work with.

"Fair enough," I agree. "I'm sure between us we can come up with something that falls somewhere in the middle. Let's keep on with our tour of performers." I'd much rather be back in my office, getting myself sorted, but "The two of you are familiar with them and their capabilities, but I'm not. I'd like to sit down to brainstorm with a better idea of what I have to work with." I barely stop myself from wincing. Dehumanizing the performers like that is probably not going to win me any popularity contests, but to my surprise, Dimi just nods, no judgment on his face.

***

It's hours and a theme park fast food lunch—which is not sitting well—later before we get back to the office. My dress shoes are not made for walking, so my feet are sore, and I'm sweaty and a little rumpled. That's okay, though, because I feel like we made some progress. And no, I'm not just talking about my quest to get Dimi to see me as someone he wants to date—or even as someone he could be friends with. I have a much better grasp now of the JU performers, and I've been thinking about some shows that might both be within their capabilities and make Dimi happy.

His plan to kick off the company with a bang is a good one. If we had access to a bigger budget and experienced performers, I'd be backing him all the way. But we want that bang to be because the show is amazing, not because it was a big fat flop. Finding some middle ground is achievable, even if it means we may need to push harder for a good performance than we would have with an easier show. I like to push, so I guess it's not a terrible thing to begin as I mean to go on, rather than easing everyone into things slowly.

We're back in the conference room. Trav grabs some bottled water from a mini fridge I hadn't even noticed and passes it around, while Dimi taps on his tablet and somehow manages to get the screen on the wall to show what he's looking at. I'm going to have to take a crash course in using technology, I think. I can handle email, web browsing, and basic—very basic—social media, but the stuff I've seen Dimi doing today with the JU app is probably beyond me. And I definitely don't have a clue how to get my phone or tablet to sync with the wall screen.

I drink deeply from the water bottle, feeling a little dehydrated. It's warmer here than in New York, and while I used to walk everywhere the subway couldn't take me when I was younger, for the last decade or so I've been dependent on cabs. I try to keep fit by going to the gym, but it's a different kind of exercise to walking around for hours.

Man, I'm getting old.

Pushing the thought aside—I am *not* old—I focus on the website Dimi's brought up. It's a directory of musical theater, from the looks of it, and he's scrolling slowly down a list of shows, pausing every now and then to flip screens and make a note.

"Let me know when you see something that might work," he says, and Trav makes an absent noise of agreement.

Fifteen minutes later, we have a shortlist of about two dozen shows. Dimi's picks are all a little on the ambitious side, but nowhere near as much as *Walk of Life* was. I'm not ashamed to admit, part of me feels a little pang of regret not to be doing *Walk of Life*. It's a brilliant show, and since it's unlikely I'll be able to direct the debut of a completely new production while working for JU, it would be a lot of fun to work on. But I'm not prepared to do a shitty job of it, so it can wait until we're ready.

Wait…

I hadn't realized, but all day I've been thinking like I'm here for good. The truth is, I have a twelve-month contract with JVTC. I wasn't ready to commit to more. If this first season bombs, I can start making inquiries back in New York and walk away by the end of the second season—or sooner.

Does that make me more willing to cave to Dimi's ambitious desires?

Hell, no. I might not be here long, but JVTC will not have a bad season because I didn't push hard enough.

With that in mind, I push *hard* as we go through the list one show at a time. I make Dimi justify each and every one of his choices, roping Trav in to discuss possible choreography choices. We'll use a professional choreographer to handle that properly, but I've worked with Trav enough to know that he's got some interest and talent in that area—plus he knows a lot of the performers and what they can stretch to. Budget is another consideration—that's Dimi's department, and I know we have a relatively healthy amount of money to work with, but I've actually directed some of the shows he wants, and I know where the secret money pitfalls are.

By the time we get to the end of the list, I'm both exhausted and exhilarated. Debating with Dimi really gave my brain a workout, and from the color in his cheeks and glint in his eye, I'm pretty sure he feels the same. Trav just looks worn out from mediating all afternoon. He'll probably go home to Derek and complain about the lunatics he's working with.

On the plus side, the list is much shorter. We have it down to four, two of which were Dimi's picks. It's actually one of those that has my vote, but I'm not telling him that yet. He's going to do some research on costs, and we'll make our decision based on that—possibly with a whole lot more arguing.

Trav stands as Dimi turns off the wall screen with a remote. "If you don't need me anymore, I'm going to head out," he says, and I look at my watch. It's after six—no wonder I'm starting to feel hungry. Lunch was hours ago.

Dimi's checking the time too. "Wow, that took a lot longer than I thought." He shakes his head. "I've gotta get going—I have plans."

Ever been punched in the stomach? I have—by an actor, interestingly enough, right after I finished critiquing her performance in rehearsals. It's a bitch—leaves you sore and gasping for breath. I'm feeling the emotional equivalent right now.

Stupid, right? I have no right to feel that way. I barely know Dimi, and he's expressed no desire to change that. Still, if the emotional brain were capable of logic, I wouldn't have been so broken up when the ex-who-shall-not-be-named decided I was a stodgy, boring bastard and left me. My emotional self has a huge crush on Dimi, and its heart is shattered by the thought that he might have a date.

The thought no sooner crosses my mind than it occurs to me that it might be more than a date. Dimi might be seeing someone. Might be in a serious relationship. Living with someone. It's Monday night, after all, not really a popular date night. But an evening snuggling on the couch with a long-term lover? Totally plausible.

I feel ill.

Forcing a smile, I say, "I still have a lot of crap to unpack. And, uh, I should find the grocery store." Even though I didn't cook a lot in New York, I *can* manage basic meals. Which is just as well, because Joyville doesn't have quite as many or varied takeout options. The JU complex has a heap of restaurants, some of them supposedly very good, but I don't know that many people here yet, and eating out alone every night doesn't appeal.

"There's one not far from you," Trav says, "but why don't you come and eat with me and Derek tonight and worry about that tomorrow?"

My smile is less forced when I reply. "That's very kind of you, but I don't want to intrude." Hell, could I sound any more like my aunt Gertrude?

Trav laughs. "No intrusion, I swear. Follow me home, and we'll drive past the store on the way so you can see where it is."

I really don't want to go back to my half-unpacked, not-very-homey-yet apartment and deal with boxes all night. "Thank you. That sounds great." I follow Trav out, very carefully not looking at Dimi, who's either got a date or some one-on-one time with his boyfriend.

Or, knowing my luck, his girlfriend. It's been a long time since my gaydar has needed to be reliable—I wouldn't be surprised if I'm wasting my energy pining for a straight man.

CHAPTER FIVE

Dimi

I DON'T BOTHER RINGING the bell—it will just get me scolded. Instead, I use my key and let myself into my parents' house. "Hey," I call, and a chorus of voices responds.

Monday night dinner is a tradition my mother implemented years ago, before I even moved back to Joyville. Attendance is mandatory for whoever is in town, and if you don't turn up, you'd better have a damn good reason. The last time I skipped was the day Derek met Trav, back in May—the day we had a murder and a massive staffing crisis. And when I called Mom and explained why I couldn't come, she made disapproving noises.

So, yeah. Monday night dinner is important.

I go to the kitchen first, where I know I'll find Dad and my grandmother cooking. "Can I help?" I ask after dispensing hugs.

"No," Gram says. "You'll ruin your shirt. Go keep your mother company. Don't let her in here."

The shirt I'm wearing isn't particularly special, but that should tell you how important it is to keep Mom out of the kitchen. She's an amazing woman, a brilliant example to us all… but she sets things on fire a lot. I don't even want to think about the roast beef debacle when I was fourteen. I mean, how the heck do you set roast beef on fire? Dad's a great cook, though, and neither I nor any of my siblings inherited Mom's firebug gene, so it's fine that she can't cook.

I track her down to her little office under the stairs. It's actually a storage cupboard, but when we were growing up, it was literally the only space in the house that she could use for doing paperwork. We're all grown and gone now, and there are three empty bedrooms, but she says she's used to it and converted one bedroom into a home gym, one into a crafts room, and the other into a spare room for when her kids who live out of town visit. Which is never often enough for her.

"Hey, Mom." I duck my head to get into the office and give her a kiss. She grabs on with the ferocity of a tiger and follows me back out into the hall.

"You look tired" is the first thing she says, and yes, while I have had a long day, she would have said it even if I'd come straight from a month at a spa resort. "Are you working too hard? Is that why I never see you?"

"You've seen me three times in the last week," I remind her. Dinner last Monday, Thanksgiving, and on Friday night at the show. It's like I'm speaking to thin air, though, because she just waves dismissively.

"You officially started your new job today, didn't you? How was it? Wait, come into the living room so everyone can hear."

I dutifully trail her into the living room. My oldest brother and two of my sisters—one older, one younger—still live in town, and they're in there along with my sister-in-law, brother-in-law, and sister's boyfriend of the month, plus two nephews and a niece. It's worth noting that my younger sister only brings her boyfriends to Monday night dinner as a litmus test when she's ready to get serious. She's weird like that.

"Uncle Dimi!" My oldest nephew, at seven, scrambles up from where they're playing Monopoly on the floor. It's really unfair for him to play with his sister and cousin, who are only five and don't fully grasp the game, but he says—with great sincerity—that every once in a while he needs to feel superior.

I accept a hug first from him, then the others—I'm kind of the favorite uncle—then wave at my sibs and wait for Sienna to introduce her boyfriend. I actually know his name—we're all pretty close, and she's talked about him—but this is the first time we've met, so an introduction isn't out of order.

By the time I settle in one of the beanbag chairs—because there isn't enough furniture in the room to seat eight adults and I'm not making my sixty-seven-year-old mother sit on a beanbag—a semblance of order has returned to the room.

"Dimi was just about to tell us about his first day in the new job," Mom announces.

Sienna looks confused. "I thought you started the new job weeks ago."

"No," Patrick interjects, "he was job-sharing the new job and the old one while the new company got established."

See what I mean? No secrets in my family.

"So you're now doing only the new job?" Ryan, Patrick's husband, asks, and I nod.

"Yeah. The director we poached from New York arrived over the weekend, so we've started planning everything now." And maybe it's not going entirely the way I wanted it, but it could be worse. Jason showed that he was at least willing to listen to me. I wouldn't really want a director I could walk all over—I *am* relatively inexperienced in this career, after all. I need someone I can learn from, not bully.

Not that I would bully anyone.

Well, not deliberately. I've been told I can be bossy and forceful, and with people who are less assertive, that can be the same as bullying.

"What's he like?" Sienna leans forward. "It's that guy who directed *Fake It 'Til You Make It*, right? You've been a fan of his since forever."

Heat rises in my cheeks, but I stoically maintain

my composure. Maybe I have been kind of a fan of Jason's work ever since I was a teenager and went to New York with the school drama club for a theater weekend. But I really didn't expect Sienna to remember, and I definitely didn't want it to come up. Ever.

"He's fine. Nice guy. Has some ideas and is trying hard to understand what we've got to work with and how it can fit his vision."

Patrick and Ryan both suck in breaths, and Caitlyn, my other sister, cringes. Sienna's eyes go wide. Mom laughs.

"What?" I say defensively, mentally reviewing my words. I didn't say anything to get that reaction.

Did I?

No.

I squint at Mom. "Why are you laughing?"

She reaches out and pats my hand. "Because I love you, baby, but you've always been a stubborn little shit, and the thought of you going head-to-head with someone just as stubborn is hilarious."

I blink. Because… what?

"I… I said he was a nice guy who was working hard and had a vision." I am so fucking confused right now. Did they maybe set up a hidden camera in the conference room? "What makes you think he's stubborn or that we're going head-to-head? We're not, by the way," I tack on, just in case they think my question is tacit agreement.

Caitlyn shakes her head, her wife, Leona, shooting

me one of those sympathetic smiles that always get my back up. "Oh, honey," Cait says. "You're a passionate guy. When you're excited about something, when it's going well, it takes an act of God to shut you up. Sienna said it, you've been a fan of this guy's work for years… but you barely said anything about him, and all of it could have safely gone into a press release."

Well, fuck.

I mean, she's not wrong. I do tend to get excited about things, projects at work or the community theater, and sometimes I share about them a lot. I've always been like that. Usually my family just tells me to shut up already. It never occurred to me that lack of a response would be a big red flag for them.

I sigh and flop back on the beanbag. "It's fine," I tell the ceiling. "I had a vision, and his doesn't quite match it. We're compromising." That's all true and should be enough to keep them happy. They don't need to know more. They *really* don't need to know that I got my feelings hurt. We're a protective kind of family, and the last thing I need is my sibs or mom turning up at my job to stick up for me.

My sibs seem to accept it, but Mom gives me a suspicious look. I keep my face as blank as possible, and thankfully, Dad calls us in for dinner right then.

It's nearly ten by the time I get home, even though I don't live far from my parents. When I moved back to Joyville, I thought about looking for something on the other side of town, away from the neighborhood

I grew up in—although really, Joyville isn't that big and it wouldn't have made a huge difference—but in the end, I decided to stick close to family. It's less than a ten-minute walk from my townhouse to the house I grew up in.

I strip to boxers and take my tablet to bed with me—no, not to watch anything interesting. I want to start researching the costs involved with the shows on our short list. Although, now that I think about it, that's kind of sad. Not that I particularly want to watch porn right now, but shouldn't it have occurred to me to take my tablet to bed so I could have some happy time rather than use it for work?

Come to think of it, when was the last time I actually had happy time? I jerk off in the shower a few times a week, but the last time I was with someone, or even spent some quality time with my hand, as opposed to treating it as a purely practical thing, was….

Huh.

When was it?

It's not that I'm a monk with no social life. There was that guy I went out with a few times who it turned out was planning to move away from the area… but we never made it to bed. And that was in June.

June.

Really? I haven't been out with anyone in over five months?

Maybe I am a monk. It seems like the only reason I have a "social life" is because a lot of my friends are from the community theater. Dinner or drinks after rehearsal are pretty common. I'm going to have to pick up my game a bit, though, both with my friends and with my dating life. I love my job, and I'm determined to forge this new career path, but I don't want to be a workaholic—not least because my mom would kill me.

So… maybe no work tonight? It's not like it can't wait until tomorrow. Ten on a Monday night is probably too late to call a friend to meet up, but I can still start training myself not to work in every spare moment. I've got a couple of books I bought earlier this year that I still haven't read, even though I was pretty excited about them at the time. Or there's always Netflix—that thriller that came out last year that I never got around to seeing is on there. Or there are a couple of series that have been recommended to me that I've been meaning to watch.

I'm seeing a pattern emerge here. I might be further down the path to workaholism than I thought.

In the end, I decide on porn—are you surprised? Like I said before, it's been a long time since I "pampered" myself, and now that the idea's in my head, I can't let it go.

I don't use my work tablet, though. I have some standards. Plus, our IT geniuses can monitor that shit, even if you do it from home. I had a very enlightening conversation with one of them at the holiday party last year, and my tablet has been strictly work-only since then—I don't even check the weather on it anymore.

So I grab my laptop from the spare room-slash-office-slash-one-day-I'll-convert-this-to-a-gym room and settle in my bed with a hand towel and a bottle of lube. I peruse my bookmarks, wondering if I should maybe go looking for something new, but finally settle on one of my favorites.

As usual, it doesn't take long for me to get into it—it doesn't take *them* long either—but this time I'm a little distracted by one of the actors. He's a little older than the other, with salt-and-pepper hair, hot in a Clooney kind of way, but something about him strikes me as familiar. I mean, what I can really see of his face. The camera isn't exactly focused on it. He's doing the younger guy from behind, both of them on their knees, in profile to the camera. I stroke myself lazily as I watch, half trying to figure out what it is about the guy that's familiar, half just enjoying the stimulation.

The younger guy with the bubble butt moans, a deeply carnal sound, and the older one says, "That's right. You love this. Tell me how you want it." He thrusts just that little bit harder, and I squeeze my cock, breath catching.

Moaning some more, the younger guy demands, "Harder. Do me harder. Make me scream."

Mr. Salt-and-Pepper pushes the guy down onto his hands and knees, grabs his hips, and goes to town. I shift so I can reach my balls, panting a little as I watch Mr. Salt-and-Pepper ream Bubble Butt, pumping my dick with one hand and squeezing my balls with the other. I know what's coming, I've seen this vid a million times, but that only makes it hotter.

Sure enough, Mr. Salt-and-Pepper leans over Bubble Butt and bites his shoulder, Bubble Butt yelps, and my dick jerks in my hand, precome leaking liberally. Mr. Salt-and-Pepper laughs darkly, straightens, and pulls almost all the way out. He's totally hung, like most porn actors, his cock thick, heavily veined, and flushed. It's shiny with lube, and in that breathless second while he pauses, my mouth waters.

He shoves back in, and Bubble Butt cries out, then immediately shouts, "Again!" Mr. Salt-and-Pepper complies, the pace of their fucking going from fast to slow but *hard*. I want to come—it's been a long time, and these two are so hot together—but I squeeze the base of my cock. I want to last a little bit longer.

It takes only half a dozen of those hard thrusts before Mr. Salt-and-Pepper yells and pulls out, shooting his load all over Bubble Butt's… bubble butt. I gasp as he pumps himself and swears, but don't let go yet.

My favorite part is next.

The scene changes. Now Bubble Butt is standing, and Mr. Salt-and-Pepper is on his knees, licking his dick, which is quite possibly the biggest thing I've ever seen.

"You want this?" Bubble Butt asks, grabbing his cock and painting Mr. Salt-and-Pepper's lips with the tip.

"I wanna choke on it," Mr. Salt-and-Pepper says and opens wide. Bubble Butt seizes the opportunity, fucking deep, and Mr. Salt-and-Pepper gags—then grabs Bubble Butt's hips and yanks him closer again.

I jack myself in rhythm with Bubble Butt's thrusts, knowing it won't be long—for either of us.

Three thrusts later, Bubble Butt jerks back and comes all over Mr. Salt-and-Pepper's face.

And I see stars.

Later, after I've cleaned up the mess—and boy, was there a mess. Definitely have to have some "me" time more regularly—I pick up the laptop to put it away, and the screen comes to life. The video has returned to the opening frame, in which my silver hottie is wearing a jock that frames things to perfection. I'm admiring him when that pang of familiarity strikes again. I tear my gaze away from his dick and study him more closely.

It's not him, exactly. I definitely don't know him, and I'm pretty sure I've only ever seen him in this video. Maybe another one, too—I seem to remember something in an office setup. It's more the look on his face and the way he carries himself—absolute confidence, but not in a forceful way. The silvered hair adds to it, giving him a distinguished vibe. If he were wearing a shirt and tie, he'd have the same overall look as Jason.

My gut seizes. Oh, hell no. I did not think that.

I am not attracted to Jason.

Well... I am. He's hot, yeah? But it's a superficial

attraction. Like attraction to a famous actor. Nobody ever does anything about that. Ordinary people who've never met him don't actively pursue Chris Hemsworth. They don't want to put him on his knees and make him choke on their dick. Not the normal ones, anyway. My attraction to Jason is like that. I recognize that he's hot, but it's not something I ever want to act on. I definitely don't want to jack off to images of him like I do with the porn guy.

I resolutely ignore the fact that Chris Hemsworth has starred in several of my fantasies in the past, unattainable actor or not.

Jason is a colleague. He will only ever be a colleague. I *am not* thinking of him that way.

I'm just tired. It's been a long day. Next time I watch this video, I'll probably wonder how I ever imagined a resemblance, no matter how superficial, between the actor and Jason.

***

By the time I get to work early the next morning, I've forgotten the incident that I can't remember—I really have—and am raring to get stuck back into the challenge of selecting JVTC's debut show. Two of the ones on our short list were my suggestions, and there's one in particular I think would align well with my goals. Am I still bummed that we're not going with

Walk of Life? Yes, absolutely. It's a brilliant show and would have set the right note for the company from the get-go. But Jason and Trav have been working in this industry for a long time, and I'd be an idiot not to concede to their expertise. It *would* be worse to put on a mediocre version of a great show than a brilliant version of a good one.

That doesn't stop the disappointment, of course, but I'm nothing if not practical, so I push it aside and focus. I've copiously researched two of the shows and am moving on to the third when someone clears their throat from the doorway of my office.

It's Trav, and he has an amused expression on his face that likely means he's been standing there for a while and I never noticed.

"Hey," I say, glancing at the time on my laptop. Shit, it's nearly nine thirty. I've been at this for over two hours. No wonder my back's starting to feel achy.

"Good morning. Come and have coffee with us—you could probably use a break."

Now that he mentions it, I would commit several felonies for a coffee. I stand and stretch, make sure to hit Save on my notes, and follow him out into the common space. Jason is unloading a tray of takeout coffee cups on the desk that will belong to one of our assistants. There's also a paper bag from the bakery here in the Village, and my stomach growls on cue. Breakfast was hours ago.

"Good morning," Jason says with a cheerful smile,

and I smile back, *not* picturing him on his knees, naked. "You've been hard at work. What time did you get in?"

"A little after seven." I'm a morning person, and since I'm up anyway, if I don't have anything productive to do at home, I come in to work.

Jason's eyebrows shoot up. "Then you'll definitely need this." He extends a cup to me. "Trav told me how you liked it."

I ignore the double entendre he didn't know he was making and widen my smile to include Trav as I say, "Thank you. Yeah, it's definitely coffee time. And I wouldn't say no to some of whatever's in the bag." I nod toward it. Normal. I'm being a normal coworker.

"You don't even know what it is," Jason protests, but there's a sparkle in his eyes. We seem to be getting along a lot better this morning, despite the dirty thoughts I'm trying to hide. Maybe because I'm not being defensive? Sure, he said dickhole things, but we need to work together going forward, so I need to let that go. I want this company to succeed, and it won't if he and I are deliberately antagonizing each other.

Or if I'm constantly picturing him in place of a certain porn actor.

"Everything from there is amazing," I inform him. "Are you going to share, or do I need to take steps?"

He laughs out loud, hearty and full, and hell, that little pang of superficial attraction stands up and waves for my attention. He has a great laugh.

Handing over the bag, he tells me, "Take what

you want. There's enough for all of us."

We're soon settled for our break, munching companionably. "What are your plans for the morning?" I ask them, and Trav holds up a finger, indicating I should wait while he chews and swallows. Jason snorts.

"Trav's been showing me how to use the app," he says. "We have a list of questions for you when you have time. And I'm going to go through the applications HR sent."

Trav finally swallows and nods. "Seriously, Dim, that app could be used to achieve total world domination, and we've only got access to the features we need. Who came up with that thing?"

I grin. "We have some scary smart tech guys working at JU. There was some talk a few years—maybe five or six?—back about bringing in a company that could develop an app to incorporate all the functions of the intranet for easier use on tablet and smartphone. Two of the guys in tech had already been thinking about it, they pitched their ideas, and the decision was made to let them run with it, since they already knew what was needed. So it was all developed in-house, and once we rolled it out, head office was so impressed they transferred those guys to California to work for the parent company."

"That's Joy Incorporated?" Jason confirms, and I nod.

"Last I heard, they've rolled out an app specific to

the needs of the animation design studio."

"Impressive."

It really is, but I bite back my enthusiastic monologue on the subject, because it gets a little technical and most people's eyes glaze over. I'll let him get used to our app first. Instead, I change the subject.

"I need to go through the HR applications today as well, but I want to finish the costings first. I should be done by lunchtime. Can we set some time this afternoon to go over them?"

"Sounds good." Jason looks at Trav. "Does two work for both of you?"

Trav agrees, and I pull out my tablet and set up the meeting. Jason looks vaguely surprised when his tablet and phone chime.

"That could get annoying fast," he mutters. "Why didn't yours ding?" He shoots Trav an accusing look.

"We'll change the settings so it only dings for stuff flagged as urgent," Trav promises. "Otherwise it will be going off all day." He takes a final gulp of coffee. "Okay, I'm going to look up some of the past choreography for the shows on the short list. Are any of them so ridiculously out of our budget that I shouldn't bother?"

I shake my head. "Not so far, sorry."

He winks and wanders into the conference room. When I was setting up office space, he told me not to bother with one for him, since most of his work will be in the theater. The conference room works fine for the occasional times he needs a desk.

I finish my coffee and Danish and thank Jason again. Time to get some work done.

***

"So we're agreed?" Jason sits back in his chair and looks around the table.

"Agreed," I say, feeling smug and victorious, even though there's no winner or loser here. I still feel like I won.

"Agreed." Trav grins widely. "This is going to be fun."

It actually didn't take us as long as I'd feared it would to go through the information and make a decision. Interestingly, it seemed like Jason's preference was the same as mine, and since that show was well within our budgetary limits—even if we do some of the more creative things Trav and Jason were casually brainstorming yesterday—it was an easy decision.

So the debut season of JVTC will be *Out of Line*. It's a lighter show, no heavy drama, but does have a few more intense scenes that give it depth. It had a very successful first season in the West End, then on Broadway, but didn't get as much attention as some of the flashier shows, so it hasn't been as widely traveled. And I'm so excited to sink my teeth into it.

"Right," Jason says, and he's grinning. "I'll leave it to

you to arrange licensing, Dimi. Now that we know what we're doing, I have thoughts about the choreography. Do we need to use the in-house choreographers, or can I bring someone in?"

I make a face. "You can bring someone in, but long-term we'll probably want to develop talent in-house. It's cheaper and better for company morale."

He stares at the table for a long moment, clearly thinking. Trav and I exchange glances. We actually had a really detailed discussion about this a couple months ago, when I was negotiating the budget. We'd both prefer to keep the choreography in-house, but ultimately allowed for the hire of a contractor because our choreographers are used to dealing with thirty-minute shows aimed at children, and we wanted to make sure we had the money to get help if it turned out we needed it.

"How about this," Jason says finally. "I'd like to talk to the choreography team, see what ideas they have. Maybe set them a scene they can use as a kind of audition. Based on that, we can decide whether it would be smarter to bring someone in this season and have the team shadow that person in prep for next season. Does the team even have the bandwidth to be taking on a project like this?"

That sounds fair. In fact, it's a lot more than I expected from him. "Not really," I admit. "In the same way that the company is increasing the pool of performers, the plan would be to add to the choreography team if their workload was going to increase."

"Pete, the head of the team, told me he's put some feelers out but hasn't actually advertised anything yet," Trav adds. "He didn't want to assume."

Jason nods. "Can we set up a meeting with him? Let's get this moving. If they can handle this, they'll need to get started as soon as possible."

I pull out my phone and make the call. Pete is happy to hear from me and agrees to come and meet with us first thing in the morning. He offers to come right away, but Jason and I both need to sort out those applications from HR or we'll be run off our feet when things start up in earnest. Assistants are a must-have.

"Done, then." I lean back in my chair and allow myself to grin. "I'll put in the licensing application this afternoon. From what I could see in my research, it should be quick." And if there look to be any delays, JU has a brilliant legal department I can utilize to push things through.

"Sounds good. If you run into any issues, let me know, and I'll lean on some of my contacts."

I knew we'd hired him for a reason.

"So," he says, and something about the way his tone is so studiously casual catches my interest, "how was your date last night?"

Date?

What date?

Shit, did I have a date I forgot about?

Nah. I would never plan a date for a Monday night.

A moment of sheer, gut-wrenching panic seizes me—*does he know about my self-care time?* Is that what he means?

I will myself to be calm. There's no way he can know. And even if he did, so what? I'm sure he's probably jerked off a time or two in his life.

But....

"I didn't have a date last night," I say calmly. He raises his eyebrows.

"Oh. Sorry. You said you had plans, and I guess I just assumed."

See? Just a misunderstanding. I chuckle.

"Monday night dinner at my parents' place. Attendance is mandatory, or face the wrath of Mom."

Trav laughs. "Your mom's awesome, but she also kinda scares me."

"How so?" Jason looks intrigued.

"She's Dimi, but with thirty-some years' worth more self-assurance and life experience."

Say what?

"What." My tone is so flat it doesn't even sound like a question. I mean, don't get me wrong, my mom *is* awesome and it would not suck to be like her... but I never thought I was. Not really.

"Oh, come on, Dimi. Think about it. You're both organized, driven, and competent in a scary way. You can both walk into any chaotic situation and get things on track and people obeying orders within minutes—and they'd be grateful to you."

I think about it.

He's kind of right.

No. He's right. No "kind of" about it.

I can't believe I've been blind to this all these years.

"I guess I should be nicer to my mother," I say finally. "Seeing as how I'm going to be her one day."

Jason chuckles. "I've got to meet your mom. The curiosity is going to kill me."

I shrug. "She'll turn up when the show premieres. She and Dad always come to my shows." I force myself not to wince. I didn't mean to refer to *that night*, I swear. Things are going well between us now, and the last thing I want is to derail that with any reminders of our previous—well, *my* previous—animosity. On the flip side, the community theater is a huge part of my life, has been for years, and it's going to come up. So maybe it's best to start making it an ordinary part of the conversation.

Jason doesn't react badly, thankfully, just smiles and says, "I'll look forward to meeting her, then."

Working with him may turn out to be a great thing, after all. As long as I stay focused.

CHAPTER SIX

Jason

THIS MOVE WAS A good idea. I'll admit now that I was more unsure of it than I let on when I first arrived in Joyville, but three weeks in, I'm confident that I made the right decision. I love New York and adored working the Broadway scene all these years, but I needed a change of pace after I broke up with the ex-who-shall-not-be-named. The last few years have been one upheaval after another—my parents passing on barely six months apart, my brother and sister squabbling like selfish brats over the estate and dragging me into it, the breakup and having to leave my home of fifteen years—getting away from all of it, working in a new environment with new people, was exactly the right thing to do.

These last weeks have been hectic. We want to start performances in March, which means we need to move fast, especially with the holidays causing their usual disruption to schedules. Dimi got the rights we need within record time, and after careful consideration and a lot of discussion, we decided to use the in-house choreography team. It's a risk, but Pete, who heads the team, has a lot of experience, some of it in a big theater company in Atlanta, even if it was a long time ago. I'm willing to take a chance on him.

Dimi and I hired our assistants, but mine quit after three days when she discovered during the course of casual conversation that I'm gay. It was a shock to all of us—JU has a solid nondiscrimination policy, and the parent company has been very open about its support of diverse minority groups. The worst part was that she was so earnest and "polite" about it. *"I'm sorry, Jason, I just can't work for a homosexual. It's not personal."*

Um... how is it not personal? Did she think it would be less of an attack on who I am because she didn't use slurs? That I would be less angry? I guess being a big deal on Broadway for so long has insulated me to a certain degree—it's been more years than I can count since the last time I personally experienced homophobia. My immediate circle is liberal, and people I came into contact with for work were all eager to impress me. So I was literally speechless with shock when she said that and then followed it up by asking for a reference. For three days' work.

Luckily for me, Dimi overheard and swooped in to save the day. He reminded her of a whole heap of JU policies that had been in the employment contract she signed and ushered her out the door within seconds. Then he got on the phone to HR and tore them a new one. Turns out the screening process is supposed to include a question on whether the applicant can work in a diverse workplace without discriminating, but somehow it got missed this time around.

So I'm currently without an assistant. Most of that is because I'm a bit apprehensive now about hiring someone new. Dimi's been pushing me to get on with it, and he's right. I'll get it done after the holidays.

And speaking of holidays, that's what we're doing right now. Literally. Speaking of holidays. Dimi just asked Trav about his and Derek's plans to spend the holidays in New York with family.

"…so we're both kind of dreading it, but in an excited way." Trav finishes explaining the sleeping arrangements at his parents' place. I have to admit, I tuned a lot of it out, but only because he and I were talking about it last week.

Dimi scrunches up his face in a way that makes his already youthful face look even younger. "I get it," he commiserates. "When I didn't live in town, I dreaded coming home for the holidays. Most of my sibs and their significant others and their kids all converged—still do—on my parents' place, and there was barely enough room for us all growing up. There's nowhere to go if you need a minute to yourself—not even the bathroom, because one year my youngest brother thought it would be a good idea to claim the tub as his bed for the week."

I laugh. How can I not? That shit's funny.

Dimi grins. "He's always been the simpleton in the family," he confides. "His logic was that it would be a bed to himself, no sharing required."

"That's... well, I can't beat that," Trav says, chuckling. "Remind me, how many of you are there?"

"Eight." Dimi sighs dramatically, and although I've gotten to know him pretty well over the last few weeks, this almost whimsical side of him is new. We've been pushing hard, and there hasn't been a lot of time for fun—which, now that I think about it, isn't good. That's how people burn out. I make a mental note to allow for more mental health breaks during the workday.

"You're one of eight?" I ask, because shit, that's a lot of kids. I thought one brother and one sister were enough to drive me insane. I can't imagine having seven siblings. "Where do you fall in the order?"

I'll bet he's the oldest. He's got that organized, managing, look-after-everyone-and-everything personality. But on the other hand, he mentioned that his siblings have kids, and since he's barely more than a kid himself, that probably means he's not the oldest.

Maybe he's the youngest? Forced to assert himself to avoid being overridden by all the rest? No, he just mentioned his youngest brother.

"I'm number four," he tells me, and boy, did I have it completely wrong. I would never have picked him for a middle child.

"So… the house was completely full while you were growing up." Man, that must have sucked for him. I've noticed how protective he is of his personal space. His office is his sanctuary—anytime I go in to discuss anything, he moves us to the conference room, claiming we'll be more comfortable. I mean, the offices aren't huge, but they're not that small.

"Yep. We were stacked in like sardines." He tilts his head, looking thoughtful. "It wasn't until I moved out that I realized a lot of people don't have siblings always in their space like that. There were days I would gladly have sold a brother or sister just to get ten minutes alone in a room, but I thought that was normal. If I could relive my childhood, I don't think I'd sacrifice any of them. They're all kind of amazing in their own way, even the simpleton. I'd never live with any of them again, though. It's bad enough some of them stay with me for the holidays." He's smiling as he says it.

"Is it really that bad?" I tease, because I don't think he means it.

"Horrible," he assures me. "The ones who are single crash with me, and we generally stay up late watching bad movies, eating junk, drinking, and talking about the shit that's going on in our lives. At some point, sins of the past usually get brought up and we drunkenly argue over things like who really broke the window that one time and who told Mom about any of the many times any of us broke curfew."

I'm hit by a pang of… envy? Maybe. I don't have that kind of relationship with my brother and sister. I mentioned their disgraceful behavior over our parents' estate, right?

"That sounds perfectly awful," I say, heavy on the sarcasm, and Trav murmurs agreement.

"I don't know how you cope, Dimi," he adds, straight-faced.

Dimi shakes his head, still smiling. "Mock all you want, until you've had to hear my sister shrieking about the state of the bathroom after either of my younger brothers have been in there, you have no idea about my pain."

I snort, because when I was starting out on Broadway in my early twenties, I lived in a two-bedroom, one-bathroom dump with six other guys. I get what his sister is screeching about.

"And that's what I'll be doing for the holidays this year," Dimi concludes. "Our big family dinner is Christmas Eve."

"Not Christmas Day?" I'm a little surprised. If the family is all coming into town especially for the holidays, they probably don't have other commitments on Christmas Day.

Dimi shakes his head. "No, on Christmas Day we all go to the party at the theater."

I look at Trav and see on his face the same combination of interest and curiosity that I feel.

"What party? At the community theater?"

"Yeah. I guess you wouldn't know, since this is your first holiday season here. A lot of the employees here at JU aren't 'native' to the area, right? And since the complex is a holiday destination, nearly everyone has a shift at some point over the next few weeks. Enough time off over the holidays to leave town is rarer than hens' teeth. So since not everyone has family to go to, about forty years ago some of the local business owners banded together and hosted lunch at the theater for anyone who was interested." He shrugs. "It's grown a lot since then, changed from lunch into an all-day party. People come and go all day from about eleven, usually bring a dish of some kind, just hang around and have fun."

Wow. I mean… wow.

That's a huge effort.

"That's amazing," Trav says, sounding just as flummoxed as I am. "I kind of wish we weren't going to New York, just so we could come. Derek never mentioned this at all. Has he been?"

Dimi laughs so hard he's nearly crying by the time he calms down enough to talk. "Has he been? He's played Santa at least five times that I'm aware of since he moved here."

I clear my throat, then bite my lip. I don't want to laugh out loud—volunteering to be Santa at a community party is a nice thing to do, and laughing at the image I have of Derek in a Santa suit and beard would be rude. But… it's an image of Derek in a Santa suit and beard.

Trav's staring at Dimi. "Please tell me there are pictures," he whispers, and Dimi grins.

"Probably hundreds of them," he promises. "The kids love him—he's been the favorite Santa for years. I'll see if I can find some for you."

Trav's grin is a little vicious. "I love having shit to tease him with."

"He's not going to be embarrassed," Dimi warns. "He loves it."

"That doesn't surprise me," Trav deadpans. "Still, I can't believe he never mentioned it. Jase, you should go."

I blink. "What?" When did this turn on me?

"Are you staying in town for the holidays?" Dimi asks, sounding a little surprised. I don't know why—I've talked about the work I plan to get done over the next week. Did he think I planned to do that from somewhere else?

"Yeah."

He looks expectant, but I don't really want to explain that I haven't been invited by either of my shitty siblings to visit them, that I lost quite a few friends when I went from being an *us* to a *me*, and that those who remain would gladly welcome me but have families of their own. I sublet my apartment when I moved down here, so I'd have to either get a hotel room—in New York, over the holidays—where I would spend most of my time alone, or stay with friends and intrude on their family time.

I sound bitter, don't I? The truth is, I have several friends who've asked me to stay with them for the holidays. I know their families well and know I would be welcome. But it's so easy to feel like the odd man out, and since the breakup, it seems like that's all I ever am.

There's no way I'm saying all that to Dimi.

"I've got momentum going here," I say instead. "I don't want to break it by leaving town. I'll take a long weekend and visit people later on."

He nods. As motivated as he is, it doesn't surprise me that he accepts that excuse. Trav, on the other hand, looks a little suspicious. But then, he knows about the ex-who-shall-not-be-named, and he was also around when I took time off from a show during the final decline of my parents.

Yeouch, that sounds awful, doesn't it? Like the title of a Greek tragedy. "The final decline of my parents." I didn't realize I was quite that dramatic.

"You should come, then," Dimi says. "It'll be a great opportunity for you to get to know people."

I smile, because I was not looking forward to spending yet another day alone in my apartment, working or watching TV shows I have no interest in. Being able to spend even just a couple of hours in the company of other people in a social setting sounds *great*. "I will, thanks. Is there anything in particular I should bring?" I'm not great in the kitchen, but I can manage basic dishes—and I'm hell on wheels when it comes to ordering stuff. There're still a few days before Christmas; I'm sure I can buy what I need somewhere in town.

"I'll ask Mom," he says. "I know last year we had heaps of desserts but not that many sides. She's on the organizing committee, so she'll have a better idea of what dishes we're most likely to need."

I'm about to thank him when I hear his assistant, John, say, "Can I help you?"

The three of us shut up, shamelessly eavesdropping. We still don't get that many visitors to the office, and John knows most of them, so this must be someone new. The door to the conference room is open, which makes it easy to listen.

"Is Jason Philips here?" a low female voice asks. Dimi looks surprised. He gets up and goes to the door.

"Kiara?" he asks. "What's brought you here?"

"Dimi, unless you're ready to come and work for me, I don't want to see you."

I can't see his face, but I hear the smile in his voice when he says, "You haven't forgiven me yet for taking the job with Derek instead of you? It's been years."

"Never. Jason here?"

I get up and go to look over Dimi's shoulder. There's a woman around my age with a truly amazing afro standing in our reception area. The tips of her hair are dyed in a multitude of colors, including metallic shades that I've never seen before in hair. My friend Brice, a stylist who changes his hair frequently, would adore it.

"I'm Jason," I say. Whoever she is, Dimi knows her well enough to have a jokey relationship with her, and that's recommendation enough for me. He moves aside, and I stroll out and stop about six feet from her.

Her sharp dark gaze takes me in, head to toe, and then she nods. "Nice to meet you, Jason. I'm Kiara James, the head of human resources." She steps forward and extends a hand. I've automatically reached out to take it before her words fully register.

"It's nice to meet you, too," I tell her. "Is there a problem?" It's perhaps a little blunt, but I'm pretty sure she's here to tell me I need to hurry up and hire another assistant, and I'm not ready.

I don't wanna.

She can't make me.

Anything else I can say to sound like a whiny child? No? Just as well. I'm sure you get the gist.

"Yes, but not for you. Can I have some of your time?" She meets my gaze steadily, and I get a really good vibe from her, so I tip my head toward my office.

"Sure. We were just slacking off, anyway. Dimi needs an excuse to get back to work."

"Hey!" Dimi exclaims, but he doesn't sound mad, and I can hear Trav laughing. Kiara grins and walks ahead of me.

I close the office door and wave her over to the couch.

We could sit at the desk, a formal meeting with me taking the seat of power, but even though I really don't want to hire a new assistant, I think Kiara could be a great connection and being an asshole isn't how I want to start relationships here.

Well, not more than I already have, anyway. Dimi's been great, but there are still moments where he seems a little wary, and that's all my stupid fault.

"So," I sit at the other end of the couch and turn toward her, "what can I do for you?"

She smiles, and again I get that vibe. It's impossible for me not to be comfortable with this woman.

"Either you think I'm stupid, or you're trying really hard to dodge the issue," she says, and I make an embarrassing sound that's somewhere between a groan and a laugh.

"Fine, I know why you're here. I promise I will get back to hiring an assistant right after the holidays. I know it needs to be done—but part of the reason I haven't done it yet is that the workload's increased because I don't have an assistant."

"A vicious cycle," she says slyly. "But that's actually not what I'm here for."

Oh.

Huh?

"It's not?"

"No. Although I'm glad you've agreed to restart the hiring process, and I *will* make sure you follow through on that promise." She's still smiling, but there is suddenly something about her that makes it obvious why she's the head of her department in a company this size.

"Okay. So... you just came down to say hello?"

"No, I came down to ask why you haven't filed a formal complaint."

Oh, right. I'm a little disappointed, actually, that this visit is just about covering her department's ass.

"You don't have to worry, I have no plan to file a complaint," I assure her, and she shakes her head.

"We just keep misunderstanding each other," she says. "I want you to file the complaint, Jason."

Well, that's not what I expected.

"Say what?"

Her grin is sharp. "File the complaint," she repeats. "Dimi already, er, explained to your recruiter that she missed some crucial parts of the process"—I snort, because I heard Dimi's "explanation," and while he never raised his voice or used any inappropriate language, I was still extremely glad not to be on the receiving end—"but until you make a formal complaint, I can't officially remove her from your brief, I can't require her to redo any training, and I can't begin an on-record review of all her previous hires."

I blink.

"I'd like to make a formal complaint," I say, and the words are no sooner out of my mouth than she's whipping out her phone and tapping away. A moment later, my phone vibrates in my pocket.

"I've just sent you the form you need to complete. Why don't I walk you through it?"

Yep, my vibe was right. Kiara's good people.

I grab my tablet and bring up the file she sent me. The form has a lot of fields, but with Kiara's guidance, it actually doesn't take too long. At first I tried to just type in that my assistant had resigned because JU's policies hadn't been properly explained during the hiring process, but Kiara had snatched the tablet away and deleted that.

"Be specific," she instructed, handing it back. "I know it's difficult. It's embarrassing and painful to relive exactly what happened, and I'm sorry to make you do it. But I *am* going to make you do it. This is a serious breach of JU policy. The recruitment process should have prevented this, and I never want you or anyone else to have to go through a similar situation. What I need to work out now is whether this was a problem with the process, with the training our recruiters receive, or with the recruiter herself."

I sigh. I never really imagined myself to be sheltered, but the fact that I don't want to type "My assistant resigned because she found out I'm gay and she didn't want to work for a homosexual" seems to imply otherwise.

"It could have been worse," I mutter, more to myself than Kiara. "I was lucky. She could have been violent." Or she could have been in a position of authority over me—or someone else. She could have hated gays but not been willing to resign.

"No," Kiara insists, and I look at her in surprise. "I mean, yes, it's good that she wasn't violent, but you're not 'lucky' because of that. This is supposed to be a safe place for you, Jason. You should never have had anyone speak to you that way here. This is not something silly. It's a serious incident." She points to the tablet. "Now type."

By the time she's satisfied and lets me send the form back to her, I feel like the equivalent of a wet rag, but I'm no longer embarrassed about it. Kiara's right—just because she was "polite" doesn't mean it wasn't an attack. I'm allowed to feel bad about it. It doesn't make me weak.

"Stay there," Kiara orders as I make to stand and show her out. "I know the way to the door. I'm gonna get this filed and start things in motion before I leave for the day. You'll have a new recruiter when you start looking for an assistant after the holidays—someone I know will carry out the process right."

"Thanks, Kiara. We should have lunch one day." I could use someone like her in my circle.

"Absolutely. After the holidays, though—who has time before then?" She waves carelessly as she opens the door and strides through. I hear her talking to someone outside, but I'm too busy flopping back on the couch and staring at the ceiling to try and listen.

A moment later, I sense a presence and lift my head to see Dimi standing in the doorway.

"Oh. Hey." I struggle to sit up straighter, but he comes in and closes the door.

"Relax. I just wanted to make sure you were okay."

That desperate niggle of attraction that I've been pushing down for weeks struggles to be heard. *He cares!*

I shove it right back down again. He's my colleague. He knows about the incident. He's just showing the same kind of concern any decent person would.

"I'm fine." I smile tiredly, letting myself sink back down. "It wasn't the most fun thing I've ever done, but I survived it. And I really like Kiara."

He studies me for a long moment, then comes over and flops on the couch beside me. "Yeah, she's great. She's been head of HR for as long as I've been working for JU."

I roll my head along the back of the couch so I'm looking at him. "Tried to poach you for HR, did she?"

"Nah." He shakes his head. "I was quietly looking for a new job when the role of Derek's assistant opened up. She had a pretty senior position open in HR at the same time, and she tried to convince me to go for it, but it was never a real option, and she knew that."

"Mmm." I close my eyes. It's not that late, not quite even close of business, but I still feel like I've been awake forever. Emotional exhaustion is the worst. I can hear Dimi talking quietly, and I try to stir myself to listen, but the warm, fuzzy feeling is just too nice to give up.

"Jase?"

There's a hand on my arm, shaking gently, and I force my eyelids up. Dimi's handsome face is smiling at me, and I smile back.

"Come on, I'll drive you home."

I pretty much just loll on the couch while Dimi goes back to his office, then he comes back in and shuts down my laptop. He's putting it in my bag and gathering the rest of my stuff before it occurs to me that I should be doing that.

I make myself sit up. "Hey, I can—"

He holds up his hand and shakes his head. "I've got it. Are you ready?"

Am I? Forcing my brain into gear, I think about it. "Yeah." I lever myself off the couch and follow him out into the reception area. Trav is there with John, and from the concerned look on his face, I figure he knows I'm not my best self right now.

"Call if you need anything," he says. "We're just a few minutes away."

I've gotta smile at that. It's nice to know people care. "I'm fine," I assure him. "I'll be a new man tomorrow." I hope. Psychological exhaustion goes away after a good night's sleep, right?

Trav says something to Dimi as I aim my feet toward the door, and I catch enough of it to know he's giving him my address. It's not until we get outside that I realize if Dimi drives me home, my car will still be here. I don't know why I didn't think of it before…

I mean, one driver plus one passenger equals one car.

"My car," I say, stopping beside it.

"It'll be fine here overnight," Dimi assures me. "It's locked, right?" I nod. "People leave their cars here all the time, so don't worry. And I'll pick you up in the morning."

How very domestic. That's a nice thought.

"Okay," I agree, because I'm tired and don't want to mess around with logistics, *not* because I like the idea of Dimi picking me up for work in the morning. I take the few steps needed to get me to Dimi's car and climb in. It feels nice to sit down again. Who knew emotional exhaustion was physically tiring as well?

Dimi starts the car and backs out. In moments, we're out of the lot and on the street. I break the silence.

"I'm okay, you know."

He glances over at me. "I know. But there's no reason why you shouldn't give yourself time to settle. It's not fun to have someone basically tell you you're not good enough, and you haven't really dealt with that. Not that I've seen, anyway."

I think about that. He's right. Ever since it happened, I've been drowning myself in work. It was easy enough to do, with no assistant to help with the load, and a great way to distract myself and pretend someone didn't refuse to work with me because of who I am. Filing a complaint with Kiara this afternoon forced me to confront that, to deal with my feeling about it—the anger, the hurt.

No wonder I'm exhausted. And it is nice to not have to think about anything right now. I'll just let Dimi drive me home, order takeout, and watch mindless TV for a while. Tomorrow will be a new beginning.

"Thank you."

"You're welcome."

"I hope it's not out of your way."

His look this time is incredulous. "Jason, it's Joyville. Nothing is really out of the way. Have you seen the size of the place?"

"It's not *that* small," I protest. I've only been here a few weeks, but I'm getting attached already. Sure, Joyville is technically a small town, but the population is over twenty thousand and growing. "It's going to get a lot bigger when the University of Georgia build their campus." Construction is due to commence sometime next year.

"True," Dimi concedes. A tiny frown plays over his mouth. "I know a lot of people are excited about it, but I wonder if it's a good thing."

I turn in my seat to face him properly, a little surprised. "You think it will ruin the town?" It's kind of a weird viewpoint. Joyville isn't a traditional small town that sprang up organically. It was designed and built for the express purpose of housing employees for Joy Universe. To this day, if JU was closed, the town would die. There just aren't any jobs in the area to sustain the population without the complex. Anything that brings in a diverse source of jobs—like a college campus—has to be a good thing, right?

"No, that's not it. I grew up here, and I always knew if I wanted to go to college, even community college, I'd have to leave, yeah? We all knew that. You either went to work in a lower-level job at JU and hopefully worked your way up, got a minimum-wage job at one of the stores here in town, or you left. I was lucky, in that I eventually got to come back to a great job here, but I think it was good that I left. I got to see bigger towns and cities, work and live there, get experience outside JU. Move away from my parents and family and learn to cope on my own in a place where nobody knew who I was and looked out for me. If the college campus had been here, maybe I wouldn't have left. I'd have gotten my degree, sure, and probably a job at JU, but I wouldn't be the same person and I don't know that I'd bring the same perspective and skills to my work."

I laugh. I can't help it, and Dimi looks a little hurt before his face smooths into a blank mask.

"I'm not laughing at you, I swear. I just…. You're worried that local kids won't be as well-rounded because they'll stay close to home?"

Silence.

Finally, he cracks a smile. "It does sound dumb when you put it like that," he admits, pulling out of JU's front entrance and onto the highway. "I guess the kids who want to stretch their boundaries will go away to college anyway, and the ones who probably wouldn't have gone will now have a chance to further their education."

"That's the spirit! It's all about perspective." I sound a little too enthusiastic, so I dial down the cheer. "You were just overthinking it."

"I do that sometimes." His voice is dry. "Another habit I get from my mom."

"It makes you a great manager, though."

"Thank you."

"And it's going to help us make Joy Village Theater Company a rousing success!"

"Jason?"

"Yeah?"

"You can stop talking if you want."

I lean my head back against the seat. "Thank you. I don't mind talking, but we should probably change the subject. I think we've exhausted all avenues of that conversation."

"What would you like to talk about?" He sounds amused now, and I'm happy I caused that.

Wow. Seriously, I've never felt so *honest* and open as I do right now. Exhaustion is better than drugs.

"Tell me about you," I demand.

"About me? There's not much you don't know already. I work at JU, love amateur theater, and have a big family. I'd be more interested in hearing about you."

I wave a hand dismissively. "Anything about me that's interesting, you can find on Google." Except for what my friends very carefully helped me keep out of the public domain. But I'm not talking to Dimi about the ex-who-shall-not-be-named. "Tell me what it was like growing up here."

He seems to think about it for a moment. "I guess it was like any small town. You've seen what it's like—the town is far enough from JU that the locals and the tourists don't mix. JU is really a separate place from Joyville."

"Did you go a lot? Since it was so close? There's a discount for employee families, isn't there?" I actually have no idea. I don't have a family who might want to know and I haven't tried to access a theme park except that first day when I was with Dimi and Trav, which was for work, so I don't know if I could get in free or for a discount or whatever.

"Sure. Employees get an annual pass every year, and any kids under sixteen are free—you just have to register them in your employee file. When you've worked here for two years, you get two annual passes. Dad and Gram and Gramps all worked at JU, so we all basically could come and go as we pleased—except you don't, when you live so close. Weekdays are for school and homework, and weekends are taken up with errands and sports and all that stuff." He chuckles. "Don't get me wrong, we came at least a few times a year, more when we got older and friends got part-time jobs here, but it's not like we spent every weekend at the parks."

"Did you get a job at one of the parks?" Part of me is delighted by the image of a teenage Dimi, maybe ganglier and not as confident, selling pretzels or something in one of those ugly uniforms.

"I did."

I wait, but that's all he says.

"What did you do?" I prod, and he sighs.

"Don't laugh," he warns, which tells me I'm going to laugh.

"No promises, but tell me anyway."

The look he shoots me vows retribution should I so much as chuckle.

"You know how the characters from Joy Inc. movies and TV shows wander around the park and take pictures with kids?"

"Yeah, of course." Oh my God, is he about to tell me that he was a handsome prince or something? Or maybe Joy Bear? I might actually die laughing if he once walked around in a bear costume, hugging kids and gesturing wildly to make himself understood.

"I was a handler for the ones who wear full headpieces."

I take a moment for that to sink in.

"You babysat for giant anthropomorphized bears?"

"Something like that." He tries to sound disgruntled, but I can tell he really didn't mind the job.

"So you held their hands and led them around and made sure kids didn't swarm them?" Man, he would have been so good at that.

"There's a bit more to it than that, but yeah."

"That's actually pretty cool," I admit. "I thought you sold hot dogs or something boring."

"I had a friend who did that. He thought he was too cool to be a handler and 'hang out with babies all day.' He regretted it when he realized he was spending his days out in the heat slinging food to bitchy customers and I was wandering around the park in fifteen-to-thirty-minute segments having kids think I was the coolest person ever."

Now I laugh, but he's laughing too, so it's okay.

"Did you have a job when you were a teenager?" He pulls off the highway onto the exit into Joyville, and I'm disappointed to realize we'll be at my place in a few minutes.

"I did," I say, wondering if we can sit in his car outside my apartment and just talk. I'd invite him up, but I'm afraid that will break the spell. We're not quite friends yet, I think, so it might be awkward. "It was nothing glamorous—I was a stock boy at the grocery store. Little kids definitely did not think I was cool. Well, not unless I was stocking candy."

He's still laughing as he turns onto my street. I like the sound of his laugh—it's deep, like his voice, but where he's so controlled and measured in everything else, his laugh is casual, a little uncontrolled. Listening to it feels like looking into a secret part of him.

Or I could just be getting dramatic.

The car comes to a stop, and Dimi says, "This is

it, right?" I look out the window, and yep, there's my building. It's a nice building, the neighbors are decent, and my apartment is comfortable, but right now I hate it.

Pushing down the irrationality of that, I say, "Yes. Thanks for the lift."

"Will you be okay?" His gaze is warm, slightly concerned still, and for a moment, I'm tempted to say no, ask him to stay.

"I'll be fine. I'm going to get a pizza or something and be slothful."

He smiles approvingly. "That sounds like a plan. I'll pick you up at seven tomorrow?"

That's a little late for him—for me, too—and I grin. "Six thirty, Dimi. I'll be fine tomorrow, I promise."

He agrees and waits for me to grab my things and get out of the car. I stand on the sidewalk, not moving an inch until he gives in and drives away. I don't need him waiting for me to go inside like I might faint at any moment if he doesn't watch me. No way do I want Dimi thinking of me as needing to be looked after.

Even if it was nice that he did.

CHAPTER SEVEN

Jason

I PREPARE FOR THE community holiday party as though it's the most important event of my life.

Small towns are foreign to me. Before now, I'd never lived in one—and I'm not totally convinced Joyville counts, since having JU right there means access to a lot of amenities and conveniences a lot of small towns don't have. Still, there's a sense of community in Joyville that I just never felt living in New York. And I don't necessarily mean that in a good way. In New York, I lived in the same apartment for fifteen years, and although I knew my neighbors well enough to smile and say hello (most of them, anyway), maybe exchange holiday cards or ask to collect mail while I was on vacation (only a few of them), I didn't actually know them. Jobs? Only if it came up in passing. Family? Same. Hopes and dreams? Please.

Here, though… within the first two days after I moved in, four of my neighbors knocked on my door to introduce themselves and ask if I needed anything. Within the first week, I'd met everyone in the building. Sure, it's not a huge building, but still. I'd also been given cookies, cake, and casseroles—which was a big help while I found my feet in the kitchen. Now, nearly a month later, I'm fully aware of what's going on in everyone's lives *because they tell me*. There's no such thing as just stopping to say hello—it turns into a fifteen-minute discussion of everything that's happened since last we spoke. Mrs. Henshall, who lives in the ground-floor apartment, likes to park her walker outside her door where she can sit on the little seat and watch everyone coming and going. I see her literally every day, sometimes twice a day, and yet she still seems to have a ton to tell me. Most of it is gossip about the other residents, which has made me utterly paranoid—what must she be saying about me?

One of the other residents, Marcus, actually caught me hiding in the stairwell once because I didn't want to face her. It was a catch-22 situation: stop to talk to her and be late for work, or hide in the stairwell in the hope she'd get distracted and be late for work. Lucky for me, Marcus knew immediately what I was doing and commiserated.

"You've timed it perfectly," he murmured as we both peeked into the lobby, being careful not to be seen. "Frank will come along soon and distract her. Then we just walk past, call hello and wave, and keep going."

"Does that work?" Would she be likely to stop us both to join the conversation? "And is that fair to Frank?"

Marcus chuckled. "Frank is her suitor."

Yes. He actually used that word. It took me a moment to assimilate, and by then I could hear a man talking to Mrs. Henshall.

"Come on," Marcus commanded, and we walked out of the stairwell and made a beeline for the front door. "Good morning, Mrs. Henshall! Hey, Frank! Talk to you later!"

I waved and called a greeting of my own, eyeing Frank, who definitely wasn't one of my neighbors. Then we were outside, free!

"Thank you," I declared fervently, checking my watch both to make sure I wasn't going to be late and also to note the time for future reference.

Marcus laughed as we went toward our cars. "No problem, man. You got plans after work? Come over for a beer, and I'll tell you about Frank."

I agreed and learned far more than I ever wanted to know about Frank (who lives down the street) and Mrs. Henshall's romance. Funny how she never mentioned *that* any of the times she accosted me with gossip.

Today, I will have no protection. Marcus has gone to Atlanta to be with family for the holidays, and Frank will be spending the day with his grandkids— although supposedly he visited this morning as usual.

And somehow I've been volunteered to accompany Mrs. Henshall to the community party.

How, you ask? Yeah, me too. I was talking to her last night, she demanded to know what my plans were for today, I shrugged and said something about being lazy, watching some movies, and maybe stopping in at the community party… and the next thing I know, she's instructing me to come and collect her at ten forty-five precisely and that she didn't mind if I didn't stay at the party all day, but I needed to let her know before I left so she could make alternative arrangements to get home.

It could be worse, right? I'm basically just giving her a lift. She could have expected me to dance attendance on her all day. And if she knows as many people in the community as I think she does, this will be a great way to meet people. Whether I'm just here for a year or for the long haul, it will be good for me to make some contacts and meet people outside of work. Maybe even start dating.

Not Dimi.

Whatever, I'm determined not to give her or anyone anything to criticize. Today, there will be no comments from me that can be interpreted as negative. I will be humble. I will be helpful. I will be cheerful.

It's all going to be okay.

Which is why I've spent an hour trying to decide what to wear. My first choice—chinos and a dress shirt—seemed like I might be trying too hard. After all, it's a community party, supposedly not formal. So I changed into jeans—nice ones—and a long-sleeved tee. But that was just too casual and resulted in a complete raid of my wardrobe. At moments like this, I really miss the ex-who-shall-not-be-named. For all his faults, as a costume designer he had an impeccable sense of style and could always put together the perfect outfit for any occasion.

In the end, I go back to my first choice. Chinos and a shirt are always a safe choice for a social occasion.

Dimi spoke to his mother, who said they would likely need savory dishes, so I made one of the few things I can actually cook well—mini quiches. The best part is that they taste just as good cold as hot and can be eaten with fingers. I grab the covered platter, check that I have my wallet, phone, and keys, and head out the door. Since I'm not trying to avoid Mrs. Henshall, I use the small elevator—the last thing I want is to develop a sudden case of klutziness and throw myself and the quiches down four flights of stairs.

Mrs. Henshall is waiting impatiently at her front door, and I check my watch just to make sure, but I'm definitely not late. It's still only ten forty-three.

"Good morning, Mrs. Henshall. Merry Christmas. You look lovely." She does. Her usual plain T-shirt and cotton skirt have been replaced with a very festive red dress that looks great against her dark skin and snow-white hair.

She looks me up and down, then nods. "Merry Christmas, Jason. You're such a handsome boy. Come and help me with this dish." She stands up from the seat on her walker and lifts the covered dish that was in her lap. I shake off the disorientation of being called a boy for the first time in about twenty years and go to take it from her. It takes us a while, since even with the walker she's not that sprightly, but we make our way outside, and I have her wait at the entrance while I go get my car. Originally I thought I might walk—it wouldn't have taken more than twenty or so minutes—but that was before I was pressed into service as a chauffeur.

Fortunately, when we pull up to the community theater, there's still plenty of parking available— probably because we're so early. It's only just after eleven. "I'll stop here and walk you in and then go park," I suggest, braking near the front door, but Mrs. Henshall shakes her head.

"Park there," she says, pointing to a space in the nearest row. "I can walk from there."

I hesitate, but the look she gives me is pretty convincing. I haven't been this afraid of anyone since I was a kid and one of the school bullies convinced me he'd trained his dog to eat people who annoyed him.

We make our slow way inside, and there are already more people there than I expected. The lobby is set up with long tables for food, and the doors to the theater are open, showing people circulating inside and what looks to be a bar area on the stage.

"Do you see anyone you know?" I ask, only belatedly realizing what a stupid question it is when she raises an eyebrow, making her forehead wrinkle even more. "I mean, where would you like to sit?"

"Go put the food down," she orders. "I can find my friends without you."

And that easily, I've been dismissed.

I'm still staring after her with my mouth open and the dishes in my hands when someone comes up beside me and clears their throat.

"You can put that down right over there."

The amused voice is familiar, so I shut my mouth and look over at Dimi sheepishly. "I feel so used."

He raises an eyebrow and glances after Mrs. Henshall. "You're her ride? Don't worry, she does that to everyone."

"Is that supposed to make me feel better?" I snort. "Let me put this down. I think I've made enough of an idiot of myself this morning."

We turn toward the food tables, and within moments I've delivered my contribution to the food table supervisor—and don't even get me started on that.

"Merry Christmas," I tell Dimi belatedly as he leads me toward the bar.

He grins over his shoulder at me. "Merry Christmas to you too. Meet my oldest brother, Patrick. Pat, this is Jason Philips." Dimi leans on the bar and waves a hand at the good-looking man screwing the cap back on a bottle of juice. There's a definite family resemblance, but this guy doesn't have Dimi's air of youthfulness. I was hugely surprised to discover that Dimi is actually twenty-nine, not the twenty-five or so I'd assumed—although it makes sense, because it would have been really weird for JU to give him this much responsibility just a few years out of college. Even at twenty-nine, he's ahead of the curve.

Patrick smiles and offers a hand. "Hey. Great to meet you. I applaud anyone who can work with this control freak." He tips his head toward Dimi and winks, and I shake his hand.

"Good to meet you too. And thanks—although I'll gladly take any tips you can give me. So far, I've mostly been letting him have his way, but that can't last forever."

Dimi laughs, which is a relief. I've never really teased him like that before, so I wasn't sure how he'd take it. Patrick snorts.

"Yeah, you can't let him win. You really need to talk to Cait or Mom. Or Jack. They were always best at handling him." He waves at someone behind me.

"I feel like I should object here," Dimi says. "Nobody needs to *handle* me. I don't get *handled* by anyone."

"You don't?" a new voice says. "Poor you. Though, it might explain why you're such a workaholic."

To my delight, Dimi huffs and rolls his eyes like a teenager. Is this what having a close family is like? If so, I really missed out.

Although I could probably live without having people comment on my sex life or lack thereof.

"Jason, meet my sisters Cait and Sienna. And Patrick's husband, Ryan." He sounds pouty and put out, but in a good way, a "this is what I put up with but I love them anyway" way. I want to kiss the smile back onto his lips.

No. No, I don't. I'm just carried away by the Christmas spirit. Or something.

I hide my panic and make myself smile and greet the newcomers. I've met half the Weston siblings now, and it's really easy to tell they're related. They all have dark hair and eyes, fair skin, and great bone structure.

I fall easily into conversation with them, first mostly teasing Dimi, but soon moving on to more general topics. The size of the group changes as people come and go, and somehow we drift away from the bar and end up grabbing food.

I'm trying to figure out what exactly is in some casserole-looking thing—eggplant or shoe leather?—when a voice beside me says, "Don't eat that, whatever you do. You must be new here to even be thinking about it."

I look over at the twentysomething woman sneering at the dish. She's wearing a fifties-style red halter dress that shows off two full sleeves of tattoos, and her hair and makeup are done to match. As she shakes her head in disgust, light reflects off the multitude of piercings in her ears, nose, and eyebrow. "Thanks for the tip."

I'd pretty much decided it was shoe leather anyway, but it's nice to have confirmation. "Although it looks like everybody else is wiser than me, and I feel kind of bad that it's all going to be left. Someone went to the effort of making it."

Her smile lights up her face. "Aren't y'all sweet? Don't worry about it, one of the committee will sneak it away soon and make sure there's only a little bit left. Irene will never know. I'm Chloe, by the way."

"Jason," I tell her. "It sounds like this isn't the first time Irene has brought… this." I don't even know what to call it.

"Every year," she says, wrinkling her nose. "Nobody has the heart to tell her how disgusting it is. She's got a heart of gold, but she's convinced herself she can cook and that this is her signature dish. And I know who y'all are."

She does? "Oh." What am I supposed to say? "Are you part of the community theater?" Who else would give a crap about an ex-Broadway director?

"Try the potato salad," she advises. "Tracey from the pharmacy makes it, and it's amazing. We're lucky there's still some left. It usually goes fast." I reach for the serving spoon as she continues, "Nah, I work part-time for Sascha Weston, Dimi's mom, and she mentioned that he was working with some big deal guy from New York called Jason something. You're the only person here that I've never seen before, and you were talking to Dimi earlier, so…." She shrugs.

"I'm not really a big deal." Not outside Broadway circles, anyway. "Do you really know everyone here?" I know it's not a huge town, but still. There have been a lot of people coming and going today.

"No, there're a lot I haven't met. But I never forget a face. Listen, you should be good with the rest of the food as long as you stay away from the chocolate mousse. It's a damn shame, because Mrs. Collins makes the best chocolate mousse I've ever tasted, but her grandkids are staying with her this week and I heard the oldest two snickering about switching the sugar for salt when she wasn't watching."

I make an immediate mental note to stay away from the chocolate mousse.

"Thanks, Chloe. Will you come and eat with me?"

She shakes her head. "Thanks for asking, but I'm here with family, and my mother will have a conniption if I don't eat with them. But it was great to meet you." She flashes me a grin and wanders off before I can say anything more.

The party really gets going as the day progresses, and even though I only meant to stay for a couple of hours, it's nearly four by the time I stop to look at my watch. I'm having fun, though, and there are still plenty of people hanging around, so there's no reason to leave—right? Mrs. Henshall already sent a minion over to tell me she was ready to go and that a friend was taking her home, so I'm officially free of responsibility.

And no, that has nothing to do with the fact that

Dimi hasn't really left my orbit all day. Or is it the other way around? Whatever, we've mostly been in the same group or conversation or within arm's reach of each other. It's purely coincidental. Probably he was looking out for me at first, since I didn't know anyone, and then since we have pretty similar tastes, it's no surprise we've gravitated toward the same conversations.

I'm talking to him and a couple of the performers from JU about our audition plans for the new year when an attractive woman not that much older than me comes over and puts her arms around Dimi from behind. He looks down at her hands on his chest, grins, and draws her around to give her a proper hug.

"Are you finally free?"

She shakes her head. "Not until the place empties, baby. You know that. But I can take a break to meet your friends." She smiles at us, and with a jolt, I realize that she must be Dimi's mother.

Who's not much older than me.

And doesn't that make me feel like a dirty old man.

"Mom, meet Sam, Parker, and Jason. Guys, this is my mother, Sascha."

Pleasantries are exchanged, but soon Sam and Parker excuse themselves and wander off, and Sascha Weston turns all her attention on me.

"It's so nice to finally meet you, Jason," she says, and I smile and hope that she can't tell I've been thinking decadent thoughts about her baby.

"You too. Dimi speaks so fondly of his family."

She laughs. "I'm sure he speaks not-so-fondly of us too, sometimes."

"You know me so well, Mom," Dimi says dryly, and she swats his arm.

"Don't be a brat. Now, Jason, how are you settling in here after living in New York? I went to college there, you know, and sometimes I still miss the convenience of living in such a big city."

We quickly fall into a discussion of our favorite places in the city. It turns out that Sascha is a little older than I first assumed and was long gone from the city before I moved there, but there are still a lot of old haunts that overlap our respective college days. It's a good twenty minutes before she sighs, looks over her shoulder toward the bar, and regretfully informs us that her break is over.

I end up staying until the very end—and then helping to clean up. There are enough volunteers that the work goes quickly, but it's still after seven before the committee shoos the last of us out to the parking lot. I look toward my car as the crowd begins to disperse, oddly averse to the idea of getting in and going home. I've been working hard this past month, plus I don't know—or *didn't* know—that many people here in Joyville, so my social life has been a lot less active than usual. I'd almost forgotten how much I like to get out and be with people.

"Hey."

The voice is almost as familiar to me as my own now,

and I catch myself smiling as I turn to look at Dimi. He's a little mussed after being in charge of folding the tables up and storing them away, and the less-than-his-usual-perfect look does something to me that I've been trying to ignore.

"You got plans for tonight?"

I shake my head. "No. It'll be me and some Christmas movies, probably."

"Great. Come over to my place. My brothers and I will be doing the same thing, but we'll add junk food and beer."

"Yes." The word comes out so fast, it surprises even me. "I mean, yes, thanks. Company would be great." What do I say next? "Uh, can I bring anything?"

He waves a hand. "Nah. My houseguests always cater Christmas night to make up for the fact that they've invaded my home and hogged my bathroom." He raises his voice for the last part, and two of his brothers jeer. I've only met one of them, but the other one has what I'm now thinking of as the Weston Family Looks, so he's gotta be a relative.

"Okay, so I'll follow you?"

"Sounds good."

We part ways to go to our respective cars. I sit in mine and take a moment to appreciate what a good day I've had. Nothing like Christmas Day last year, which was the first holiday in fifteen years that I'd been single for. That was a miserable day. Today's been full of cheer, and it's not done yet.

I start the car and pull out of my space to follow Dimi onto the road. He lives in the opposite direction from me, but it's still not that far, and I make mental notes about which streets will get me home the fastest later. Soon we're pulling up outside a cute townhouse with a postage-stamp-sized front garden and a bright blue door. Dimi parks in the garage, then waves for me to take the driveway.

"Nice garden," I comment when I meet them in the garage a moment later. "Do you look after it?" After living in Manhattan for so long, I have a tiny fascination with actual yards and gardens, rather than balconies and rooftop gardens.

The brother I haven't met yet laughs. "Dimi, garden? No freaking way. He gets someone out every couple weeks to weed it." He sticks out a hand. "I'm Mike, by the way. Number six."

"Number six?" I shake his hand, then realize what he means. "Oh! You're the third-youngest sibling."

"That's me."

"Jason Philips. I work with Dimi at JVTC." The garage door starts rolling down, and we head toward the inner door.

"Oh, I know who you are. I was there for the *Fake It 'Til You Make It* obsession."

I blink. Mike seems to have a skill for throwing me off-balance with his conversational gambits. "Obsession?"

"It wasn't an obsession," Dimi says as we enter the

kitchen, which is immaculately tidy except for an open bag of chips on the counter that he's glaring at. "Brody, are those yours?"

Brody grabs the bag, tips his head back, and pours the chips into his mouth. Chips scatter everywhere, and I can almost see Dimi's blood pressure going up.

"It was an obsession," Mike insists, not relinquishing the conversational thread. "You played the soundtrack at all hours of day and night and read the reviews *obsessively*—and it only got worse after you actually saw it."

Aww. Dimi's a fan of my work? That makes me feel all warm and melty inside. I sneak a glance his way and find him red-faced and staring at his brother like he wished his eyes shot laser beams.

"That's the kind of reaction we were hoping for," I say as smoothly as I can. Really, it is. And that show is a great one, one of the best I've ever directed. Plus, anything to make Dimi not regret inviting me tonight. "Did someone say something about junk food and movies?"

Mike smirks but falls into line. "Sure. Brody and I stocked up yesterday. We've got six flavors of popcorn, chips, about thirty different types of chocolate and candy, and beer, wine, and soda. What's your poison?"

I feel vaguely ill just thinking about all that food, especially after the way I ate today. "Uh, I'll have soda for now. Maybe popcorn later."

"Did anyone have the chocolate mousse today?

It was so bad. Is Mrs. Collins sick or something?" Brody crumples up the chip bag and tosses it into the trash can tucked neatly beside the fridge.

"Her grandkids switched the sugar for salt," I say automatically. "Sorry, I should have warned you."

"How do you even know that?" Dimi asked, getting out glasses for Mike to pour the soda into.

"Someone overheard them joking about it and told me. Chloe." I feel vaguely embarrassed, and I'm not sure why.

"Chloe who works for Mom sometimes?" There's a note of interest in Mike's tone, and I notice Brody has perked up too.

"Uh, that's what she said." I bite my lip to keep from laughing. Dimi's gaze meets mine, and I can see the merriment there. I guess Chloe *is* an attractive young woman. I just didn't really notice, what with being gay and nearly old enough to be her grandfather.

I studiously ignore the fact that she's not really *that* much younger than Dimi. Maybe seven or so years?

"I didn't get a chance to talk to her today." Brody actually sounds pouty, and Dimi can't hold back his laughter anymore.

"Please, like she'd ever look at you twice."

"Hey, women are into me! I get plenty of action, fuck you very much. I just have to snap my fingers to have chicks swarming."

Dimi points at him. "That's why she'd never look at you twice. Because you think of women in terms of snapping fingers and swarming. And don't ever let Mom hear you talk like that, either."

Brody opens his mouth to retort, but Mike steps in. "Movies," he announces, handing around the glasses of soda. "Brody, grab the popcorn and candy."

***

"So wait… she knows it's a haunted house and that there was something fishy about the guy's death, and she's been creeped out by other stuff that's happened, but she still goes to see what the weird noise was?" Brody, otherwise known as the simpleton, shoves more popcorn in his mouth and shakes his head.

"I don't think you can really call it a haunted house," Mike says thoughtfully.

"Of course it's a haunted house," Brody argues, spraying popcorn everywhere. I sneak a glance at Dimi, mostly to see the expression on his face. It really wouldn't surprise me if he murdered Brody before the night ends. His house is immaculate except for his brothers' crap. "A ghost lives there. How can it not be a haunted house?"

"Well… he's not really haunting it, is he? He just lives there. Most of the time people don't even know about him. And he owns it, too, sort of. And he's corporeal sometimes. A haunted house has nasty ghosts who make their presence known."

"Dude, no way." Brody sits up and grabs the remote. On the TV, *The Spirit of Christmas* freezes midscene. Dimi huffs and reaches for the wine, which he went to get about half an hour ago, and I hold out my glass for a refill. This is the fourth time Brody or Mike has paused the movie to debate something stupid.

I love it.

I'm sure it would get old if I had to put up with it every time I wanted to watch a movie, but tonight, with good company, too much sugar, and alcohol providing a pleasant haze, it's the best thing ever.

"A haunted house is any house that has a ghost in it," Brody declares. "And he doesn't own it—that's why they're going through all this bullshit in the first place. If he owned it, the lawyer chick wouldn't be trying to sell it."

Mike opens his mouth to respond, but Dimi gets in first.

"Whether it's officially a haunted house or not, it doesn't change the fact that weird stuff has been happening and she still went to check out the noise on her own. *But*," he hurries on as both brothers look like they're going to say something, "we all know that nothing bad happens, so can we unpause the damn thing and get on with it?"

"Dimi!" they both exclaim at the same time, shooting horrified looks my way. "Spoiler alert!"

I laugh, because they're just that precious.

I may have had more to drink today than I realized.

"It's okay, guys," I assure them. "I'm pretty sure this movie ends happily, since it's a Netflix Christmas movie."

"Still," Mike says, shaking his head disapprovingly at Dimi as he picks up his beer, "most of the fun is in the journey."

"Soooo… maybe we can *get on with the journey*?" Dimi gets up from his armchair to snatch the remote from Brody. "I want to watch that really bad movie after this."

"Which one?" Brody asks.

"Does it matter?" Mike counters.

Dimi just hits Play. The screen unfreezes, and I smile as I immerse myself back in the movie.

***

"Are they asleep?" Dimi's whisper is exaggerated, and I turn my head to meet his laughing gaze.

"If they're not, they're the best fake snorers I've ever heard," I say at a normal volume, and he snorts.

It's the wee hours of the morning. *The Spirit of Christmas* finished hours ago, and since then we've watched two movies that were so horrendously bad I don't even want to remember their titles. On the plus side, Brody and Mike decided the best way to get through a bad movie was to take a shot every time something cheesy happened or was said. The tequila came out, and needless to say, they were beyond plastered before we got halfway through the first movie.

I'd like to take a moment here to recommend you get some friends drunk and then watch bad movies with them. It enhances the experience tremendously.

They passed out a bit ago, and now it's just me and Dimi. In the semidark. In the silence of the night. Pretty much alone. Intelligence and inhibitions fuzzed by sugar and alcohol.

The butterflies in my stomach are going nuts. Sure, I know nothing is likely to happen. Dimi hasn't given any indication he wants it to—and why would he? We work together. I'm much older than him. I know that he's gay because of a conversation he and Trav had that I overheard, but he's never flirted with me or anything.

Well… not really. Just in that joking way.

So… yeah, there's no reason for butterflies. But it's been a long time since I've felt this will-he-won't-he-does-he-doesn't-he type of attraction. A long time since I've sat (sort of) alone in a darkened room with a man I was attracted to and wondered what was going to happen next. So if you don't mind, I'm going to let the butterflies have their way and enjoy this crazy attraction while it lasts. I loved being in a committed relationship for so long, loved the ex-who-shall-not-be-named (until I didn't), but I never expected to have to face the dating world again. I'm twenty years older than the last time I was single, a lot grayer, a bit softer, and a lot less inclined to hit the clubs. If I'm being strictly honest, after the breakup, I expected to spend the rest of my life alone. Not because I feel like I'm not lovable, but because everything felt so raw. It's hard to have your trust smashed. I didn't want to make that kind of commitment, put myself at that kind of risk again. I didn't feel attracted to anyone, even men I'd admired in the past.

So the butterflies are nice. It feels like healing. Like maybe I've got my old self back—just a little wiser.

"Come into the kitchen," Dimi says. "We can talk without waking these two morons."

He's not going to drop hints that I should go home? Because I was about to get moving—the administrative functions at JU have the day after Christmas off, but I planned to do some work anyway. I don't know how effective I'll be, though, what with being fuzzy from lack of sleep and slightly hungover.

I get up and follow him to his kitchen, which is lit only by the light above the stove. His townhouse is a little bigger than my apartment, but mine was renovated more recently and is a bit nicer. His has a more permanent feel, though—which makes sense, since he's been settled here for years, and I've just been here for a month.

He gets two glasses from a cupboard and fills them with water, then hands me one.

"Thank you." I didn't realize how thirsty I was until he gave me the glass. I drink and then lean against the counter beside him. "Are you going to leave them in there?"

Dimi shrugs. "They've slept worse places than my couch. Waking them is a pain in the ass, and then they'll be all grumpy." He smirks. "Plus, it's kind of my duty as their older brother to make sure they're as uncomfortable as possible. They're lucky I'm not taking advantage of this situation."

I laugh. I guess that's one reason to be glad my relationship with my siblings isn't that close.

"That leaves the guest room free, though, if you want to crash there. I'm not sure exactly how much you drank, but you probably shouldn't drive. And it's late."

I don't even hesitate. "Thanks, that's really kind of you." I hold back the wince. Once again, I sound like Aunt Gertrude. I set my water glass down beside me on the bench, mostly as a distraction, and when I look up again, Dimi's standing right in front of me.

My breath catches in my throat, and I nearly choke. I'm still trying to regulate my breathing when he leans in and kisses me.

It's quick. Just a press of his mouth to mine, a taste. By the time I get over my shock enough to kiss him back, to raise my arms to hold him, he's pulling away, stepping back.

"There are clean towels in the bathroom and extra blankets in the guest room wardrobe in case you get cold."

And then he's gone, leaving me half-frozen in shock in the dimly lit kitchen. It feels like hours before I can get my wits together enough to move, but it's probably only minutes. Numbly, I go down the hall to the guest room, close the door behind me, and collapse on the bed. It's neatly made, and I suspect that's Mike's doing—it wouldn't even occur to Brody.

Yes, I really am wondering who made the bed. Because if I don't think about the mundane, I'll have to think about the fact that Dimi kissed me.

Kind of.

Well, barely.

Was it a kiss? I mean, of course it was a kiss. Lips touched. That's a kiss. But was it a *meaningful* kiss? Or was it just a friendly kiss goodnight between two guys who work together and are becoming friends?

Does such a kiss exist?

It was over awfully fast. If it was a kiss that was supposed to mean something, to signify sexual or romantic interest, wouldn't it have lasted longer? Maybe included some tongue or touching?

I'm overthinking this. I haven't obsessed this much over a kiss since I was a teenager.

The question is… what do I do now?

Am I supposed to pretend the whole thing didn't happen?

Or is this the opportunity I've been waiting for?

It's not a secret (well, not to me or you—I really hope it's still a secret from everyone else) that I've been crushing hard on Dimi. Things started roughly between us, my fault, but over the last couple weeks they've gotten better. We're definitely friendly, and I think becoming friends. Especially after today. Today was a great day. So combine that with Dimi's kiss, and maybe the universe is giving me a great big flashing neon sign that I should be making a move.

Sighing, I lean back against the pillows. My brain is muddled by alcohol and sugar and exhaustion, and I really don't have the capacity to make a sensible decision right now. Or any decision. Best to get some sleep and think about it in the morning.

When I'll wake up in Dimi's house and have breakfast with him.

My dick perks up at just the thought and suddenly I have something else to concern myself with.

CHAPTER EIGHT

Dimi

WHAT THE HELL HAVE I done?

I barely slept at all last night. Who am I kidding—I *didn't* sleep at all. After I made that asinine comment about towels and blankets and left Jason in the kitchen, I fled to my bedroom to hide from my own abject stupidity.

What was I thinking?

Jason's hot. I'm not an idiot, I know that. Remember the first night we met when I could barely speak to him without tripping over my tongue? Not to mention the porn fantasy that I may or may not have revisited a few times in the last couple weeks. He's also intelligent, talented, amusing, and an all-around nice guy. I still don't know what prompted him to be a dick at our first meeting, but after seeing him all day, every day for a month, I'm inclined to say it was an aberration, not the norm. So if I had a list of things I look for in a man, he'd check all the boxes.

Except we work together and he's never really indicated that he's interested in me *that way*. Which means kissing him constitutes sexual harassment, made worse by the fact that on paper, he works for me.

I want to bang my head against my desk. Except it's not actually my desk—not anymore. I snuck out of my place before the sun was up because I wasn't ready to face Jason, especially not with my idiot brothers watching, but I only got halfway to the office before I realized that he was probably planning to work today like I was. So I came to the main administrative building instead and set up camp at my old desk outside Derek's office. His new assistant isn't likely to come in today, not with the offices officially closed and Derek away.

Let's sum up, shall we? I sexually harassed a subordinate, then ran away instead of dealing with the situation and am currently hiding in someone else's space.

I give in to the urge and bang my head against the desk. It hurts. It also sends nausea spiraling through me, because hello, hangover. I didn't drink as much as my brothers did last night, but I drank enough.

Slumping back in the desk chair, I sigh and rub my forehead. I can't even say what prompted me to kiss Jason. No, that's a lie. I'd been thinking about what it would be like all night. All day, really—since he turned up with Mrs. Henshall, proving what a great guy he is, looking utterly delicious in an amber-toned shirt that made his sherry-brown eyes almost golden. I've always been aware of how attractive I find him, but in a background kind of way. Remember the famous actor analogy? Yesterday, though, seeing him in a purely social environment, with no work to distract us, seeing how well he fits in with my life… that attraction crossed the line from theoretical to very real. It wasn't helped at all by my goddamn brothers and sisters and their innuendoes every chance they got. Seriously, you admire a guy's talent and drive for half your life, and when you finally get a chance to work with him, your siblings make a huge deal about that admiration. You should have heard the things Brody and Mike said in the car when I told them Jason would be joining us for movie night. And then Mike had to go and bring up my fascination (*not* obsession) with *Fake It 'Til You Make It*. They're both lucky I didn't shave them bald after they passed out.

So yeah, I was thinking of him in a nonprofessional context all night. Then we were standing in the dark kitchen, all alone, and he was smiling for whatever stupid reason, a bit mussed, less guarded than usual, and I just had to know what he tasted like.

Delicious, in case you're wondering.

The worst part? I feel like an utter shit, but I don't regret kissing him. How I did it, yes, absolutely. If I could go back and get some kind of sign from him first that he wanted a kiss, I would. But I will never forget how amazing that kiss was—and it was barely even a kiss.

I've gotta fix this, don't I?

Groaning, I drag myself away from the desk where I'm not doing any work anyway. I could sit here procrastinating and mentally beating myself up all day, but it won't change the facts—and tomorrow I'll have to go to my own office, where I work with Jason, and *work with him*. Better to get the awkward, uncomfortable part out of the way now and give myself a head start on any paperwork that needs to be done if he wants to file a complaint. Or worse, quit.

Shit.

He wouldn't do that, would he?

Suddenly I'm not just the fuckup who harassed a subordinate, I'm also the fuckup who flushed his career down the toilet. Finding another director at this stage will mean starting from square one—but I probably won't be the one who has to worry about that.

I want to hide under my old desk.

Instead, I suck in a deep breath the way Derek taught me, decide it's the stupidest thing ever and doesn't work, and trudge toward the stairs. I could take the elevator, but the stairs will take longer and I'm all about delaying the inevitable for as long as possible.

***

Unfortunately for my desire to procrastinate, I find Jason in the first place I look. He's in his office, sitting at the desk, staring into space, so distracted that he doesn't hear me come in. When I knock on the doorframe, he startles, then flushes dark red.

Great.

"Uh, hi. Got a second?"

He clears his throat. "Sure. Do you… um…. Have a seat." He doesn't get up or even look toward the couch, and I resign myself to this being painful. We don't often meet in each other's offices—mostly because they're really small spaces for two men our size and I needed more breathing room—but every time I've come in here to discuss something, he's abandoned the desk for the more informal couch.

I sit in the visitor chair and try to decide how to begin. I've been rehearsing what to say the whole way over, but now that it's time to actually speak the words to him, they seem wrong. He's looking at me, though, waiting for me to tell him what I want, and so I open my mouth and hope the right words will come out.

"I'm sorry." Okay, that's not a bad start. His expression becomes a little guarded, but not overtly disgusted or upset. "I… I overstepped the bounds of…." No, that's stupid. "I mean, I… I shouldn't have kissed you like that. I'm sorry."

There's a long silence. My heartbeat hammers in my ears, and a wave of heat rises from my chest into my face. I can't read his expression at all—he's totally blanked it, which is so unlike him that it freaks me out. This is it.

Do you know the worst part? Right now, at this moment, I actually don't care about my career. I don't care that I'll likely never get a dream job like this again. That I'll probably have to leave JU and Joyville, my home, my family. That I've let down so many people who believed in me, who put their necks on the line to get me this job. Instead, what I care about is that I've killed the seeds of friendship that were growing between me and Jason. That I've destroyed any chance there might possibly have been of that friendship one day organically growing into something more. I never even realized I'd been harboring those secret hopes, but now that they're gone… it's devastating.

"You're sorry you kissed me?" he asks, and his voice is so sharp in the silence that I jump and blurt, "No. I mean, yes."

Fuck. This is not going well.

He raises an eyebrow, and after all these weeks, I finally see the asshole director he's reputed to be. "Yes or no?"

I struggle to respond. What can I say that won't make this worse? If I say no, I'm a creepy guy who takes pleasure in harassing his colleagues. If I say yes—

Wait.

"Why does it matter?" I ask. A tiny, teeny, almost nonexistent flame of hope has flared to life inside me.

We stare at each other across the desk.

It seems like neither of us is willing to lower defenses. I guess since I'm the one who preempted this whole fucked-up mess, I should be the one to give first.

Right?

At least it'll end this stalemate. And maybe I'll stop sweating.

"I'm sorry I kissed you without making sure you wanted that, and I'm sorry I've made things awkward and disrupted our working relationship, but I'm not sorry I kissed you." Instantly, I want to add another hundred disclaimers, but I force myself to shut up. Babbling is not going to help this situation, and I think I was clear enough.

I hope.

He blinks, and it seems like it's in slow motion, his lids lowering, lashes sweeping down, then up, until I'm once again staring into those golden-brown eyes.

He sighs. "I'm not sorry you kissed me, either."

It takes about a week and a half for his words to sink in, and then I surge out of the chair, adrenaline exploding through me…

…and stand awkwardly in front of his desk, not sure what to do next.

So I sit back down.

He's smiling now, and even though it's kind of at my expense, I'm glad.

"If you'd asked me if I wanted that kiss, I would have said yes. And I think we're both old enough and professional enough to not let this fuck up our work."

Right. That's an opening.

"I agree."

The words hang in the air as we continue to look at each other across his desk. I should do something. Say something. Lunge across the desk and kiss him.

No. Wait.

I stand abruptly. "Come on." I don't wait, just turn and stride out of his office, through our reception area, down the hall, and out into the street. The area behind the theater is abandoned, what with nothing happening inside. I wait until Jason steps out to join me, a baffled look on his face, then pin him against the side of the building and kiss him.

Properly, this time.

I'm not really a romantic person, but I swear, music soars, birds sing, and colors explode. His lips are so soft and warm and wet, and his body against mine is nothing but temptation. Neither of us shaved today, and the friction of our morning beards is the sexiest thing I've felt in a long time.

By the time we break apart, we're both breathing hard, and I'm flushed hot all over. His cheeks are pink and his eyes glassy. It's a great look on him, and I love that I made him look that way.

"No kissing, no sex, no anything in the office," I pant.

He stares at me blankly, then nods. "Only outside the office." He hesitates, then surges forward to kiss me again.

This time when we break apart, I can barely remember where we are.

"Uh… were you working on something important?" *Please say no*.

"Nothing that can't wait." His lips are puffy. I made them that way.

"Do you want to…?" I jerk my head toward where our cars are parked, this time hoping he says yes.

"My place. Your brothers were still unconscious on your couch when I left."

Oh hell. I forgot about them. "I'll follow you," I promise, literally doing so as he begins walking. My eyes are on his ass, so I nearly run into him when he stops abruptly. "What's wrong?"

"I need to stop at the drugstore."

Being an intelligent man, I catch on quick. "Oh." I guess that makes sense—he's only been in town a month, and he's been working all hours. I have stuff at my place, but if I stop by there to grab it, my brothers… well, let's just say, I'll never hear the end of it. "I'll go," I offer, "and meet you at your place."

Three minutes later, I'm in the car and on my way to the store. It'll take me two minutes, tops, to get in there and grab what I need. Even if there's a line at the register, I should still only be five or six minutes behind Jason. We can be naked a minute after that.

So of course I run into my grandmother and sister at the store.

"Dimitri!"

I get called Dimitri by my grandmother, occasionally an employer, or when I'm in trouble, so even if I didn't recognize the voice, I would have known who was behind me. I close my eyes. Running into Gram does not bode well for my plans to be naked in the next ten minutes—or for my erection.

Turning with a very fake smile pasted on my face, my spirits dive even further when I see Sienna with Gram. "Hi," I say and bend to kiss Gram's cheek. "How are you today? Not too tired from yesterday?" Gram is a force of nature, but she's nearly ninety-two. She didn't stay for the whole party, but it's still been a busy few days. I'm actually surprised Mom didn't try to stop her going out today.

Although, knowing Gram, Mom probably did try to stop her—and failed.

Sure enough, she waves her hand as if my question was ridiculous. "What are you doing here? You said you were working today." It's almost an accusation, and I immediately feel guilty.

"Yes, I, uh, just need to pick up some things and then Jason and I will be… brainstorming for the rest of the day." I mentally eviscerate myself but keep a bland expression on my face. I can't show weakness in front of Sienna—or Gram, for that matter.

Sweat trickles down my spine.

"We won't keep you, then," Gram declares. "You work so hard."

Could she have said anything to make me feel worse?

I muster up a sickly smile. "Thanks, Gram. I'll see you on Monday. You too, Sienna." I'm actually a little afraid, because Sienna hasn't said anything yet.

She knows.

Impossible. How could she?

She meets my gaze, and the wicked gleam there is all the proof I need.

"See you Monday, Dimi."

I give a weird little wave and stroll away as nonchalantly as I can. Now I have to somehow get what I need and get out without running into them again, because I do not want Gram to realize what I meant by "brainstorming."

By the time I make it out to my car, I'm sweating profusely and having flashbacks to the time my mom walked in on me watching internet porn when I was fifteen. I'd just decided that being gay was no longer a possibility but a definite when she opened the door. Needless to say, I came out to myself and to her that day.

It's something I still occasionally have nightmares about.

I drive to Jason's feeling a lot less sexy than before, but sure that just seeing him will help get the mood back.

Until I walk into the lobby of his building and see him talking to Mrs. Henshall.

Or rather, trapped by Mrs. Henshall.

I sigh, then wade into the fray.

"Hey, Mrs. Henshall."

She looks up as I join them and narrows her eyes. It makes her dark brown skin wrinkle even more than it is already. "Dimi, what are you doing here?"

"I came to talk shop with Jason—and to say hello to you. I barely got to see you yesterday, you were so popular."

Her expression tells me I'm not fooling her, but she sniffs and nods. "It was a lovely party. Your mother and the committee work so hard."

"They do," I agree, because it's true. It takes a shitload of effort to pull it off, but the community party is an essential part of Joyville.

We chat for a few minutes more, and then she says, "It's time for my show. I'll see you boys soon. Don't go causing any trouble."

The look Jason gives me over her head is agonized, but we merely agree, wish her a good day, and then watch in silence as she shuffles with her walker into her apartment. The door closes, and Jason grabs my arm and drags me to the elevator. Neither of us say a word until we're in and the door is safely closed, and then we collapse in fits of laughter.

"I'm fifty-three years old," he gasps. "What the hell kind of trouble am I going to cause?"

The elevator door opens, and we get ourselves under control enough to exit and get into his apartment.

And an awkward silence descends. We stand there, looking at each other. What is wrong with us? We've both had sex before.

Screw it.

I grab the front of his shirt and yank him to me. Our mouths collide, and suddenly the awkwardness is gone. Everything is right.

Jason loops his arms around me, and without pulling away from the kiss, tugs me back—presumably toward his bedroom. Or the couch. Or a bare patch of wall. I'd be fine with any of the above, because I have my hands and mouth on him, finally. I yank his shirt out of my way and fumble with his belt. We stumble, and our mouths break apart for a second before he pulls me back in.

It might be a minute or an hour later when we collapse sideways onto his bed. I've managed to get his pants open, and he's stripped off my shirt and is currently licking his way across my chest. I've always had sensitive skin, but I feel like I'm on fire right now. I thread my fingers through his thick hair, trying to resist the urge to clench a fist, and he moans and lifts his eyes to my face.

"Get naked."

I jackknife off the bed and get my clothes off so fast, it leaves me dizzy. When I look back at Jason, he's still lying there, a startled and impressed expression on his face.

"I think I'd throw my back out if I tried that," he muses.

"Less thinking, more stripping," I order, and he grins and rolls off the bed.

"Did you get what we need?" he asks, and I look around. Where the hell is the bag from the drugstore?

"Yes. Wait." I leave him to get out of his clothes and retrace our path from the front door. Sure enough, I dropped the bag right around the time I grabbed him. By the time I get back to the bedroom, Jason is naked, sprawled on the bed, and stroking a mouthwatering erection.

I take a flying leap toward the bed, making him yelp and scramble to get out of the way.

"What is wrong with you?" he scolds, but he's laughing as he slips a hand behind my neck and pulls me down for a kiss.

We get distracted for a little while—he just tastes *so damn good*—but then the bag crinkles beside us, and he breaks the kiss and reaches for it. A second later he tosses the box of condoms to me.

"We should probably have discussed this before, but top or bottom?"

"Anything that will have us both coming," I declare, gaze fixed on his nipples. His chest hair is surprisingly sparse, given how thick the hair on his head is, and his nipples are dark pink and hard and look like little candies I want to suck.

"You're versatile?" he asks, and I hesitate, because… not really. But I don't *hate* bottoming, and I really will do anything this afternoon if it means being with Jason.

He's watching me now with a sneaky smile on his puffy, delicious lips. "What's your preference?"

"Topping," I admit. "But I don't mind bottoming occasionally." Fuck, this really is something we should have discussed. Jason's used to being in charge at work, just like me—does that carry over into his sex life?

"Good, because I love to bottom." He nods to the condoms. "Get one on," he commands, bossy bottom that he is, opening the bottle of lube, but I'm frozen, watching with my mouth open as he pours lube onto his fingers and slicks himself up.

He's. So. Fucking. Hot.

It's not until I feel myself beginning to drool that I snap back to reality. He wants me to do him. I want to do him. What the hell am I just sitting here for?

I tear into the condom box and get myself suited up in record time. Jason's eyes are on me as he fucks himself with his fingers, and I'm so hard I almost can't bear it, but there's one thing I want—really want, desperately want—before I fuck him.

I lean down and lick his dick.

His groan is deep, guttural. "Don't," he warns. "I'm so close, and if I come, I'll be too sensitive for… and I really want you to…." He seems unable to finish sentences, and I love that.

"I just wanted a taste," I promise. "There's plenty of time for more later. We have all day."

His movements falter, and a shadow crosses his expression.

"What?" I ask, concerned. "What's wrong?"

He hesitates, and I move back a few inches and straighten.

"Do you not want…?"

"No, I do," he hastens to assure me. "But… I'm not thirty anymore. You said we have all day, but it might *be* all day before I can…."

Oh.

Is that all?

"Then we spend the day kissing and fooling around until you can," I say, shrugging. "It still feels good, right, even if you take longer to—"

"Yes," he interrupts.

"Right, so I can still lick you all over. It's better this way, actually, because I'll have time to really explore and get my fill. I love the taste of you and—"

This time he cuts me off with his mouth on mine.

I've said already how amazing kissing him is, but it bears repeating. I honestly don't care if he goes off like a rocket right now, because it means I can spend a couple hours kissing him until he's ready to go again.

Although….

I break the kiss and bend again to lavish some attention on his hard, leaking cock. It's a little longer than mine, not as thick, maybe, and leans a little to the left. It's also the best thing I've ever tasted, except maybe for Jason's lips, and I can't get enough, licking around the head before taking it into my mouth for a couple of hard sucks.

The noise that explodes from Jason makes me feel like a superhero, and I'm seriously tempted to keep going… but he's already slicked himself up, and I also want desperately to be inside him. There are going to be plenty of opportunities to suck him dry. This first time we're together, I want to be buried in his ass.

I give him one final lick and draw back. He's panting, lips parted, eyes glazed, looking hot as fuck. "You got a preferred position?" I don't care how I do him.

He blinks a couple times, then draws his knees up and opens them wide, displaying everything he's got.

I swallow hard. His hole is pink and glistening with lube, and I've never seen anything so inviting.

Leaning over, I steal another kiss from his lips, then kneel between his legs and position the head of my cock at his opening, tracing along his crack. His indrawn breath is like music to my ears.

Slowly, so slowly because I want to savor every second of this, I breach him, feeling the initial resistance and then the give as I slide inside. He's hot and tight, and it's honestly everything I can do to keep myself from coming right this instant. I keep my movements slow, both because I don't want to hurt him and because I don't want to go off too soon.

"Dimi," he grits out through clenched teeth, "I'm not a virgin and I'm not delicate. Get a move on."

Huffing a laugh, I adjust myself, draw back a little, and thrust home.

We both groan, and it feels so good that I do it again. And again.

Soon I've established a nice rhythm that has us both panting and moaning. I alternate between the incredible sight of my dick sliding in and out of Jason's ass and the incredible sight of his face as I fuck him. I'm a convert to the missionary position, because watching his every reaction while he's wrapped around me is hotter than anything else, ever.

Except maybe…

"Touch yourself," I gasp. I'm not going to last much longer, and I want to see him come.

He opens his eyes and focuses on me for a moment, and something he sees makes him smile, a secret, smug little smile. He reaches between us and grabs his cock, squeezing, his eyes rolling back, and suddenly I feel him tightening around me.

"Ungh… Jason," I manage, and he lets out a breathy chuckle, then moans when I change angles and nail his prostate.

Moments later, he's spraying cum over both of us, and just the sight of his O face is enough to make me lose it.

***

I'm lying half on Jason, half on the mattress, sated, sweaty, and drowsy, enjoying the repetitive stroke of his fingers through the hair at my nape, and I think I've been ruined for sex with anyone else, ever.

That must have been a fluke, right? A one-off thing as a result of the weeks of slowly escalating tension between us and the adrenaline of the day?

Maybe we should go again to make sure. I can make good on my promise to lick him all over.

As soon as I can move again.

"Dimi?"

"Mmm?"

"Can I ask you something?"

I stir and roll a little reluctantly off him and turn so I can see his face. Soon we'll need to go clean up, but I like this quiet time with him. "Sure."

"It's about your name."

That gets my attention. I don't know what I was expecting him to be thinking about right now, but my name isn't it.

"What about my name?"

He moves, propping himself up on an elbow, and blinks lazily at me. "I like it, but none of your brothers and sisters have names like it."

Oh. Is that all? I smile at him. "My great-grandfather's name was Dimitri. He died about six weeks before I was born, and Gram asked my parents if they'd give me his name as a middle name or something to show respect. They liked the name, so…." I shrug. "The shortened form is because Patrick and Cait were too lazy to say it properly when I was a baby, and it stuck. My siblings' names were all just picked from a baby name book or whatever TV show Mom was watching."

Jason looks fascinated. "So your gram is, what, Russian?"

"Ukrainian," I correct. Gram's quite sensitive about that. "Her father, who I'm named after, was some big deal diplomat in Berlin in the years after WWII. Gramps was stationed there with the army at the time, and he and Gram met. This was before East and West Berlin were so strictly separated. They fell in love, and by the time he was due to come back to the States, they'd already been married for months."

"So she came with him and said goodbye to her family?"

"Yeah." I always feel a pang when I think how Gram must have felt, leaving behind everything to come to a new place where she knew only one person. "They didn't know then how difficult it would become to stay in touch with her family. At the time, they planned to visit back and forth—not often, of course, but a couple times a decade, maybe."

"But the Cold War got in the way?"

I nod. "Gram never got to see her family again after she left Germany. They managed to exchange letters for a while, so she knew they'd moved back to Kiev, but things got sketchy for a long time. They did make contact again after the end of the Cold War, and she spoke to her parents on the phone quite a few times before they died."

He lies back down. "I wasn't paying a lot of attention to politics back then, but I still remember what a big deal it was when the wall came down."

I say nothing. I literally wasn't born then, so I have no story about where I was when I heard and what it meant to me. I asked Patrick once—he was nearly ten at the time, and even though he was too young to realize what it really meant, he knew that Gram had family he'd never met because of the Cold War, and he was aware of how excited Gram and Gramps and Mom and Dad were.

Jason seems to realize why I've gone quiet, because he turns on his side and his gaze searches my face. "Is it weird for you that I was partying and beginning my career when you were an infant?"

I actually take a minute to think about it, because before this moment, it never occurred to me exactly how many years there are between us.

"No," I say finally. "I hadn't thought about the fact that your growing up experiences will have been very different from mine, but couldn't that be the case even if we were the same age?"

"We're not talking about socio-economic or regional differences," he warns. "We're talking about me watching Live Aid on TV and sulking because my parents caught me trying to sneak out to hitchhike there with my friends, while for you, it's something you studied in school."

I decide not to mention that we barely even studied it. His meaning is pretty clear, but it doesn't change my mind. "What that means is that there are going to be things we see from a different perspective. That's not a bad thing. We'll find out as we go if it's something we can't deal with." I raise an eyebrow and wait for his nod before continuing. "If you're worried that I have a daddy kink or something, don't."

He suddenly looks incredibly vulnerable. "It's… it didn't escape me yesterday that your mom is only a little older than me."

"I'll tell her you said that; she'll be thrilled." I smirk. "Mom's sixty-seven, and Dad's nearly seventy. Sure, you're closer in age to them than me, but I don't think of you as being a parental figure—or even as being in their age bracket." I lean forward and kiss him. "This honestly is not weird for me. Our ages are not a factor here. You're just a smart, handsome, talented guy who I'm attracted to." I kiss him again, and he grins against my mouth.

"I guess I'm okay with that."

***

My fingers itch to smack the smirk off Trav's face. I'd regret it, of course, because Trav's a good friend, but there would also be the satisfaction of wiping away that smirk.

"Let me make sure I understand," he says, sounding insufferably amused. "You and Jase hooked up. Despite the fact that you're now in the position to live out every workplace porno ever made, you've made a strict pact to keep all personal interaction out of the office. And you want me to act as your safety net-slash-referee."

"It's not a pact," I mutter, "and we just want you to warn us if you think we're letting our personal stuff affect work, not be a referee." Jesus, what would he even be refereeing?

I deliberately don't let myself think about the whole workplace porno thing. Well, not much, anyway.

"Of course it's a pact. You both agreed to do something. That's a pact."

"Stop calling it a pact. It's not a pact. It's just an agreement."

"Sure." His tone says more clearly than anything else that he's still thinking of it as a pact. I think that irritates me more than the smirk did.

There's really no reason for me to be irritated. In the four days since Jason and I first hooked up, we've been fucking like bunnies. I'm so blissed-out sated that most of the time I float around with a stupid-ass smile on my face. And so far, we've been totally succeeding at keeping sexy times out of the office. We (eventually) talked it out and decided we weren't going to do anything as "formal" as dating, but that this was more than just fucking. No sex, groping, kissing, or personal stuff during work—although we agreed that short conversations along the lines of "my place tonight" or "what do you want for dinner" were okay—and it was Jase's idea to ask Trav if he'd pull us up if we slipped.

Wait—if it was his idea, how did I end up being the one who had to ask?

Pushing the thought aside for now, I say, "So? Will you?"

"Of course, but I don't think you guys will have any issues." He grins broadly. "Congrats, by the way. I wondered if there was something there, but you're both fucking closed books."

"To each other, as well," I muttered. "Uh… could you maybe keep this to yourself?" The gossip circuit at JU is highly developed, and I'd really rather not be fodder for it.

The look Trav gives me tells me I'm shit out of luck. "I'm telling Derek," he insists, and I nod, because I never expected to keep this secret from Derek. "You know it's going to get out," he warns.

"It's probably already out, but I just haven't heard the rumors yet." That makes me feel rather glum.

"Are we ready?" Jason calls as he comes across the theater to where we're standing. I guess lunch break is over.

"We're ready," Trav confirms, and we take our seats again as John goes to call in the next lot of performers.

It's day one of auditions, and so far things are going really well. We have to do these auditions in stages throughout the week, since the performers are all JU employees who have shifts in the parks, but the scheduling turned out to be less of a challenge than I'd expected. And the turnout has been great—not everyone is interested, of course, but the numbers align with what I projected. Trav and I have our secret wish list of performers for the major roles, but Jason just rolls his eyes and insists he doesn't want to know so his decision making won't be influenced. He's so adorable when he's pretending to be exasperated.

Er. I didn't just say that. Working hours. Sorry.

Anyway, we're already building a short list of people to call back for a second audition. Watching the performers, I can finally let go of the final niggle I had about *Walk of Life*. There was a secret part of me, way deep down inside, that still wanted to produce it for our debut show, no matter how logical and sensible I was being about giving it up for *Out of Line*. But now I can see that Jase and Trav were right. We have some amazingly talented young performers, but the key word there is young. They haven't had time yet to develop the performance maturity they would need for a show like *Walk of Life*. *Out of Line* will give them the opportunity to exercise their ability while still letting us put on a brilliant show.

By the time the end of the day rolls around, I feel a deep sense of satisfaction—and a minor dread. The satisfaction is because the auditions went really well. The dread is because Kiara sent me a message and wants me to nag Jason into picking an assistant. The original plan had been for recruitment to begin in the new year, but she apparently didn't have enough to keep her occupied over the Christmas break and not only assigned a new recruiter to the job, but that recruiter—Sean, who is scarily efficient, even for me—has already rescreened the previous applicants and picked some contenders that the old recruiter discarded despite their being qualified. From the undertones of the message, I got the impression that the recruiter had some definite prejudices and is now unemployed.

Sean sent the newly selected candidate applications to Jason this morning, at which point Jason thanked him politely but said he was too busy this week to look at them and would get back to him in the new year—which is three days away. That's apparently not good enough for Kiara, and I'm not fool enough to argue with her.

So now, as Trav gets up and gathers his things, I clear my throat. "Jase, can you hang around a second? I need to talk to you."

He looks a little surprised but shrugs and settles back in his seat. Trav smirks. "I guess it's after hours, but no funny business in the theater. I'm counting it as part of the office."

I flip him the bird, and he laughs as he leaves.

"What's up?" Jason asks. There's a sparkle in his eye that tells me he's considering "funny business."

"Have you looked at the assistant applications yet?"

The sparkle disappears, and I hate that I did that. My job should be to put it there, not take it away. Maybe we can bend the rules and "christen" the stage?

I push the thought aside. That's an idea for later—if I can overcome my own conscience.

"You need the help, Jase. Leaving them for later won't change anything." I try to sound gentle without being condescending. I don't blame him for being a bit nervy about this, but he does need an assistant.

He sighs. "Yeah. I know. Today's been busy, but I could probably have made time. I'll do it now." He's distinctly unenthused.

"Want me to help?" It might mean being late to Monday night dinner, but I'm willing to do that if it makes Jason happy again.

He brightens. "Would you?"

"Sure."

He pulls out his tablet and with a few taps manages to bring up the applications. He's really mastering the JU app.

Sean has sent four applications, and they all look good. We scan them to see if there's anything obvious that would disqualify the candidates, but there isn't, so we go back to review more thoroughly. Jase makes notes on the first two, but I can tell he's not particularly excited about either. The third one is going much the same way until I see a note about part-time work the applicant has done recently, and something clicks in my head. "Oh, this is Chloe. You met her at the Christmas party, remember? She worked for my mom whenever she was home on break from school."

He pauses in the middle of making a note and skims back to the top of the form to read her name. "This is Chloe? Tall, blunt-spoken, dresses like a pinup and has tattoos?"

I look at him. "Why do you seem surprised?"

"I shouldn't be—shame on me for passing judgment. Her education is fantastic. You're right, I liked her. Do you think she'd fit with the team?"

I consider it. "Yeah, but I don't know her that well, so don't decide to see her based on my opinion. Want me to ask my mom?"

He nods. "Please. I'll get Sean to set up an interview anyway, though." He flips to the next application and makes a face. "I may as well interview all of them. Sean seems to know his stuff, and I'm just wasting both our time sitting here. It's going to come down to personal impressions."

"Probably," I agree. "But it's not a waste of time."

His smile is indulgent and loving. "You need to get to dinner with your family. I can do this on my own. Come on, let's get out of here."

"Are you sure?" He's right, but….

He kisses me quickly, so quickly I don't even have time to enjoy it.

"Hey, that was barely a real kiss!"

"Which means it doesn't break the rules." He winks.

Who can argue with that?

***

I'm only a little bit late for dinner—everyone's just settling in at the table when I get to the house. Mom raises an eyebrow at me but only says, "If you want beer, it's in the fridge."

"Nope, I'm good with water," I tell her, detouring to drop a kiss on her cheek before I slide into my chair. Brody, beside me, passes me the green beans, smirking like an idiot. His school doesn't go back until next week, so we're unfortunately stuck with him until then. Fortunately, though, the rest of our visiting sibs have gone home, so he's out of my place and staying here with Mom and Dad as of this morning.

The smirk is worrying, though. It means he's probably planning to mention the fact that I pretty much abandoned him and Mike and disappeared from my own home for four days. That's the kind of thing the simpleton does—it doesn't occur to him that I *will* exact revenge.

We get about halfway through dinner on pleasant conversation before Gram asks me if I took any real time off or just went right back to work after Christmas. "Don't be that 'all work and no play' cliché, Dimitri," she warns, and I groan internally because she's just given Brody the perfect opening.

"You don't need to worry about Dimi, Gram,"

he announces gleefully. Could he be any more of a child? I shoot Patrick a look. Clearly we failed in our responsibilities as older brothers if he's still this dumb. "He's been playing *plenty* since Christmas."

There's a momentary lull as conversation and movement cease. Heads turn in our direction, expressions a mix of surprise and sheer dumbfoundedness, because nobody can really believe the simpleton just made a sexual innuendo about me to Gram. She's never been prudish, but some things you just don't say to your grandmother at the dinner table. Even the kids have gone quiet, no doubt sensing the mood.

Brody, of course, is the only one who's oblivious. "When a man doesn't come home for four days except to pack a bag real quick, you've gotta assume he's having a real good time, am I right?"

Patrick shakes his head slowly. "Did we drop you on your head too many times when you were a baby?"

"What?" he protests, all wounded innocence. I really want to pinch him, but with all eyes on us, Mom would never let me get away with it.

Fuck my life. I'm twenty-nine years old, forging ahead in my career, respected at work… and reduced to wanting to pinch my younger brother at the dinner table.

"I'm just saying, it's good to know Dimi's not a complete workaholic. He's just as capable as anyone of having a four-day sex marathon."

I give in to temptation and pinch him. Hard.

Luckily, everyone is too busy telling him what an idiot he is to notice. He glares at me, rubbing his arm, but from experience knows better than to try pinching back. At least I managed to drum something into his head while he was growing up.

Finally, Gram's voice rises above all the rest. "All right, we've wasted enough time talking about this. Brody, if your brother had wanted to share about his personal life, I'm sure he would have. It's not your job to do it for him." The look she levels at him has him squirming in his chair. He mutters an apology, and the room falls silent for a few glorious moments as we resume eating.

Until a little voice says, "Uncle Dimi, what's a sex marathon?"

CHAPTER NINE

Jason

I THINK I'VE ALREADY mentioned that Dimi could probably take over the world if he wanted to, right? Well, the person at his right hand would be Sean, the recruiter assigned to find me an assistant. I didn't send him a message about setting up interviews until after six last night, but when I checked the app at seven this morning, he'd sent me the schedule of interviews... all for today. It's New Year's Eve!

So now I'm sitting in my office, three interviews down, feeling a little more confident about it all. The candidates were good, professional, and easy to talk to, and when I made a point of saying I was gay—which I've never done before during a hiring process, and frankly, it made me feel a little dirty—one blinked and said, "I don't know how you want me to respond to that—um... that's nice?" Another grimaced and replied, "Coming out all the time is a bitch, isn't it?" And the third smiled and said, "Cool. Is there a significant other who gets access to you at all times, no matter what you're doing?" My takeaway from that is that Sean did a thorough job of screening.

John, who has been single-handedly doing the tasks that he should be sharing with my assistant, including acting as receptionist, knocks lightly on the door and sticks his head in. "The last applicant is here."

"Thanks, John." I owe the guy a bonus.

He disappears, and a moment later, the door opens properly and Chloe walks in. Her dress this time is blue and has cap sleeves, but the style is similar to what she was wearing at the holiday party, and her smile is just as friendly. I get up and walk around the desk to shake her hand.

"Hi, Chloe. Nice to see you again." It really is.

"Nice to see you, too. I was kind of surprised when Sean called."

I blink, a little taken aback. "Why?"

She shrugs. "The woman who interviewed me the first time made it clear that I didn't meet JU's hiring standards. Did you have Sean call me because we met at Christmas?"

Not for the first time, I curse the recruiter who got me into this mess. "Partly," I admit. "But I didn't know you'd applied until Sean sent me your résumé. We had some… difficulty with the original recruiter, and when Sean took over, he rescreened all the applications. I was glad to see yours, but you're not the only person I've interviewed today." I match her bluntness with my own—I get the feeling she'll respect that, and if we're going to work together, I need someone I can be totally honest with. That's my New Year's resolution, by the way. I'm taking back my confidence. The ex-who-shall-not-be-named left me feeling insecure and shaken—that's my fault. He was a dick at the end, but I let his words and actions get to me and crack my confidence. That's done now. No more second-guessing myself.

Chloe nods, seemingly satisfied, and I gesture toward the couch. It might be more "appropriate" to hold job interviews at the desk, but I decided not to. I'm starting my interactions with my prospective assistant, whoever I choose, the same way I plan to manage our working relationship.

We sit, and it takes only a few minutes for me to confirm what I suspected all along—Chloe would be the perfect assistant for me. She's qualified, has some experience in administration, but more to the point, is used to dealing with people. And most importantly of all, we get along. Her candid, open manner and ability to go with the flow are exactly what I need. Plus, she has tech skills that I do not. I may be much better at using the JU app now, but I still manage to screw it up sometimes.

She's just asking me about what her duties would be when there's a brief knock and Dimi opens the door and leans in.

"Hey, Jase— Oh, sorry. I didn't realize you were still interviewing. Hi, Chloe. How're you doing?"

I concentrate on keeping the fatuous smile off my face, since I don't want to seem like an adolescent in the throes of a crush. He just looks so good, dressed casually and slightly rumpled.

"I'm good, thanks, Dimi. You?"

"Yeah, great. I'll leave you to it. Jase, can I have a word when you're done? It's not urgent."

"Sure. We won't be much longer."

He smiles at us both and then withdraws, closing the door. Chloe turns to me and tilts her head, narrowing her eyes.

"What?" I ask.

"Nothing. You were saying I'd need to share receptionist duties with John?"

By the time I walk Chloe out, I'm pretty sure she's the right choice. The other candidates are all great, but she and I really click. I'm feeling peppy about it as I knock on the open door to Dimi's office.

He grins at me. "That wasn't so hard, was it?"

The expression on my face must tell him what I think of that comment, because he laughs.

"Did you need something?" I ask.

"Just to let you know we've been invited to a last-minute thing at Derek and Trav's place tonight. Do you want to go?"

I think about it. We'd planned to take advantage of

the New Year's Eve activities and celebrations here at JU—there's a whole bunch of stuff going on at the various parks and resorts—but it might be nice to do something a little more low-key. Plus, I'm still making connections here, and Derek and Trav have some good ones.

"Sure, sounds good. Do we need to bring anything?"

"I'll take care of it. Meet at your place? We can walk from there."

"Good plan." If I know Derek and Trav, they'll have allowed for drunken revelers to crash at their place, but there'd be no privacy, and Dimi and I are still, er… exploring things. Walking home is a better idea.

***

A laughing, tipsy woman plonks herself on my lap, nearly upsetting my drink, and declares, "Take me to bed or lose me forever!"

Beside me, Dimi laughs so hard that my slightly fuzzy brain worries he's going to rupture something. It's not *that* funny, but then again, he's probably as tipsy as she is… as I am.

I plant a kiss on her mouth and tell her, "I would, but that would ruin you for any other sexual partner ever. You'd have to move to Argentina and become a nun, cloistered from life and forever mourning the loss of sexual pleasure."

She screws up her face as though she's thinking about it. "Never mind, then. It would probably be great, but I've never met a man worth giving up sex for. I like you, though. Come and talk to me later." She lurches to her feet and throws herself into someone else's arms. "Take me to bed or lose me forever!"

"I like her," I tell Derek, who's perched on the arm of the recliner beside me. I do know who she is, by the way—her name's Gina, and she used to work on Derek's team. He claims he still hasn't forgiven her for leaving him. Dimi swears she's the best colleague he's ever had, including me. She and I had a long conversation earlier about the best way to tell someone they were an idiot without burning bridges.

"I like her too, traitor though she is," Derek agrees. "Why Argentina?"

Dimi goes off in fresh gales of laughter. I'm beginning to wonder if I should cut off his liquor intake.

"What?"

"Of all the places in the world where she could become a nun, why did you choose Argentina?"

Wow, that's a good question. Isn't it?

I'm not sure.

"It was just the first place that came to mind." Huh. I tilt my head. "I wonder why? I've never been there."

"Who knows how the mind works?" he asks dramatically. "Maybe it's a sign. Maybe your subconscious is telling you something. You're supposed to go to Argentina to fulfill your destiny."

I blink, confused. "My destiny to become a nun?" I don't think that would work. I'm not religious. And I like a sex. A lot.

"You can't become a nun. They wear those ugly robe things, and I don't think they make them from quality fabrics. You like high-end cotton too much to become a nun," Dimi informs me, and he's right. I have a weakness for really nice cotton shirts.

"Not your destiny to become a *nun*." Derek sounds exasperated, like we've missed the point or something. "Your destiny to live in Argentina and reinvent yourself and fall in love with a con artist with a heart of gold who plans to betray you but ends up loving you back and dies tragically when he double-crosses his bosses so he can be with you."

Silence.

"Have you been watching daytime TV?"

He shrugs and looks away shiftily. "Maybe. But sometimes those storylines are based on *real life events*."

"You can't move to Argentina," Dimi tells me firmly. "I will not allow you to fall in love with a con artist. Or anyone."

"Plus it would be bad if I was the cause of someone's death," I agree, because it would. Realization strikes, and my eyes widen. "Is that why I become a nun? Because Edoardo's death fills me with guilt and remorse?"

"Who's Edoardo?" Derek sounds confused now,

and I roll my eyes.

"My Argentinian lover."

"You're dating an Argentinian?" a new voice asks right before a guy I met briefly earlier sits in the armchair Derek's perched against. "I thought you and Dimi are a thing?"

"We are," Dimi says, even as I wonder how the hell so many people know that already. "And I think I might be the reason Edoardo dies. Because I kill him." He looks fierce, and while my sober inner self knows it should be appalled by the talk of murder, my drunk moving-to-Argentina-and-becoming-a-nun self melts at the thought that Dimi is jealous of my make-believe lover.

The new guy, whose name I cannot remember, gives us a weird look, then hands his phone to Derek and says, "Did you see this? Head office is not going to be happy to be associated with this."

Derek takes it, and a crease forms between his eyebrows as he reads aloud, "*Caught on the Casting Couch?* Director Jon Reynolds, best known for Joy Incorporated box office hits *Bongolicious* and *Let It Happen*, was today caught with his pants down in the on-set trailer of actor Bret Weiss. Reynolds, who only last year married renowned Broadway costume designer Rick Henessy, has declined to comment, but Weiss advised *Bonjour Celeb* that their love is real and they plan to be together in the future."

My whole body goes ice-cold, and the pleasant

alcohol haze disappears, leaving me absolutely sober and slightly nauseated. Derek squints at the screen and says, "Why do I know—"

His eyes widen. His gaze darts to me for a split second, and I know Trav has told him the whole messy story. It's not exactly a secret—most of Broadway knows—but we managed to keep it out of the gossip pages with some clever half-truths.

"It's not like head office isn't used to dealing with publicity crap," he says dismissively, handing the phone back. "I think we need to change this music and start dancing!" He shouts the last and is met by a chorus of cheers. There aren't that many people here—maybe twenty—but they're all enthusiastic.

I'm glad for the distraction he's providing, because I'm still numbly processing.

"Hey, you okay?" Dimi leans over, and I force a smile on my face. What am I supposed to say? *My ex who I found out was cheating on me when he married someone else just got publicly humiliated when his new husband cheated on him?*

When I think of it that way, I'm actually not sure why I'm upset. I mean... he got what he deserved, didn't he? But on another level, it was almost easier when I thought he'd done that to me because he'd found his soul mate—a "forever love." Knowing that he threw away what we had and shattered my life for just another fallible relationship *hurts*.

"I'm fine. I guess the alcohol just hit me. Let me

get some water, and then we'll dance." Derek and Trav are loudly arguing over which playlist would be better. I don't know what Derek's taste in music is like, but Trav's leans heavily toward the 80s—the music of my youth—so I hope he wins.

Dimi gives me a kiss and says, "I'll get it. I've gotta use the bathroom anyway."

I use the time while he's gone to get a grip. The fact is, nothing that happens to Rick matters to me anymore—not really. I've moved on and am rebuilding my life. It was just a shock to hear about him again. But at some point, I'll probably have to mention him to Dimi. He's casually referred to a couple of his exes, and it will be weird if I keep avoiding talking about Rick, especially since we were together for so long.

He comes back with a bottle of water just as Trav wins the music battle, and a moment later, classic Bon Jovi blares through the sound system.

It's time to dance.

CHAPTER TEN

$\mathcal{D}imi$

WATCHING JASON DANCE IS a revelation.

A hot as fuck revelation.

Maybe it's the fact that he's drunk, but he's a lot looser than I ever expected him to be. Jase usually has this *contained* air about him. He's got a reputation for being a real hard-ass director, which I haven't really seen from him yet, but the guy I know is actually a little... I don't know, shy? But not really. I get this sense that he can take on the world, but that he's afraid to. I don't know. Maybe I should stop drinking.

Anyway, all hints of that reticent, contained Jason are gone right now. He's the best dancer in the room, and considering fully half the people here are professional dancers, that's really saying something. The other half of the group have stopped to watch, me included.

His body moves in a sinuous, sexy way that turns

me way the fuck on. I spent a lot of time in clubs when I lived in Atlanta, but I've never seen anyone's hips move that way.

Hoo, baby.

The music changes, and we must have switched playlists because the song that starts is not from the eighties. It's got a low, thrumming, repetitive beat, and the dirty dancing factor ramps up immediately, which I wouldn't have thought possible.

Jason starts twerking, and I'm immediately forced to rethink my stance that twerking is ridiculous, because I can't breathe.

His *ass*.

My God.

This is why twerking is "popular." People are trying to look like *this*. Too bad most of them fail.

Lucky for me, my lover is one of the successful few.

I wonder if he can move his hips like that while we're fucking.

Or while I'm sucking him.

I'm still contemplating all the possibilities when he straightens and turns, catching sight of me. The slightly lost look he had before is gone, and he grins wickedly, crooking a finger in my direction.

"Ooooh, Dimi, you're being summoned," someone teases, but I don't care. I don't even care that I'm only a mediocre dancer and will look like an idiot amidst the highly talented group. I stride over to my guy and grab him by the hips, pulling him close for a big, wet kiss.

And the crowd goes wild.

Amidst the whistles and catcalls, Jason and I make out to the bass rhythm of a song I don't recognize, gyrating against each other in a way that can't be called anything but foreplay.

By the time we finally break apart, everyone is dancing, and if a stranger walked in right now, they might well think it was the early scenes of a dirty movie.

"I didn't know you could dance like this," I murmur, biting Jason's earlobe gently. "You're so hot. I wanna do filthy things to you while you dance."

He makes a sound halfway between a chuckle and an explosion of air against my neck. "Maybe if you're lucky, I'll let you."

My dick, which was already half-hard, perks right up. "Really? Will you dance naked for me?" I already have a song in mind. Imagine him twerking like that, naked….

Uhhhhhhhh.

He pulls back a little, gaze searching my face. "You want me to dance naked?"

I nod emphatically. "Hell, yeah. I'll bet I can get off just watching you."

That smug little smile comes back. "Well, then, we'll definitely have to see if that's true." He drags me even closer, if that's possible, and grinds his groin against mine. For the next few minutes, I lose myself in the music and movement.

"How do you even know how to dance like this, anyway?" I finally ask. Jason shrugs, which should look weird while he's dancing, but doesn't.

"I took a few classes in college, and then when I started working, I thought I'd be a more effective director if I had an idea of what I was asking of the performers, so I took a few more. Plus, I've always loved to dance and been kind of decent at it."

Kind of decent? Talk about an understatement.

"I say this in the best possible way," I say solemnly. "You could make a fucking fortune as a stripper."

A startled laugh bursts from him. "Uh, thanks? It's nice to know there are other career paths open to me."

I leer at him. "If you like, you can try it out for me, see if you like it." I slide a hand down over his ass and squeeze. "I promise to tip well."

He leans in to kiss me. "Do I get a bonus if I give you a lap dance with a happy ending?"

"Oh, hell yeah."

CHAPTER ELEVEN

Jason

WALKING HOME IN THE wee hours, the streets are both busier than I expected and quieter than I'm used to. In New York, walking home from a New Year's party at three in the morning (or nine, because the best parties end with breakfast), the streets would inevitably be almost as busy as on workday. In a town as small as Joyville, there's a lot less traffic, but we still see more cars and people than I thought we would.

"Are you still tipsy?" Dimi asks, swinging our arms. We're holding hands, something I haven't done with a lover in years, and I'd forgotten how much I like it. It's such a simple intimacy.

"Yeah." I am. Once the dancing started, I quickly let go of my shock and tension. I haven't been clubbing in a long time, and I've missed dancing. Moving here and being with Dimi have allowed me to rediscover a lot of the things I love.

"Good. I plan to take advantage of your lowered inhibitions." A delicious thrill runs through me, and I'm just contemplating the implications of that when he continues, "What was bothering you before?"

There goes my erection.

I sigh. "That article Derek was reading?" There's no point fobbing him off. I may as well just get it over with. "Jon Reynolds is married to my ex."

Dimi's silent, and I sneak a glance at his face to see a thoughtful expression. "I think I remember hearing about that when it happened," he muses. "They eloped overseas somewhere, didn't they? It's never easy to hear news about an ex," he commiserates, and I wince.

"It's a little more complicated than that." I take a deep breath and go for broke. "We were still together—living together—when they eloped. I found out he'd been cheating on me when someone saw the news on a gossip site during rehearsal one day. I thought he was visiting his mom in Indiana." I shrug. "Turns out he'd been cheating on me for years. He met Reynolds when he consulted on costumes nearly three years ago for the film adaptation of a show he'd worked on. They'd been fucking behind my back ever since, every chance they got." I don't mention the horrible, hurtful things Rick said when he got back from his honeymoon and came to collect his things. What's the point?

Dimi swears a blue streak. "What a complete fuckwad turd."

I laugh. Come on, you did too.

"Yeah. I'm lucky, though, because we managed to keep it out of the tabloids that he'd been cheating on me. He'd been away a lot—I thought his mom was sick, the bastard—and so we hadn't been out in public together for months. A friend of mine is a publicist, and he spun it so it looked like we'd broken up and the thing with Reynolds had been a whirlwind romance. Neither of them disputed it, probably because it looked better for them that way, and that made me completely uninteresting to the gossip rags."

He's quiet for a minute, then asks, "Is that why you took this job?"

"Partly," I say honestly. "I mean, it's a great job anyway, but I was looking for a change. Everyone who knows me well knows what happened, and there's been a lot of speculation from others within the industry. I'd rather be talked about for my work than because I'm an idiot who couldn't see what was going on under my nose. I figured getting out of town would do me good."

"I'm glad you came." He squeezes my hand.

I squeeze back. "Me too."

***

Dimi and I spend New Year's Day snuggling on the couch in my apartment watching Netflix and nursing our hangovers. This is the second time I've been drunk in a week—and also the second time I've been drunk since the night Rick picked up all his stuff. My friend Brice took me to a bar that night and gave the bartender a hundred-dollar tip upfront to make sure my glass was never empty. I still can't think of tequila without shuddering.

January 2, we're back to work. More auditions today, but luckily, recruiter Sean is brilliant and arranged a temp contract for Chloe until her permanent paperwork can be processed, which means I once again have an assistant. I swear, I thought John was going to cry tears of joy when I told him.

Chloe and I run through the plans for today and my expectations of her through it all. I grab what I'll need from my desk so we can head into the theater, but when I turn toward the door, she's standing there with a weird look on her face.

"What?" I ask, feeling a strange kind of déjà vu. She had that same look during her interview the other day.

She hesitates. "I don't want to piss you off," she begins, and wow, that's not a good sign. Did anything good ever come from a conversation that started that way?

I blow out a breath and lean back against my desk. "Okay, just get it out."

"Are you and Dimi seeing each other?"

There. Are. No. Secrets. In. This. Place.

Seriously. Dimi told me—and so did Trav—that the JU rumor mill was crazy efficient, but Chloe's been working here less than an hour. Has the news spread through town as well?

Oh fuck. Chloe used to work for Dimi's mom.

I can actually feel the blood draining from my face, which is just as unpleasant a sensation as it sounds. It's not that we're keeping this a secret—in fact, for all I know, Dimi's already told his family that we're kind of seeing each other. But if he hasn't, I *do not* think it would be a good idea for them to find out from gossip.

"Whoa, are you okay? I'm sorry, I didn't mean to freak you out. I just didn't want to fuck anything up because I didn't know." Chloe comes toward me, her eyes wide.

"It's fine," I manage. "It's… not widely known, that's all. How did you find out?"

She eyes me carefully, seemingly concerned, but must be satisfied by what she sees, because she shrugs. "I guessed."

"You… guessed."

"Yeah. I don't know, there was just something between you the other day."

I think back to her interview. "You mean in the three seconds when he stood in the doorway, said hello, and asked me if we could talk later?"

"Yeah."

"Can you read minds or something?" I'm only partly joking, but she laughs.

"No, but you looked at each other and… I don't know, I got this feeling."

Who am I to argue with a feeling?

"Well, your feeling is spot-on. It's new still, and we're not advertising it, really, but people know. I'm not sure if Dimi's told his mom, though, so…."

"Don't worry, I can keep my mouth shut." She mimes zipping her lips.

"We're also trying to keep it out of the office, so if you think we're getting too personal on company time, feel free to drop a quiet word in my ear." It can't hurt to have someone else in our corner, right?

"Sure." She hesitates again. "Does that mean John and Trav don't know? I'm not asking because I plan to gossip," she hurries to assure me, "but it helps to know who knows, you know?"

"Trav does. John hasn't officially been told, but he's sharp, so I wouldn't be surprised if he's worked it out. On the other hand, it's only been a few days, and one of them was a vacation day, so he might not have."

She nods sharply. "Cool. Don't worry, I've got your back. Let's get moving; those actors won't audition themselves."

***

Our first fight comes sooner than I expected.

To be honest, I don't know why I'm surprised. We've already clashed several times over work, and although we resolved to keep our personal relationship out of the office, we forgot to make a similar resolution about bringing work home. So when we argue over auditions, it's not really surprising that it spills over into our personal life.

He's in the wrong, of course. He gets a certain amount of say in casting, but the ultimate decision is up to me—I *am* the director, after all. The creative side of this company is my domain.

He, Trav, Pete the choreographer, and I are in the conference room, hashing out casting choices. We all agree on the leads—Trav is one of them—so that was easy. But some of the supporting roles are causing some strife.

"Okay," I say thoughtfully, staring at the screen. The character names are at the top, with the casting choices listed in columns beneath. We've been discussing this for a while, and everyone's put in their two cents. It's time for me to make a decision. "For Minnie, let's go with Simone. Tim, Parker. Janie, Lena. And for Josh…" I study the screen again. This one is a really close call on paper, to be honest, but my gut is pulling me strongly in one direction. "Mitchell."

"Ummmmm…." Dimi makes a face. "I don't know about that. I think Sam would be a better fit than Mitchell."

I shake my head. "No. It's Mitchell." Sam is good—excellent, even—and I really like him, but I very strongly feel Mitchell is the one who should be Josh. Maybe my tone was just a little too abrupt, though, because Dimi goes kind of red.

In the next moment, he takes a deep breath and says, "I can see why you're leaning toward Mitchell. He's great, and he has an affinity for the role. But I think his performances tend to be a little uneven—"

"No, Dimi. Mitchell will be Josh." Honestly, I should have let him finish his argument, at least. Or been more polite about interrupting. But he could talk all day and I still won't agree, plus I have a ton of other stuff to do. He looks like he's going to keep arguing, so I add, "The decision is mine to make. Creative control is completely in my hands as long as I stick to the budget and JU's code of conduct. You need to accept it."

The room is deathly quiet. It seems like everyone is afraid to breathe.

"Fine. Mitchell is Josh. I'll arrange the paperwork and have the casting choices posted in the app."

We sort out a few more details, and then the meeting wraps up. I need to grab Dimi, apologize for being so abrupt, but he's the first one out the door.

My stomach sinks. This can't be good.

I hear a sharp thud, and when I step out into reception, both Chloe and John are staring at his firmly closed office door.

"Is Dimi okay?" Chloe asks, and I hide a wince.

"Sure. Uh, I think he had some stuff to do urgently." I smile weakly, and Pete mutters something about having to leave, then makes his escape. Trav prudently withdraws back into the conference room.

This is *not* good.

I go to my own office to work through the piles of crap on my to-do list, trying not to be distracted by thoughts of Dimi being pissed. He'll get over it. We've argued a lot, professionally, and though in the past we usually managed to compromise, that couldn't last forever. I'm pretty sure he's going to shut me down hard on some of the things I want that will strain the budget, and though I'll argue hard for them, if he still says no, I'll accept that. He's in charge of the business side of things, and for good reason. Once he gets over the way I shut him down in the meeting—which I will definitely apologize for—he'll accept that I have creative control for a reason. It's all going to be fine. He just needs time to be mad.

Maybe I should go apologize now. It's been nearly an hour, and the longer I leave it, the less sincere it will look.

I'm just about to get up from my desk when my phone dings with a text message.

Dimi: *Going to HQ for budget meeting. Don't bother coming over tonight.*

I stare at the screen. What the fuck?

The sound of the main office door closing brings me back to my senses. He's left? And he told me he was going via *text message*? My office is right fucking next door to his, and he couldn't lean in the door to say he was going?

I'm tempted to race out and chase him down before he gets to his car, demand to know what the fuck, but I don't want to cause a scene. Plus, that last sentence is playing through my head on repeat: *don't bother coming over tonight*.

What the hell is that supposed to mean? We agreed no personal stuff at work, and I figured that would cut both ways and we'd leave work out of our personal relationship. Clearly, though, Dimi plans to punish me for our disagreement at work by… what? Cutting off sex?

Oh, hell no.

I was ready to apologize. I still *am* ready to apologize, because I shouldn't have cut him off like that. Our working relationship has always been about mutual consideration and respect, even when I'm right and he's wrong.

But this is not okay.

That text really pisses me off.

Also, I've just started having sex regularly again after a drought of nearly a year, and I'm not willing to give that up just so he can sulk tonight.

I settle back in my desk chair and get on with work. I have a lot to do, after all, and I'm not dropping the ball just because Dimi has a bug up his ass. I'll deal with him later.

Don't bother coming over tonight. He's fucking high if he thinks I'm just accepting that.

Should I text him back? Something snarky so he

knows he's being a complete dickweasel and maybe pulls himself together enough to take it back?

No. Why should I give him warning?

By the time I finish up for the day, I'm completely amped up on adrenaline. I am *ready* for this battle.

So I go over to his place.

I have to lean on his doorbell for nearly three minutes before he opens the door. It's childish and petty—clearly he doesn't want to see me—but it gives me an immense feeling of satisfaction after that text.

"What?" he demands, and I push past him—or try to. He seems determined to block the doorway, so we do this pushy-shovey thing with our bodies that's definitely juvenile.

Eventually, I tell him, "Your neighbors are probably watching, and this is going to be all over town by morning." I *think* I'm exaggerating, but from the speed with which he stops shoving and steps back, he obviously considers it a valid possibility.

Hmm.

He closes the door behind me. "What do you want, Jason?"

I cross my arms over my chest. "You can't freeze me out because I made a decision at work that you don't agree with."

He glares. "You don't get to say what I can and can't do."

We stare each other down. I am not going to give in on this. I'm in the right, dammit.

He looks so fucking sexy when he scowls. How did I never notice that before?

I'm still pondering if he'll let me lick the crease between his eyebrows when he lunges forward and kisses me. I'm not ready, so I stagger back and we slam into the door. The handle jabs me in my right kidney, but I don't care, because Dimi's hands are in my pants (when did he undo them?) and his mouth is on mine.

What follows is a frenzy of grunting, grabbing, and clothes flying, until we're both seminaked, our pants around our ankles, our dicks rubbing together in the tight circle of Dimi's hand. We're dry, so it's a little uncomfortable, but not enough to stop the pleasure. That, and the adrenaline from our fight, means that we're coming in record time, spurting all over ourselves and the entranceway.

My knees give out, and Dimi comes down with me, both of us panting and sweaty.

Much later, lying on the floor near his front door, half-naked with clothes strewn around us, he begrudgingly says, "Fine, no personal life at work, and no work stuff at home."

"Agreed. I'm sorry I was so short-tempered today. I should have let you explain why you think Sam is a better choice."

Out of the corner of my eye, I see his face turn toward me, and I roll my head to the side so I can meet his gaze. "Would it have made any difference to your decision?" he asks.

I don't hesitate. We need to be honest with each other if this is going to work. "No. They both look good for the role, and they both have strengths and weaknesses, but my gut says it should be Mitchell, and I've learned to trust my gut on these things."

His lips thin slightly and he turns his head back to stare up at the ceiling. "Fair enough," he says finally. "Not saying I like it, but you do have creative control. This is your department. I have to trust that you know what you're doing and accept it even if you're making a mistake."

Oho. Did you notice that little dig? Dimi's a cheeky bastard sometimes.

I let it slide, because I *know* I'm right and he's wrong, and time will prove it. In the meantime, I want to address something else.

"That text you sent really pissed me off." I gather all my energy and drag myself up to a sitting position, then shuffle back to lean against the front door.

He winces and sits up. "I thought it might. That's why I sent it. I was being a dick, and I should never have let work cross over to home... but I was so mad."

"No more texts like that. Well," I say, thinking about it, "not because of work stuff, anyway." I'm sure we'll fight again, and that text was a *very* effective weapon. Plus, the make-up sex after....

"Work stays entirely professional," Dimi agrees. "Although one day we might want to negotiate a temporary pause in professionalism so I can do you on the stage in the theater."

Hmm. I pretend to consider it, even though just the mention has my cock stirring slightly, something I didn't think it would be able to do so soon.

"If you really want to."

He leans over and licks my cheek. "I really, *really* want to."

CHAPTER TWELVE

Dimi

IT TAKES ONLY ANOTHER week for me to admit defeat and concede that Jason is my boyfriend. To be honest, I've never really been a fan of that word—it seems so ageist. I'm not even thirty yet, so I can't by any stretch of the imagination be called old (unless you're my nephew, who thinks *thirteen* is old), and yet for the last five or so years, I've felt foolish referring to the guy in my life as my boyfriend. And now that I'm with someone twenty-four years older than me, it seems especially stupid.

What are my other options, though? Partner? That could easily label us lawyers or accountants, not lovers. Significant other? What a mouthful. Plus, neither fits right for me. So I'm sticking with boyfriend for now, even if it seems weird.

Anyway, by mid-January Jase and I have spent

exactly zero nights apart. I've been to two Monday night dinners, and both times have had to bite my tongue to keep from mentioning him. I think my sibs know something is up, though, because I'm getting a lot of weird looks. Honestly, they could already know and just be waiting for me to tell them. I've already said that the gossip mill at JU works in overdrive, and it often spills over into Joyville. Jason and I haven't exactly been hiding at work—it's widely known that we're together, especially after Derek and Trav's New Year's Eve party. There weren't that many people there, but if gossip were an Olympic sport, they'd all be champions.

It's a Wednesday afternoon when Derek knocks on my office door, looking his usual smiley, relaxed self. The only time I've ever seen Derek look even slightly ruffled was last year when his reputation was being dragged through the mud in the national media. Ordinary crises just don't faze him.

"Hey, Trav's in the theater," I tell him, but he shakes his head and comes in, closing the door behind him.

"I already saw him. Jason kicked me out for being a disruptive influence. I felt like a naughty schoolboy." A reflective look passes over his expression, followed by a wicked grin. "I think I like it."

I laugh and gesture for him to sit down. "Do you want a drink? We've got soda and water, I think, but for coffee we go to the Arabica Bean." The coffee shop in the Village is damn good. I'd gotten used to drinking the stuff from the coffee cart in the HQ building, which was more than decent, but clearly the stuff we sell to guests gets a higher priority.

"Nah, I'm good. I just wanted a quick word." He slouches into the chair and stretches his legs out in front of him. "You know I think you and Jason are great together."

I raise an eyebrow. This is not what I expected. "Sure." Jase and I had dinner with Derek and Trav last week, and it was a great night. I've known Derek for nearly four years—I would have known if he wasn't feeling it.

"Right, and because you've been so open about being together, the betting on you guys has been fairly restrained."

I groan and roll my eyes. "I heard. There are odds on if we'll have a screaming fight in the theater and *when* we'll break up. I'm pissed about that one."

"I would be too," Derek agrees. "Although we wanted an option about *whether* you'll break up, but we couldn't get any takers. I mean, if someone bets that you stay together, there's no way for them to ever collect unless one of you dies."

"Thanks," I mutter, not sure whether to be glad or not. Although…. "Wait, *we*? You're running the pool?"

His gaze slides away. "No, of course not."

I open my top drawer, pull out the Joy Bear-shaped stress ball inside, and throw it at his head. He ducks, but it still glances off his ear.

"I probably deserve that," he admits. "Anyway, what I was saying was, given how public you are about being together, you need to suck it up and tell your family. Tracey nearly gave it away to your gram the other day—it was just dumb luck that I was there and could distract them both."

"Pharmacy Tracey?" I ask, mind racing. Crap. Gram would really be unhappy to find out I'm seeing someone through the gossip mill.

Derek nods. "You know what she's like. It would never occur to her that maybe you want to keep part of your life private."

"Yeah. Okay. You're right. I'll tell them tonight." I'll stop by after work; that way next Monday, I can bring Jason to dinner.

Hey, that works out great.

"Really?" Derek sounds kind of surprised, and I focus back on him.

"Of course. Jase and I are happy together. I don't really know why I haven't already told them—probably because it's easier not to answer all the questions. But I can't keep pretending Jason and I are just casual, can I?"

He smirks. "Nah. Good for you. I'm glad you've found someone."

We talk for a few minutes more before he heaves himself out of the chair and declares he's going to the park to do some surprise visits to new staff. I wave him off, thinking about how different he's been over the last five or six months. Derek has always been a "happy" person, never without a smile, but since he and Trav settled down together, that happiness has taken on a new dimension, gained a depth that made it evident how superficial his previous happiness was.

I get happy butterflies when I realize I feel that way about Jason. It's still so early in our relationship, but everything seems brighter and more meaningful now.

Ugh. I'm turning into a lovesick fool.

***

After work, I wait until we're in Jase's car, headed back to my place, before I raise the topic of telling my parents.

"So, I thought I'd go round to my parents' house and tell them about you."

The car swerves slightly.

"Oh."

I look over at him. "Is that a good 'oh' or a bad one?"

"It's a surprised one, but I think I like it." He sounds considering now. "I haven't had to meet a boyfriend's parents for… hell, nearly thirty years, I think." He paused. "Is boyfriend the right word?"

"I have no idea," I say honestly. "I've been using it in place of anything better. The meaning fits, anyway."

He takes his eyes off the road and shoots me a smile.

"I think so." Returning his attention to the traffic, he adds, "You're right, it's time they know."

So after we've eaten, I leave Jason watching TV, get in my car, and go to the house I grew up in. As usual, I don't bother ringing the bell, using my key to let myself in.

"Hello?" I call.

"In the living room." That's Dad, and I close the door and go to find them. They're settled comfortably, Mom and Gram watching TV and Dad reading, but they all look up when I come in.

"Hello, baby," Mom says, holding her cheek up for a kiss. "What are you doing here?"

I kiss her and Gram on the cheek and drop a kiss on Dad's head and a slap on his shoulder, then take a seat in an armchair.

"I wanted to tell you all something. It's good," I tack on, just so they won't worry.

They exchange glances, and Gram mutes the TV.

"We're all ears," Dad quips.

"I'm seeing someone, have been for a few weeks, and it's pretty serious."

"That's great, Dimi," Mom declares, sounding a bit surprised but grinning wide. "What's his name? Do we know him?"

"Actually, yeah. You met him at the holiday party. It's Jason."

Dad laughs. "Jason, the director you work with? The guy you've had a professional crush on for fifteen years?

That's fantastic!"

Gram claps her hands. "It's like a movie! I didn't get to meet him at Christmas; you'll have to bring him to meet us."

"If it's okay, I thought I'd bring him Monday night," I suggest, and Gram nods approvingly.

"Of course it's okay," Dad says. "You know you can bring a guest anytime you like."

I stay and chat for a little while longer, but when Gram suggests we have coffee, I make my excuses. "Jason's waiting at my place," I explain, and she and Dad get these smug little smirks.

It's not until I'm nearly home that I realize Mom didn't say much.

***

Monday night, Jason and I get out of my car and start up the front walk. Well, I do, and then I realize he's not with me. When I turn around, I see him still standing beside the car, looking at the house.

O-kay.

I walk back to him. "Hey. You okay?"

The smile he pastes on is a little forced. "Yeah. Just nervous, I guess. It's been a long time since I've done this."

Aw. I kiss him lightly, because we don't have time for a proper kiss, and squeeze his hand. "It'll be fine.

You met Mom, Pat, Cait, and Sienna already, so it's just Dad and Gram, really. And they're excited to meet you." It's true. Gram's rung me three times since last Wednesday with questions about Jason.

He takes a deep breath and squares his shoulders. "You're right. Let's do this." He doesn't let go of my hand, though, and I can't say I mind.

I let us into the house, but I don't need to call out—Sienna and Ryan are hovering in the entryway, waiting for us.

"Hi," I say dryly, but am completely ignored. Instead, Sienna swoops on Jason and hugs him.

"Thank you so much for taking him on!"

What.

Fuck my life. I hate my sister.

Jase laughs, a startled little sound, and hugs her back. "Uh… no problem? It's kind of a pleasure, really."

She pulls back and rolls her eyes. "You say that *now*. Just… when he starts to drive you insane, we have tips. Don't just dump him."

Really. Hate. My. Sister.

"Thanks, Sienna. So glad you're here." My tone is completely flat, and I take Jason's arm and tug him past her. Ryan steps into our path. "What?" I sound very unfriendly, and that makes me wince. Ryan's good people. "Sorry, but…." I shrug and tip my head toward Sienna.

Ryan grins. "Just wanted to congratulate you both on hooking up. And to let Jason know that he'll get used to the Weston family insanity, and if he ever needs it, I have a great ear and a fridge full of beer."

That's actually helpful, and I smile gratefully at my brother-in-law. "Thanks."

"I might take you up on that," Jase adds, smirking.

By the time we make it into the living room, I've almost forgiven Sienna—though not really—and Jase is feeling more confident. Our entry prompts a wave of people standing—it's pretty funny. Have you ever seen meerkats popping up?

"This is Jason," I announce. "Jase, my gram, Alina, and dad, Carter. You've met Mom."

"Well," Gram declares, studying him. "Don't I feel foolish? I didn't realize how old you are. I should have. Dimi has talked about you."

In other circumstances, this would have been followed by an awkward pause, but Gram counters that by stepping forward, hand outstretched. Jason takes it and is promptly pulled down for a smacking kiss on the cheek.

"I have questions about the theater industry. Mostly I'm interested in the gossip. We have good gossip around here, but I imagine it can only be better in New York."

"I don't know about that," Jase says thoughtfully. "It's pretty spectacular here."

"We'll talk later," she tells him, smiling. "Welcome."

Dad comes forward to shake Jason's hand. "It's good to meet you," he says sincerely. "Dimi's been talking about you for about fifteen years. I should have known it was more than just professional interest."

Seriously, can my family embarrass me any more? I thought my dad, at least, was above that. He winks at me so I'll know he's doing it on purpose.

Jason laughs and shoots me a sidelong glance. "Mike and Brody mentioned that he's been a fan of my work for a while. I'm completely flattered."

"I'm sure you are," Mom says. "Dinner's ready."

There's a general flurry as everyone moves toward the dining room, but I hesitate. What was that? Mom sounded… well, less than welcoming. And since when does she call everyone in to dinner? Meals are Dad's domain—and Gram's, now that she lives here.

I have a bad feeling about this.

Sure enough, by the time we're halfway through dinner, I'm genuinely ready to strangle my mother. On Christmas Day, Mom seemed to like Jason. They talked. They laughed. That's not to say they found life-long besties in each other, but they definitely got along. Tonight? Not so much.

For one, Mom's been decidedly uncommunicative. She's normally quite outspoken and chatty, especially a family dinner, but tonight she's spoken only a few times.

Dad's been completely normal. He's treated Jason the same way he's treated every guy I've brought home since I became an adult—not that there have been that many. Remember the man drought brought on by workaholic tendencies? I think Dad's just so relieved I'm not going to be a lonely old man á la Scrooge that he would have been glad to meet anyone I brought home, no matter who. And Gram's been hitting Jase up for theater gossip since we sat down. I think that might actually be contributing to Mom's attitude, because every time Gram asks Jason a question, Mom's mouth tightens.

Does she not want anyone to include him in conversation? Does she not like him? What? I just don't get it.

Worst of all, though, is that the few times she speaks without being spoken to first, it's to make sly little comments intended to make Jason—and me, and everyone else at the table—uncomfortable. Like when Patrick and Cait were talking about the new version of *Teenage Mutant Ninja Turtles*, which their kids are addicted to, and she said, pseudo-fondly, "I remember when you kids used to love watching that. Did you used to watch it too, Jason? Oh, sorry—you would have been too old for cartoons then."

Cue awkward silence. Luckily, Jason is an expert in being "on" in social situations, and he just laughed and made a comment about never being too old for cartoons, then changed the subject.

Which brings us to now. Honestly, the only fly in the ointment is Mom. Dad and Gram, as I've said, have been great. My sibs and their significant others have made a few cheeky or embarrassing comments, but I expected that. It's what we do. The kids really don't care. Jason is just another face at the table for them. So if it weren't for Mom's inexplicable behavior, things would be going great.

I've given up on trying to work her out, but plan to chase her down in private and ask her what the problem is. Jason, bless him, is still trying. I feel bad that he's being subjected to this after I convinced him everyone would be welcoming.

"Sascha," he begins, "I don't know if Dimi told you, but Chloe is working for me now as my assistant. She's amazing—I can't imagine it was easy for you to let her go."

Mom looks at him coolly. "I usually prefer my kids' partners to call me Mrs. Weston."

Ryan chokes.

Sienna drops her fork.

"Really, Mom?" I ask, dumfounded, because that is a blatant lie. Even when we were teenagers, she always let all our friends and anyone we dated call her Sascha.

Mom pastes on an innocent look and says, "What?"

Patrick glances up from where he's trying to get his husband breathing properly again, and the expression on his face says he's wondering if Mom's on crack.

Leona, who was one of those teenage girlfriends and has been in the family for twenty years, clears her throat. "Does that mean I can't call you Mom anymore?"

Mom's expression turns stricken as she seems to

realize what she's done. "Oh—no, you and Cait are *married*, sweetheart. It's different." Then that sinks in and she turns wide eyes on Sienna's boyfriend, who looks like he wants to sink into the floor. He hasn't been around for *that* long, and he's still getting used to us. "Uh… I guess it's okay if everyone calls me Sascha."

Jason stayed scrupulously silent through the whole exchange, his face that blank mask I've learned means he's either seriously pissed or really hurt. It's probably both right now. Maybe we should just leave.

Cait catches my eye and shakes her head slightly, her mouth set into a grim line. My big sister is pissed, and I'm not willing to be the one who riles her further. Cait's a law unto herself sometimes, but you definitely want her on your side.

"You were saying that Chloe is your assistant, Jason?" she asks. "That's great. I don't know her very well, but whenever I see her, I'm so impressed by her energy."

Jase relaxes a little. "She runs circles around me," he admits. "I always considered myself to be a reasonably organized person—not like Dimi, of course," he adds slyly, sliding me a sideways look, "but Chloe knows what I need almost before I do."

"That's great," Patrick puts in, still lightly patting Ryan on the back, even though he's mostly breathing normally, with just a hint of a wheeze. "I used to babysit for her and her brother, and she's always been that way. Bossiest little kid I ever met—after Dimi, of course." He smirks.

"She was like that at school, as well," Sienna adds. She's been quiet the last few minutes, and she's a little pale. I think Mom shocked her. "On pretty much every committee we had." She snorts. "Mike and Brody both have huge crushes on her."

Jase quirks an eyebrow. "I know. It came up at Christmas."

Pat shakes his head. "Neither of those dumbasses stand a chance with her."

"That's what I said." I'm keeping an eye on Mom, just in case she decides to say something else. If she manages to behave herself, we might be able to make it through dessert.

And speaking of.… Dad gets up and begins gathering plates. "Anyone want chocolate cake?"

***

We get into the car, and I immediately turn to Jase.

"I am so, so sorry. I have no idea what got into Mom."

He smiles a little and shakes his head. "Nothing to be sorry for. It's not your fault." He shrugs. "I even kind of get it. When you were born, I was already several years out of college and establishing my career. She's your mom, and you'll always be her baby."

"That's really sweet of you, but it's still not right. I'll talk to her."

"Don't." He reaches out and puts a hand on my thigh. "Let's give her time to get used to the idea."

I'm reluctant—avoiding issues is not my jam, aside from my mini crisis the day after Christmas—but I agree. After all, this affects him more than anyone else, so he should get a say.

But as understanding as my boyfriend is, Mom had better get used to the idea fast. I'm not prepared to allow her to treat him that way indefinitely. She doesn't have to love him, but she does need to extend the same courtesy to him that she has to all the other partners my sibs and I bring home. Hell, one time when I was a kid, Jack brought home an evangelical Christian girl who prayed aloud before we ate, asking God to please forgive the heathens she was about to break bread with. Mom never blinked, just waited until she was done and asked if she wanted potatoes. Sure, she had a few choice words for Jack when she got him in private, but she was completely polite to the girl.

My mom is better than this. Maybe she was just having an off night. Maybe Jase is right and she just needs to get used to the idea. Next week will be better.

Except it's not.

Not even close.

In fact, one could call it a disaster.

It starts out okay. Mom smiles and says hello when we arrive, which is an improvement on last week. I'm feeling hopeful as Dad calls us in to dinner. Cait winks at me, and I wonder if maybe she had a word with Mom.

Probably.

I love my big sister.

Then, halfway through the lasagna, the conversation turns to Ryan's upcoming fortieth birthday. Pat's planning a big party, which Ryan halfheartedly complains about.

"It's not that I'm really worried about turning forty," he says, "but it feels like such a landmark event. I mean, aren't I supposed to have a midlife crisis or something?"

"How is having a party going to have any impact on that?" Sienna teases, and Ryan snorts.

"Don't ask me to be logical. We middle-aged people are allowed to be unreasonable. It just feels like if we don't celebrate it, it will slide on by with all the associated furor, including the midlife crisis."

Pat's laughing so hard he's almost crying, and I can't blame him. I guess technically with life expectancy what it is, Ryan's not wrong about being "middle-aged," but I have never met a person less "middle-aged" in attitude than him.

My brother finally gets himself together enough to lean over and kiss his husband. "It's all right if you have a midlife crisis, babe. I'll still love you."

"As long as you don't find a boy toy like Jason did. Although does it still count as a midlife crisis when you're clearly past midlife?"

"Sascha!" Gram sounds horrified. The shocked silence from everyone else speaks volumes. Even the kids are quiet.

I push my chair back and get up. "We're going, Jase."

He stands, his face blank, not saying a word. My heart aches for him.

"Thanks for dinner, Dad." I nudge Jason toward the door and follow him out, but we don't say anything until we make it into the car.

"I am so, so sorry. I can't believe she said that." I literally can't. That's not my mom.

He sighs. "I want to say it's okay, but... it's really not. But it's not your fault. She obviously has an issue with the age gap between us, and there's nothing we can do about that." He looks suddenly vulnerable. "Unless this is a deal breaker for you?"

"No! It absolutely isn't," I say forcefully. "She's going to get over this, and if she doesn't, she'll pretend she has and be decent to you." No matter what I have to do to make it happen. "Jason, you're the best thing that's happened to me, ever. That's not going to change just because my mom's got some kind of issue."

His face goes all soft. "I can't imagine my life without you anymore."

Huh. Are we admitting to deeper feelings and a long-term commitment in a car outside my parents' house after my mom insulted him?

I grin. "Let's go home." Together.

***

It's the end of the week before I can bring myself to deal with Mom. I was just too angry right after dinner, even with Jason's declaration and our sweet, romantic sex marathon that night. It's been a crazy week, emotionally, because I've swung from being incredibly happy to so pissed off I can't see straight and then back again more times than I want to consider.

Still, overall my life has never been this good.

Have you ever had everything go so well that you wondered if maybe you were dreaming? That's how I feel during the last days of January. I wake up every day in a great mood and go to sleep in that same great mood—next to Jason. I have a fantastic boyfriend, my career is going gangbusters, the show fully cast, choreographed, and in rehearsals, and it looks like this going to be the Best Year Ever.

If not for Mom.

Which is why on Friday, I rearrange my schedule for the day and slip out of the office to visit Mom at work. Jase is at rehearsals, so he'll probably never notice—he gets so incredibly focused. It's really hot. And wow, I get it now why Trav says he has a reputation for being an asshole to work for. He's not mean, not abusive or anything, but he gives no quarter. The performers better get it right, or they'll keep doing it over until they do.

I stroll into Mom's store, hearing the bell chime discreetly as the door opens. Mom spent forever trying to find the right bell—I'm not joking. It had to be loud enough that the staff could hear it if they were in the back room, but not grating. I was about ten that year, and I remember she brought home about six different bells and put them over doors throughout the house. "Whichever one has annoyed us the least but proven most effective by the end of the week is the one I'll use," she declared. By day three, my sibs and I mutinied and took all the bells down and buried them in the backyard. As far as I know, they're still there.

Kelly, who's been Mom's assistant manager since the beginning, grins at me. "Dimi! C'mere and give me a hug, sweetheart. What brings you here on a workday?"

I squeeze her tightly, still marveling after fifteen years that I'm now taller than her. "I came to talk to Mom for a bit. Is she in the office?"

"Yep. Go on back—she'll be thrilled to see you."

I give her one last squeeze, then head through the store to the back room, and through it to the tiny, closet-sized office at the back. For whatever reason, my mom is doomed to always have closet-sized offices. I rap my knuckles against the open door—it's always open, the place gives her claustrophobia otherwise—to get her attention, and when she looks up, she smiles wide. I marvel at that. Given how we left things on Monday, shouldn't she be a bit wary?

"Hey, baby boy. What are you doing here?"

I step in and lean down to kiss her cheek, then perch on the edge of her desk. There's literally nowhere else for me to be, and even that is kind of tight. We'd be more comfortable at the little café table in the back room where the staff has lunch, but there's just a smidge more privacy here.

"I came to talk to you about Jason."

Her happy smile is instantly replaced by fierceness. "What did he do? I knew this would turn out badly! Just wait—"

"Mom, stop." My tone is a little edgier than I intended, and it stops her short. I make myself take a deep breath. I don't want this to turn into an argument. I don't want bad feelings between me and Mom. We're going to have a calm, rational discussion, and she's going to see reason.

If not, *then* we'll have the argument.

"Jason's done nothing. He doesn't know I'm here. I want to talk to you about your behavior toward him."

Her jaw sets in a way I recognize. This may not go well.

"It really hurts me that you feel the need to be so rude to Jason." Sneaky and underhanded? Maybe, but I'm willing to try whatever works.

Sure enough, her expression softens. "Dimi, I don't want to hurt you. I just… I genuinely don't see this going anywhere. It's going to end, and I'm so afraid that you're going to end up hurt."

"Why?"

She blinks. "Why? What do you mean?"

"Why are you so afraid I'm going to end up hurt? You've never worried so much about any of my boyfriends before. Or anyone else's."

"This is different."

"Again, why?"

Mom hesitates. She's not a stupid woman; she knows that what she wants to say is wrong. "You need to consider the very different stages of life you're at," she tries.

I raise an eyebrow. "How so? We're both adults—and it's not like I'm a barely legal adult. I've been working full-time for nearly eight years and running my own life for even longer. I have a lease I'm paying on my own. I'm involved in the community. I'm respected at work. Sure, our careers are at different stages, but the fact that his is firmly established means that we can focus on mine."

"Work isn't the only thing in life, Dimi. You grew up in different eras—he wouldn't have had a cell phone until his late twenties or thirties, but you got one the second we let you."

"Really, Mom? This is because of cell phones?" She's reaching now.

"The cell phones are just an illustration of how very different your growing years were," she insists, and I sigh.

"Mom, remember how much you loved Chris?"

He was my boyfriend sophomore and junior years at college. "You cried when we broke up because you were convinced we were perfect for each other."

She smiles slightly. "I remember. Do you ever hear from him?"

"Yeah, we stayed friends on Twitter. My point here is, Chris was raised by missionary parents and spent most of his 'growing years' in tiny communities in third-world countries. When he moved back to America for his last year of high school, he had only a very basic understanding of technology. Even after four years, he was still appalled by our consumer-driven society. Chris and I are the same age, but our 'growing years' were arguably just as different, if not more so, than mine and Jason's."

Mom's lips thin. "You're still at different stages of life now. He's literally old enough to be your father, Dimi. He's old enough to have grandchildren. You're at an age to be thinking of children. I know people are having kids older now, but there are differences to your energy levels when you're in your fifties to when you're thirty. I've been there. I wouldn't have wanted to have a toddler underfoot when I was in my fifties. It was hard enough in my late forties."

"I don't want kids. You know this. As much as I love being the favorite uncle, I don't want to be a dad."

"You might change your mind later." She has the grace to wince and look ashamed as soon as she says it. Mom has always hated when people spout crap like that. "Okay, maybe you won't. But it's not just kids. He's getting to an age where health issues are going to crop up. Even if he's perfectly healthy, routine wear and tear is a thing."

"Are you listening to yourself?" I'm getting really exasperated now. "You're telling me that I should make a decision about my love life based on the health of my partner? What would you tell Pat if Ryan told us tomorrow that he had cancer? Would you suggest Patrick leave him because of his 'health issues'? For that matter, we know bowel cancer is a thing in his family—did you warn Pat against him when they started dating? Come on, Mom. This isn't you."

Her cheeks are pink with embarrassment, her eyes glassy with unshed tears. I know my mom. For whatever reason she's chosen this hill to die on, it's completely foreign to everything she's ever espoused—to the way she raised us.

"I'm allowed to have my concerns, Dimi. This is not what I envisaged for you. It's going to end badly."

My head starts to throb with a tension headache, but this needs to be done.

"You're right. You're allowed to have concerns. And I'm sorry you're so attached to whatever you dreamed for me that you can't let it go even when I'm happy doing something else. But ultimately, none of what we've talked about matters. This isn't about Jason's age, our respective upbringings, kids, or health. It doesn't matter if this ends badly tomorrow, by mutual consent in a year, or lasts for decades. This is about my mother not having enough respect for me to be polite to my boyfriend."

My words hang in the air. Mom looks like she's been slapped.

"You don't need to like Jason. You don't need to want him in my life. You do need to treat him the way you've treated everyone else any of us have ever brought home. He won't complain about you to me, but the way you've acted the last two weeks makes all of us uncomfortable and makes him feel unwelcome. I won't subject him to that anymore, and if he's not coming to dinner, I'm not either. It's up to you, Mom. Do you love and respect me enough to accept my decisions, or are you going to force a rift in our family?"

"I can't believe you can even suggest that," she whispers, two crystalline tears trickling down her cheeks.

"I can," a voice says, and we both turn to see Pat and Cait hovering just outside the office door. "Looks like you beat us to it, little brother," Patrick continues.

"What are you two doing here?" Mom asks warily. "Is today National Visit Your Mother At Work Day?" Her attempt at joking falls flat.

"I wish it was, Mom," Cait says, her face solemn. "Pat and I thought we should come and talk to you—again. I really thought after last time, you realized you had to let it go, but…. We should have known Dimi doesn't need our help." She smiles briefly at me, but it's a little sad. I don't blame her. It doesn't feel good to have to tell your mother she's being an asshole. And based on what Cait said, this isn't the first time she's stepped up on my and Jase's behalf.

"This is absurd." Mom stands abruptly, squeezes by me, and then pushes past Patrick and Caitlyn to pace in the back room. I follow her out and stand next to my brother.

"It is," Pat agrees. "We shouldn't have to be here. If you'd asked me as recently as a month ago if we'd ever need to do this, I would have laughed. My mom would never be so shallow. My mom would never be so rude. My mom would never make a judgment for such stupid reasons."

"I get it," Mom snaps.

"Mom, we love you," Cait says. "It worries us that you're so adamant about this. Especially since it's so contrary to everything you've ever taught us. If I'm being bluntly honest, yeah, I was a tiny bit weirded out thinking of my baby brother hooked up with a guy who's so much older—but then I reminded myself that judgments like that are wrong. That's what you've always taught us to do. Why is it suddenly so different?"

Mom presses her lips in a thin line again and turns away. She could repeat all the things she said to me, but Cait and Pat will just react the same way I did—because that's how she raised us. "None of you understand."

"What don't we understand?" I ask. I'm still hoping there's some magical way to make this better. Maybe if

I get what her problem is, I can… fix it?

She doesn't say anything.

Pat sighs. "Okay. We don't want to cause strife, but the thing is, the kids are old enough now to notice when things are tense. Ryan and I already didn't like how the last two Monday night dinners went. Cait and Leona feel the same. If Dimi stops coming, the kids will want to know why. What are you going to tell them, Mom?"

"It's not up to me to tell your children anything," she snaps, and Cait shakes her head.

"Oh, Mom."

Patrick isn't as gentle. "That's fine. What I'll tell them is that you were mean to Uncle Dimi's boyfriend, and so Uncle Dimi doesn't want to come to dinner anymore."

I wince internally. It's not really any harsher than what's already been said, but it feels like it is.

Mom takes a deep breath. "I don't appreciate you threatening me." She holds up her hand before Patrick can respond. "But I understand why you're doing it. Let me process this."

It worries me that she needs to process something that should be so simple, but at least this is better than her blunt refusal to listen before.

"Take what time you need," Cait tells her. "We're trying to raise our kids the way you raised us, Mom, because there are no parents in the world that we admire more than you and Dad. When we were kids, if someone behaved in a way that you felt was harmful, you removed us from their sphere of influence and explained why so we would know not to emulate that behavior. How can we do any different now?"

As gently as she says it, it's still a gut punch wrapped in pretty packaging. Does Mom need to hear it? Yeah. Do I wish she didn't have to? Absolutely.

"I love you, Mom." I think she really needs to hear that right now. "It would hurt me to stop coming to dinner every week. But it also hurts me to see you treating Jase this way."

She nods curtly, and I say, "Okay," and go to kiss her on the cheek. It's damp. Life really sucks sometimes—like when the right thing to do means making your mother cry.

Pat and Cait kiss her too, then we all walk out together. Kelly, thankfully, is distracted by a customer, so we get away with just waving.

Out on the sidewalk, I heave a huge sigh. "Well, that was awful."

Pat slings an arm around my shoulders. "Yep."

I hold out a hand to Cait, and she comes in for a hug. "Thanks for this, you guys," I say, my voice muffled by her hair. "I appreciate it."

Cait pulls back and pats my cheek. "Older siblings are supposed to look out for younger ones."

I smile at her, because no matter how often I say I don't have a favorite sibling, Caitie has a special place in my heart. She was the one I always ran to when I needed a Band-Aid.

"Now we wait, I guess. Hopefully Mom will call me soon."

"If she doesn't, we talk to Dad and Gram," Pat declares. "Neither of them looked happy the other night. I don't want Mom to feel like we're going behind her back to gang up on her, but when she comes to her senses, she's going to feel awful about this. Let's make sure there's as little as possible for her to be ashamed of."

***

I'm at Jase's place that evening, cleaning up after dinner, when my phone rings. Jase holds out his hand for the plate I'm about to slot into the dishwasher. "Grab it. I'll finish up here."

He's being kind of careful with me tonight, and it's my fault. I'm trying to act normal, but I'm really on edge after today. I absolutely do not want a rift in my family… but even if Jason and I weren't serious and practically living together, it would not be okay for Mom to act like he has the plague. Like I told her, this isn't as much about Jason as it is about her respecting me and my choices.

I haven't told him what I did today. I'm not sure if I'm going to. I guess I'm waiting to see what the outcome will be, as it will have a pretty big impact on what I say.

It's Mom on the phone, and my stomach takes a sharp nosedive. I go into the bedroom, trying to make it look ordinary and not like I want privacy.

"Hello?" I can't bring myself to greet her more casually.

"Hello, Dimi."

"Hi, Mom." Should I ask how she is? Normally I would, but it seems stupid, considering.

"I've been thinking about what you said today."

Okay, she's just going to jump right in. That's good. No suspense.

"While I'm still not happy about this relationship and have serious concerns that it's going to leave you a wreck, I understand your point. I've always tried to let you kids make your own mistakes with relationships, and this should be no different."

That wasn't quite my point. Was it?

No. Definitely not.

I open my mouth to tell her that, but she's still talking.

"So I'm not going to be a bitch to him anymore. Jason is welcome to join you at all family gatherings and events, and he can expect to be treated with the same courtesy and respect as everyone else."

I didn't realize exactly how tense I was until she forces those words out and every muscle in my body relaxes. I exhale quietly.

"Thank you, Mom. That means a lot to me."

"I love you, Dimi."

"I never doubted that," I assure her. "I love you too." I hesitate. "I still wish I understood why you feel this way."

"Will we see you Monday?"

Okay, so she's just going to ignore the implied question. I can live with that.

"Definitely."

We say goodbye and end the call, and I go to find Jason, feeling a million times better than before. Don't get me wrong, I still wish my mother could like my boyfriend, but I'll happily settle for her not being nasty to him.

Jase is on the couch, channel surfing, but from the distant look on his face, he's not actually paying attention.

"Hey." I settle beside him and lean against his side. He turns his head and smiles at me, then leans in for a kiss.

"Hey." He hesitates, and I know he wants to ask about the call, but he won't because I left the room to take it.

"That was Mom. I went to see her today, and we talked about how she's been acting toward you."

He looks at me sharply. "I don't want to be the cause of problems between you and your mom."

"You're not, she is," I say bluntly. "She's still not happy about us, but she agrees that she's been out of line and she promises not to be a bitch going forward."

Studying my face carefully, he says, "Okay. But I

wish you'd talked to me before confronting her."

"I thought about it," I admit, making a face. "But you would have said not to, right?"

His silence speaks volumes.

"It needed to be said, Jase." I give him a recap of what Mom and I discussed. He winces a couple times at her arguments, but overall just seems resigned. When I mention that Pat and Cait turned up, he brightens a little. "It's not really you," I conclude. "Sorry if that punctures your ego."

He laughs, looking a lot brighter. "My ego is solid enough not to be punctured," he assures me. "You're right, though. If you'd told me, I would've tried to talk you out of it, and ultimately this is between you and your mom. So… I'm glad she's going to try to get along with me, and I promise not to make it harder than it already is."

I snort and steal the remote from his hand. "Like you would. Anything good on?"

CHAPTER THIRTEEN

Jason

I'M NOT GOING TO lie, the first Monday in February is a difficult one for me. Tonight, we're going to dinner at Dimi's parents' place, and we'll see if his mom really meant it when she said she wouldn't be a bitch.

I really hope she did.

I'd never tell Dimi this, but the way she acted those first two Monday night dinners devastated me. It felt like being kicked in the balls. On paper, I'm the ideal boyfriend: mature, responsible, respected, with an established career and a history of charitable works. I don't do anything to excess, and my previous relationship lasted for nearly seventeen years and ended through no fault of mine. Not only am I every parent's dream, I'm almost too boring.

The thing is, I was already feeling a bit insecure

about the age gap. Dimi assures me it's not a problem for him, and I believe that, but that doesn't mean it's not going to be a problem in our relationship. Case in point: it's the reason he was pissed as his mother last week. The reason she's feeling ganged up on and threatened by her kids. This can't be a good thing for us.

So I have all my fingers and toes crossed that she's actually willing to give me a chance to impress her with how much I adore her son.

I spend the day alternately feeling confident that I can handle this and wondering how I'll cope if things go bad. What if Dimi decides this is a deal breaker after all? Or worse, what if he doesn't, and then blames me down the track for causing a rift in his family? There are so many ways this can go bad. By the time the end of the day rolls around, I'm emotionally exhausted. And we still have to actually go to dinner.

No way am I letting Dimi know, though—he's already worried about me. I know he hated that his mom wasn't warm and welcoming, the way she was at the holiday party before she knew I was dating her son.

With a bright smile pasted on my face, I stick my head into Dimi's office. "Ready to go to dinner?"

He looks up me, then laughs. "Fuck's sake, Jase, don't ever smile like that at anyone. You could traumatize kids."

I guess the bright smile was more a terrifying grimace. I sigh and go to sit in his visitor chair.

"Sorry. Long day."

Studying me, he says, "If you don't want to go tonight, we can stay home."

Oh, hell no. "No." I shake my head for emphasis. "If we don't go tonight, that sends a message, Dimi, and not the one we want. I want things with your family to be good." Plus, if we don't go tonight, I'll be on tenterhooks for another week—and have to go through this all over again next Monday.

He stands. "Okay, let's go, then. Delaying will just make you feel worse."

Huh. I guess I didn't hide my feelings so well. I pull a rueful face as I get up and follow him out. "It's not that I don't want to go," I begin, and he laughs.

"Jase, *I* don't want to go. I have really high hopes, but I'm also terrified that tonight is going to be just as bad as the last few weeks." He holds the door to the parking lot open for me. "So let's just go, get through it, and then go home."

That sounds like a plan to me, and I tell him so.

I spend the drive compulsively flipping through his playlists—I don't think we hear more than twenty seconds of any song. Dimi's a saint, because he puts up with it and says nothing. By the time we pull up in front of his parents' place, I'm convinced I have the best boyfriend in the world.

We sit.

"Everyone's here," Dimi says, looking around at the other cars parked nearby, but he makes no move to get out of the car. Neither do I.

Another minute passes. We should go in. They'll be waiting for us to start dinner. But….

Yeah.

Movement at the front of the house catches my eye, and I turn my head to see Patrick come out the front door and close it behind him. He strolls down the front walk, gaze on us, then opens the back door of the car and slides in.

"Hey, guys." He props an arm on the back of each of our seats and leans between them so he can see us. Dimi and I both half turn to give him our attention.

"Hi, Pat."

"How are you?" I ask politely, then feel like an idiot.

He grins. "I'm well, thank you, Jason. And you?"

Yeah. I definitely feel like an idiot. I snort self-deprecatingly.

"Good. Thanks."

"Feeling a bit tense, maybe?"

Have I mentioned before that I like Dimi's oldest brother? I do. Even when he's making fun of me.

"Don't be a dick, Pat," Dimi chides, but he's smiling.

"Are you going to join us inside?" Patrick asks, tone still light.

"We haven't decided yet," Dimi tells him. "We plan to, but…."

"You're worried. Well, I can't change that, but you know the only way to fix it is to come in and see what happens."

"You're such a dad," Dimi grumbles, and Patrick laughs.

"I know, right? I've become the sitcom dad I never wanted to be. I even tell dad jokes. Want to hear some?"

"And on that note"—I open the car door—"we should go in."

"Works like a charm," Pat says smugly as we all get out the car. Dimi waits until we're halfway up the path to shove his brother, and then they engage in a shoving match that would do any child proud. The mood is a lot lighter by the time we reach the front door, but I'm still nervous.

Dimi takes my hand.

Who knew just holding the hand of the man I love could make such a huge difference?

Wait…

Did I…?

Fuck.

Okay, this is not the time. I'll deal with that later. Lots later. After this deal with his mom is sorted.

I mean, it's not like I didn't already know, deep down. I just wasn't ready to admit it. And I don't know if he is, either.

But I know the feeling is there. A man doesn't threaten to cut his beloved mother out of his life if he doesn't love you.

Right?

Fuck.

We're in the living room. How did that happen?

When? I need to stay focused, not get distracted, because there she is.

Sascha Weston.

I almost wish she hadn't been so nice the first time we met. If I'd only known her as the witch who hated me being with her son, I could dislike her. Instead, I know she's an amusing, interesting, community-minded woman who's usually very open-minded—just not when it comes to me. Which makes it worse.

"You're here," Dimi's gram says, getting up from her chair and coming over to hug Dimi tight. I smile, seeing how he bends to kiss her. He's such a caring, loving man. How can I not love him?

Alina turns to me next, hugging me as well, though maybe not so tight. "It's good to see you, Jason," she says, looking me right in the eye, and I know that whatever her daughter is struggling with, she's not going to let this strife tear apart the family.

Dimi's dad comes over next. This personal greeting is not the norm, not based on what I've seen before, but it seems they want to make it very clear how welcome we are here. How welcome *I* am here.

Too bad they weren't the ones I was worried about.

"Well, now that you're here, let's eat," Carter announces, thankfully preventing the need for me to greet Sascha. Although it makes me wonder if he did it so she wouldn't have the chance to say something nasty. From the nervous glance Dimi shoots me, he's thinking the same thing.

As dinner progresses, though, I relax. Sascha's not exactly friendly, but I can see that she's trying. There are no snide comments, she's participating in general conversation, and twice she actually directs a remark to me—the first time to explain who she's talking about in an anecdote, and the second to ask if I'd like more green beans. I don't think we're destined to be lifelong besties, but it's a start—and way better than it was last week. I can live with this.

Dimi feels the same way, I can tell, because his tension has all drained away. He's smiling widely, happy and vivacious and outgoing, and so beautiful I can barely take my eyes off him. He's in full favorite uncle mode tonight, planning a day at JU with the kids, and he's having such a great time that it takes me a while to realize he intends for me to go with them.

My nerves come rushing back, and I wait for a break in the conversation and lean over to whisper, "Dimi, I don't think I've ever spent any time with kids without their parents there." *Translation: I've never been responsible for small children before and I'm terrified at the very idea.*

"Don't worry," he murmurs back. "I'll be there, and the kids are good."

Um... not exactly the response I was hoping for. Still, seeing how excited he is, I guess I can handle it. He'll be there, and he's done this before. My job will be to follow them around all day, right? I can do that.

I can do anything for him.

Later that night, after we've left his parents' house, made out in the car because the adrenaline was still racing through our veins, and then had slow, loving sex in his—our?—bed, we lie in the dark, holding hands. I'm not sure when or how that happened but having Dimi's hand in mine is an intimacy I'll never get tired of.

"I'm so glad tonight went well." I break the silence.

Dimi squeezes my hand. "Me too. I really wanted to give you my family."

Oh. I take a deep breath, my lungs suddenly feeling tight.

"I really want to be part of your family."

***

Ever taken three kids to a theme park? No? Consider yourself lucky.

Don't get me wrong, the kids were well-behaved… mostly. Two five-year-olds and a seven-year-old are going to get tired and cranky, right? *I* get tired and cranky, and I'm fifty-three.

But it was a long day, and by the time it got to midmorning, I already understood why Dimi had said no when I suggested the kids sleep over and give their parents the night off. "Day out *or* sleepover, Jase," he told me. "Not both. Not with all three kids, anyway." And when the kids were arguing over which park they wanted to go to and I suggested we could do more than one, he just smiled and said, "Let's see how we go."

I get it now. He has more experience being a hands-on uncle, and I bow to his superior knowledge.

Not to mention, it was super cute the way he sang along to all the songs in the shows. And I do mean *all*. He knows all the lyrics. No wonder the kids adore him.

Now, though… I'm beat. We dropped the kids off with their parents just after five. Originally I thought we might want to have dinner at the park and stay for the fireworks, but even if the kids hadn't been too tired, I changed my mind by midafternoon. My feet hurt, I'm exhausted, and even though I had a hat and sunglasses on all day and the day was really not hot, I have a headache. I've been slumped on my couch since we got here, trying to gather the energy to get up and go get some water.

Dimi comes into the room, freshly showered and looking edible wearing only a towel. Too bad I'm too tired to do anything about it. My dick wants to be interested, but only if I take a nap first.

He takes one look at me and chuckles, then goes into the kitchen and comes back with a glass of water and a small chocolate bar. I don't know where the chocolate came from.

"Drink," he says, sitting beside me and handing over the glass. I sip cautiously at first, because the hot dog I had for lunch is sitting poorly, and then when my stomach doesn't revolt, I gulp. "In a minute, you can go shower. You'll feel better." He offers the chocolate.

"Where did you get this? It wasn't in the kitchen." I'm surprised to find that I actually wouldn't mind some chocolate, and I give him the glass to hold and peel open the wrapper. The smell hits me first, and suddenly I'm ravenous. I attack the chocolate like I haven't eaten in a week.

"I bought it for in case the kids started whining. A small piece of chocolate makes a great distraction, and usually holds them off until I can arrange better food."

"I don't know why I'm so hungry," I say around a mouthful, and he shrugs and takes a sip from my glass.

"We walked around a lot today, and you just had the one hot dog the entire day. Plus, when you've got kids with you in a busy public place, you're always on high alert, and that eats up a lot of energy."

I think about it while I chew, and he's right. The whole day, I've tried to keep my eyes on all three kids, the people around us, and anything that could be a potential hazard. That's hard work.

"How do parents do it?" I marvel, immensely glad I don't have kids. Dimi shrugs.

"I guess they get used to it. I got used to it—the first couple times I had the kids were a nightmare. It's much easier now." He pauses. "You'll get used to it."

I can't help it—I grin. Because, yeah, I will.

"A shower helps, you say?" I actually wouldn't mind a shower, now that I no longer feel like my brains are leaking out of my ears.

"It does," he assures me, and then he smiles slyly. "But you still look tired. I wouldn't want you to get dizzy and slip."

Huh? Fuck, I'm tired, not sick.

"Why don't I come with you, help you out?"

Ohhhhhhhhhhhhh.

Well.

"But you just showered," I point out as innocently as I can manage. He raises a brow, and my straight face falters. "Okay then, if you insist." I slowly heave myself off the couch, adding a theatrical moan as though I'm in pain and putting my hand to my forehead. "Oh, you're right. I'm a bit dizzy."

The look he gives me nearly sends me into gales of laughter. "It's a good thing you're a brilliant director, Jase, because your acting skills need work."

"Everyone's a critic," I sigh, and follow him to the bathroom. Halfway there, I say, "Hmm, I'm going to need a towel," and snatch his from around his waist. He laughs, but says nothing and doesn't turn around, which is *very* disappointing. At least the view from behind is nice.

In the bathroom, he winks at me and says, "Strip," then goes to turn on the shower. I consider taking my time and turning this into a striptease, but to be honest, I really do feel sticky and sweaty and in need of a wash… plus, me and Dimi naked in the shower is always a good thing. So I'm out of my clothes and under the stream of water before it even finishes heating up.

Dimi joins me and reaches for the body wash before I can, squeezing it into his hand and then rubbing his palms together. "Let's see if we can make you feel better."

And he does.

It starts with his soapy hands on my body, ostensibly cleaning away the day. Then, as the hot water cascades over us, washing off the suds, and steam builds around us, his mouth replaces his hands, kissing, licking, biting. My knees go weak as he works his way lower, and I prop myself against the cold tile wall.

Later, when he's sucked the energy from me (literally), and I've jerked him in return, we both sprawl on the shower floor, panting, the water around us turning cool.

"That was epic," he says, and I bite back my smug pride.

My stomach growls, and he laughs and reaches up to turn off the water.

"Come on, let's get you dinner."

***

I'm at work when the call comes in early March.

Does that sound ominous? I meant it to. We're literally days away from opening night. Everything is crazy right now, and everyone's stress levels are through the roof. Dimi and I finally had to impose a moratorium on all work talk at home so we'd have time to decompress.

This is normal. There are a million details to take care of right now, and it doesn't seem like we're anywhere near ready. We are, of course. I've been here before, and though it feels like disaster is looming, it's all going to come together in the end.

The stress is amped up a little by the fact that this is A Big Deal for Joy Universe and for Dimi—and me. Last year, a woman murdered her husband here at JU and then tried to implicate the company and some of the staff. There was a huge kerfuffle that Derek got dragged into, and even though the evidence (so I've been told) all firmly points to the woman being guilty, things looked really bad for JU for a while. So they decided to start this theater company as a distraction.

It worked, because lately the press has been full of talk about our upcoming debut production, which is good. On the flip side, lately the press has been full of talk about our upcoming debut production, which means all eyes are on us. Opening night is going to be a huge event. Aside from the bosses of Joy Incorporated flying out from LA, there are going to be several A-list celebrities and a few Broadway theater critics.

Why is that, you may ask? After all, JU is nowhere near Broadway. But it seems that when a company like Joy Incorporated opens a theater division, then employs a Tony award-winning director (that's me) and a widely renowned performer (Trav), it attracts attention. So here we are, slightly panicked but inwardly confident that it's going to be okay come opening night. Well, that's how I feel, at least. I think Dimi might just be at the "slightly panicked" stage.

Where was I? Oh yeah, *the call*. I'm not actually worried when I look down at my cell and see my friend Brice's name on the screen. I'm actually a little excited. I haven't talked to him for a while.

"Hey."

"Don't you 'hey' me after you moved to Georgia and practically ghosted us." He tries to sound pissed, but I can hear the smile in his voice.

"I'm a terrible friend," I admit. "Things have been insane here. But I didn't ghost you—we texted just a couple days ago."

He sniffs. "You missed our New Year's Eve extravaganza."

"I know, and I can only hope you'll forgive me."

"Maybe. First I have to meet this new man of yours, make sure he lives up to the pictures."

Yeah, so I sent Brice a couple of pictures of Dimi. He was nagging me about getting out, meeting people, maybe dating again. The word Grindr came up, and so I sent him the pictures and told him I had a boyfriend. That was back in the early days before we were really announcing anything, and since then, he's asked about Dimi in every text.

"I don't think we'll get up to the city anytime soon,"

I caution.

That's when I get the first hint that something is wrong. Because Brice hesitates.

Uh-oh.

"What?"

"Nothing. It's just, David and I were thinking we might come down for your big opening, meet your guy, spend some time at JU. Can you get us tickets to the show?"

"Sure," I say automatically, my brain racing to catch up. "Uh, what?"

"Don't you want to see us?" There's a pout in his voice, and that more than anything causes my mind to clear.

"Of course I do, and I'll get those tickets plus VIP passes and book a room for you—I get a great rate. But I still want to know what you aren't telling me." It's not that the idea of Brice and his husband coming to Georgia is weird—though it is—as much as the fact that this is the first time he's mentioned it. And he's right in the middle of a project himself.

He huffs.

I wait—although I do shoot a glance at my tablet, which has lit up with an alert. It doesn't look urgent, so I leave it.

Finally, he breaks. "Okay, so... did you know that Laurie Henderson and Mitch Craig are coming down to cover your show?"

"Yes." Mitch Craig is a hardass critic, while Laurie

Henderson focuses on Broadway-related journalism with the occasional review.

"Right, so... I didn't mention this before because it didn't seem important, but he-who-shall-not-be-named moved back from LA in January."

I wait for myself to react to hearing about Rick. There's a tiny stab of satisfaction that he had to come back to New York with his tail between his legs, publicly humiliated, and if that makes me a bad person, well, I'm not sorry. There's also a small pang of remembered hurt and a dash of nostalgic regret for all those good years. But it's nothing like the vicious agony I used to feel.

"I figured he'd come back at some point" is all I say.

"Did you also figure he'd immediately hook up with Mitch Craig?" Brice asks tartly, and shock echoes through me. Clearly Rick wasn't that heartbroken or humiliated by his husband's infidelity.

"Oh," I manage. "No, I... that's a surprise." Then it sinks in why Brice is calling. "Oh fuck." Rick is coming to JU with Mitch Craig, who's attending as a VIP and will be at the pre-show cocktail party *and* the afterparty... and likely will bring his date.

"Yep."

"Are you sure he's coming?" I ask hopefully, reaching for my laptop. I have the guest list somewhere, I'm sure. If not, Dimi does, but I really don't want to ask him.

Although... if Rick is coming, I'll need to tell

Dimi everything. No way do I want him blindsided if Rick says something snide.

"I'm sure," Brice says grimly. "I ran into the slimy bastard the other day and he took great pleasure in telling me all about the amazing suite he and Mitch Craig are being put up in. I hope you don't mind, I already told him David and I were coming and may have gushed a little about your hot young boyfriend."

My wince is automatic. I don't love hearing Dimi referred to that way—it's true, but it makes our relationship sound sordid, for want of a better word.

"That's fine," I tell him. "But maybe don't describe Dimi that way to anyone else."

"Never! To be honest, it made me feel kind of dirty saying it. You've got a guy who rubs your temples when you've got a headache—his age and looks are the least important thing about him. That's not going to stop me from perving on him," he tacks on, and I have to laugh.

"Okay, so I guess I'll see you this weekend."

"We'll be there," he promises. "It's going to be okay, Jase. He can't ruin this for you."

Then why does my stomach feel like lead? "I know."

We say our goodbyes and end the call, and I stare at the guest list that I finally managed to find. The latest update timestamp is from this morning. I skim down to where Mitch Craig's name is, and sure enough, where it says "guest" is a notation with Rick's name.

Great.

Sighing, I get on with what I was doing when Brice called. I'm going to need to tell Dimi about Rick tonight, but there's no point worrying about it now.

I'm concentrating hard when Chloe comes in and closes the door behind her.

"What's up?" I don't think we've closed that door more than three times since she started working for me.

"I did something and I'm not sure if it was right or not." She winces. "Probably not."

Well, that gets my attention. "Should I expect the cops to come barging in here?"

She huffs a halfhearted laugh. "Nothing like that. There was a call for you on the main line."

I glance at my cell. JVTC has a main landline phone, but Dimi and I use our cells for all calls rather than having landlines in our offices. It's apparently quite simple to transfer a call from the main line to our cells if necessary.

Which Chloe clearly didn't do.

"It wasn't business," she races to assure me. "He said it was personal but that he couldn't get through on your cell."

"That's weird." I pick up my cell and activate the screen. Full bars. "I was just on it less than an hour ago. Did you get some kind of error message when you tried to transfer the call?"

She makes a face.

"Just tell me all of it, Chlo."

"I got a strange vibe off him and told him you were

out of the office and that I'd have him call you back." She holds out a Post-it Note. "I'm sorry if that was the wrong thing to do."

I take the small square of paper. Technically, she's done nothing wrong. It's not uncommon for assistants to act as gatekeepers, and she made sure that I'd still be able to contact… whoever it is. Plus, if it was a personal call, she didn't even have to do that much.

Personal call? Who could it be? Brice calling back? I glance at the paper, and nausea rolls in my stomach.

Rick Henessy is written in Chloe's neat handwriting, along with a number that's as familiar to me as my own.

"It's fine, Chloe," I say automatically. "Thank you."

She looks at me for a moment longer, and I meet her gaze steadily. Eventually she says, "Let me know if you need anything," and leaves.

I stare at the note. That explains why he couldn't get through on my cell. I blocked his number after he left New York—not that he'd been calling or anything. It just felt like something I could do. A cathartic act.

What do I do now? More to the point, what the hell is Rick doing? After the things he said when he left, I never would have expected him to call. There's no doubt in my mind that if the opening this weekend wasn't getting so much attention in the media, he wouldn't leave New York to attend, new lover or not.

So…?

The only way to find out what he wants is to call

him back. But that feels like a concession.

I slump in my seat. To call or not to call?

This is ridiculous.

I snatch up my cell and dial the number. It barely rings once before it's answered, which means I don't have time to change my mind and hang up, damn it.

"Hey, Jase."

Really? He has the nerve to greet me so casually after everything he said the last time we spoke? Everything he *did*?

"Did you want something?" My tone is so cold, icicles would shiver.

"You're still mad."

Oh. My. God.

I say nothing.

"Okay, no small talk. I figure Brice has called you and you've heard that I'll be there with Mitch Craig for your opening night this weekend."

I still say nothing. If I hadn't heard, this would be a real dick way of telling me.

"I just want you to know that there are no hard feelings on my part. I'm coming to see what I'm sure will be a great show, and I'm sorry if that's going to be difficult for you. I.... The way we ended our relationship is a regret for me. If I had it to do over, it would be different."

I'm no longer ice-cold. In fact, my blood is boiling. There are no hard feelings on his part? What the fuck right would he have to have hard feelings? And he *regrets* how *we* ended our relationship? There was no fucking *we* involved, just him making selfish, hurtful choices!

I clamp my teeth down on my tongue to keep from saying anything.

He sighs. "Brice said you're seeing someone. I'm so happy for you."

Condescending prick.

"So… that's all I wanted to say. I don't want strife between us."

"That's… very kind of you." I almost choke on the words. "Thank you for calling." I don't bother to say goodbye before ending the call.

I bang my head against the desk. This day is not turning out how I expected.

I stay with my head down for a few minutes, then decide this is technically a work issue, since my ex's new boyfriend is a critic who will be sharing his views on our show. That means I need to discuss this with Dimi ASAP, right?

That's my story, and I'm sticking to it.

I get up and go out into reception. Dimi's door is closed, and John's not at his desk. Damn.

"Are they meeting?" I ask Chloe, gesturing to the door, and she nods.

"Yeah, but they should be nearly done."

I mentally weigh it up. Technically, this can wait, but I'm already dreading the forthcoming conversation and would rather get it over and done with ASAP.

Luckily, the door opens before I have to make a decision. John comes out, then stops dead when he sees me standing there, presumably with an expression of agonized indecision on my face.

"Is something wrong?" he asks.

"Yes. No. It's fine. Has he got time now?"

"About half an hour, but I can move things if you need more."

I smile tightly. "Half an hour should be plenty." I really just need to give him a heads-up. It's not like we can do anything.

I go into the office and close the door. Since we started seeing each other, Dimi has relaxed his rule about meeting in our offices. I asked him about it once, and he blushed bright red and mumbled something about not wanting to be in close proximity. I took that as a compliment.

Dimi's standing next to the desk, waiting for me, likely having heard me talking to John. "What's the matter?" He looks concerned.

"Sit down," I tell him, dropping gracelessly into his visitor chair. I don't deserve the comfort of the couch. Plus, this needs to be an "official" meeting.

He warily takes a seat behind the desk. "Is this going to freak me out?"

"Maybe. It's not bad, exactly, but potentially could be." I take a deep breath. "You remember I told you about my ex?"

"The dickbag who cheated on you and married

someone else while he was still living with you?"

"That's him," I confirm. "Brice called earlier to tell me that he moved back to New York and hooked up with Mitch Craig."

I see the lightbulb go off.

"The critic coming this weekend? Fuck. His assistant called and asked us to add a plus-one, but I never thought…. That's your ex?" He turns to his laptop and taps a few times on the keyboard. "Rick Henessy?"

I nod. "That's him."

Dimi blows out a long breath. "Okay. That's… not ideal, but it's not a disaster. Unless you think he's going to cause trouble?"

"That's the thing, I don't know. There's more." I tell him about Rick's call, and his face goes grim.

"I don't like this," he says. "That he called you, and that he's clearly rewritten your breakup to suit himself. I especially don't like that he'll be here this weekend and in a position to cause trouble. But there's nothing we can do except make sure everyone on the team is alert—and maybe keep him away from you as much as possible."

"I'm okay with that." I feel a little calmer passing this into Dimi's capable hands. I know how much he has riding on this weekend—he told me about his "probation" months ago, and how he feels like if this first season isn't successful, he'll have not only failed himself, but all the people who believe in him. He's especially determined not to let Derek down. He pretty much thinks the sun shines out of Derek's ass—and I know Derek well enough to say the feeling is mutual. I'd be jealous, but anyone who's ever seen them interact can see that they're just friends and colleagues, mentor and mentee, with maybe a little older-brother-younger-brother dynamic thrown in. "And when I do need to be in the same space as him, I think it would be 'normal' to have you or someone with me."

"I agree." He gives me a searching look. "Are you okay?" His tone has changed; this is no longer business Dimi. It's my boyfriend, Dimi.

This is the first time I've seen my boyfriend at work.

"I'm angry," I say honestly. "Mostly because I didn't ever want to see him again, but also because he's dragged up all those old feelings of betrayal and changed them to suit himself and could possibly fuck up every good thing going on in my life right now."

"Not every good thing." He glances at the door, then gets up, comes around the desk, and leans down to kiss me quickly. "He might fuck up work, but he can't fuck us up."

Something settles deep inside me.

It's going to be okay.

I hope.

***

That night is Monday night dinner, and I'm dreading it.

Dimi's mom has been fine since "the day of the intervention," as I've been calling it. She and I will never be besties, and we've never regained the casual friendliness we had at the holiday party, but we're cordial and polite, and there are no more barbed comments.

Still, I can't quite relax when I'm in her company. I try my hardest, because I know how important his family is to Dimi—plus his dad and gram and siblings have been great—but I always feel like I'm waiting for the other shoe to drop. She very clearly doesn't like me for her son. On the surface, that seems to be about the gap between our ages, but what if there's more to it? A little voice has whispered that it's entirely possible Rick was right about my complete and utter unsuitability to be a good boyfriend. I've been pretty good about pushing those thoughts away—new beginning, new life, etcetera—but then Rick had to call and drag all my insecurities out into the spotlight.

So… yeah, the thought of facing Monday night dinner after this dumpster fire of a day does not make me happy.

"We don't have to go tonight if you just want to chill."

Holy crap! I jump about three feet, making a squeaking noise that I didn't think my vocal cords were capable of.

"How long have you been standing there?" I demand,

hand to my chest where my heart is racing.

He shrugs, a tiny smile playing on his mouth. "I just got here. Sorry, didn't mean to scare you."

"You may have taken a decade off my life," I joke, getting my pulse rate back under control. "What did you say? I was too busy trying not to piss my pants to pay attention."

"I would pay money to see that," he informs me, chuckling. "I said we don't need to go tonight."

Wow. Is he a mind reader? For a second, I'm very tempted to take him up on that.

"No, let's go," I say instead. "Your family is so excited about this weekend. They're going to want to talk to you. Plus, your dad said he was making apple pie for dessert."

Dimi's face lights up. "He did, didn't he. Yeah, we can't miss that. Okay, are you nearly ready to go?"

"I need ten minutes, then I'm done," I promise.

"I'll come back in ten, then. Oh—before I forget, I noticed you marked two of the VIP passes as taken this afternoon. Did you convince some of your friends to come?" He sounds vaguely hopeful. He's mentioned a few times that he wants to meet my friends, and I know he's been a little worried that I have so little contact with them. He sees his friends from the community theater twice a week, although this is the first season in several years that he hasn't been producing the show. He didn't want to commit so much time while we were in the middle of getting the company going. Instead, he acts as assistant to the producer and general consultant. I go with him at least once a week to be social and also lend my expertise. I know he loves that I get along with his friends, but he also wants to be sure that I have my own circle to fall back on, separate from him. I get it—we haven't had any big fights yet, but that time will likely come, and it would be weird if I bitched about him to his friends.

"Brice and David are coming. Brice wants to run interference if Rick decides to be an asswipe. Plus, they love JU and they've always come to my opening nights. This would have been the first one they've ever missed, so I'm glad they changed their minds, even if it wasn't for a great reason."

"I can't wait to meet them. Are they staying a few days? A private meal on the weekend is probably not going to happen, but maybe early next week?" He's smiling, and my heart melts just a little bit.

"They go back Tuesday, so I thought lunch on Monday?"

"Perfect," he declares. "And they'd be welcome to Monday night dinner," he adds. "It would do Mom good to see you with your people. And I think you'd enjoy having Team Jason at the table."

I wince. "Have I been that obvious? I'm so sorry."

"Don't be—you haven't. Not so anyone else would notice, anyway. I just know you so well. Anyway, mention it to Brice. I'll be back in ten minutes, and we can go destroy Dad's pie."

I watch him go and wonder if it's too soon to say the L-word out loud. Maybe it's been "understood" for long enough and now needs to be explicit.

***

Later in the week, we have a team meeting to run through the plans for the weekend, beginning with the promotions, preshow events for VIPs, the show itself, and the afterparty and post-show events. Dimi and I discussed it and decided to tell our team that there could potentially be some trouble. We kept the details sketchy, just sharing that an ex of mine would be accompanying Mitch Craig and that we weren't sure if he had any intentions other than the obvious. Trav was shocked and appalled but hid it well until after, when he cornered me and asked if I wanted him to put out feelers. He assured me he'd word Derek up and that he'd keep an eye on things.

"Derek's great in awkward social situations," he promised. "If Rick's planning to cause trouble, Derek will charm him out of it before he knows what's happened."

That's reassuring. I'm hoping it won't come to that, but it's nice to have backup just in case.

Derek calls me a little later to reiterate that he'll run interference, and I ask him to remind me to introduce him to Brice and David.

I was right when I said everything would come together. The details are all falling into place. Rehearsals are going really well—the performers have all been intimidated into acceptable showings. It took me a while to find the right groove with them—I'm so used to working with highly experienced actors who have egos to match that I was a little too abrasive to begin with. These performers are good, talented, but lacking the experience and recognition that thickens their skins, and they took my critiques a little too much to heart at first. I was never going to be their best friend, or a gentle, coaxing kind of director, but I found a compromise between getting what I wanted from them and giving them the feedback they need to boost their confidence. And once that happened, things really started moving. They're used to working together, so there was already great chemistry between them.

We're three days from opening and we're ready.

And I've never been more freaked out in my life.

I just can't stop thinking about the fact that Rick will be there. About his call. There's something about that call that really bugs me.

Why make it in the first place? Because he wanted to set my mind at ease? That's bullshit—he must know that after the way we ended, calling out of the blue to say "no hard feelings" would stir up a hornets' nest.

Worse, that attempt to make it sound like we ended amicably by mutual agreement… there's a lot wrong with that.

There's also nothing I can do. Just wait.

CHAPTER FOURTEEN

Dimi

JASE AND I ARE in our respective offices early on Saturday morning when I hear someone banging on the (locked) main door. I glance at my watch. We've locked ourselves in because the cleaning crew is in the theater this morning and we don't want to be distracted. As soon as they leave, we'll do a walk-through to check in on things, and then I've got a last-minute meeting with the coordinator from the events department who's looking after all our VIP functions. Jase is going to the airport to pick up his friends. I'll hopefully get to meet them before the first party, because I don't want our first encounter to be when I'm distracted by work.

Am I nervous about meeting Jason's friends?

Yes. In fact, I'd go as far as to say hell, yes. So far, our relationship has been very easy for me in terms of having to impress people. Jase is it. All his friends down here were my friends first—except Trav, but Trav likes me, and we didn't meet in the context of me being Jason's boyfriend. Even Chloe, who is indisputably Jason's right arm at work but occasionally comes over for a meal, knew me first. Jason isn't close to his brother or sister, and his parents are gone, so his friends are his only emotional connections in the world—except me. And worse, he lost a lot of friends when he and the dickbag broke up. It's not even like they chose the other guy over Jason, because he moved to LA right away; it was just a case of them not wanting to hang out with him once he wasn't part of a couple.

So I really want Brice and David to like me, and I want to like them. Even if we only see them once or twice a year, it'll be a connection that grew from Jason's side of the relationship.

Did you notice the "once or twice a year"? Did you get the hint that this is now A Serious Relationship? It is. I mean, that's kind of obvious, since Jason and I haven't spent a night apart in about six weeks, but it's now at the "I want to tell him I love him" stage. Because I do.

I've said it to boyfriends before, and it was easy. Almost casual. This… isn't. This feels too important to just… say. I feel like I need to make a big deal about it, but that's kind of douchey—and anyway, it's not about any kind of elaborate ceremony or fuss. It's about the feelings, and I know he returns them. So it should be easy to say.

I'll just keep telling myself that. Maybe eventually I'll come up with a way to say it. Probably not today, though. I'm trying to keep it all together, but tonight is going to be a pretty good indication of whether I'm going to keep my job or not.

Ticket sales for the next few weeks are great—in fact, completely sold out. That's entirely due to the hype and publicity. I've alternated between friendly and polite and total asshole in my behavior with marketing. The first guy they allocated to the project was brilliant, and I was completely confident it was going to be great, but then he was in a car accident and had to take time off work. He's okay, by the way. Broken arm and a serious concussion. He's due back at the office this week—unfortunately too late to resume work on the opening night events, as selfish as that sounds.

The woman who took over from him is… fine. She's competent. She does a decent job, and in any other situation, I'd probably have no issue working with her. But this is a special case. My job is literally dependent on how this goes. So are other jobs, potentially, because although JU may not decide to close down the company on the basis of this first season, the public perception will be set, and if it's bad, it will take a lot of effort to claw back into a good place. First impressions are vital.

So Denise and I have a very controversial relationship. I push hard. She thinks I'm an asshole. I am, but I want out-of-the-box thinking, not the same generic stuff that happens at every opening night. The VIPs have to be feeling positive and excited before the show even begins. They need to remember this weekend fondly—even after the critics have written their reviews, weeks or months from now, I want them to be at parties and talk about how fabulous their time at JU was and how they can't wait to get down here again. New show opening? I want them to scramble to be included on the guest list.

And so I pushed Denise hard, and she complained about me to her boss, who came for a chat and ended up agreeing to directly oversee the project. That way someone else is pushing Denise and she doesn't hate me.

Well, not too much, anyway.

The banging comes again, and I huff and get up. I'm not going to be able to ignore that. Jason's coming out of his office too, an annoyed look on his face.

I unlock the door and snatch it open—

—and am shoved aside by a five-foot-seven whirlwind of spiky bleached hair and rhinestone sunglasses. I stand there, stunned, as he swoops on Jason, crying "I'm here at last!" and snatches him into a huge hug.

I just blink like an idiot. Another man comes in, stops beside me, and says, "Don't worry, it takes a while to get used to him. You must be Dimi. I'm David."

I shut my mouth and shake his hand, dredging up a smile. "Sorry," I apologize. "We weren't expecting you yet. Were we?" I'm sure Jason planned to pick them up from the airport.

"We got an earlier flight, and Brice decided to surprise Jase."

I glance over to where my boyfriend is talking a mile a minute at the same time as Brice. They're gripping each other's forearms and look like they might start jumping up and down like teenagers any second. There's a wide grin on Jason's face that makes every tense muscle in my body relax. Who cares about anything else when he's that happy?

Okay, so that might be taking it a bit far. I still care about other stuff. But I'm so, so glad to see him happy.

"I'm glad you guys came," I murmur, then turn to look at David properly for the first time.

Don't hate me, but my first reaction is terrible. He's not who I expected a guy as vibrant as Brice to be with. Isn't that an awful thought? But where Brice is all glitter and squeals and jumping around, David is dressed in brown tweed—I didn't even know you could still buy jackets like that—and looks like he'd happily settle into a wingback chair with his pipe and slippers and some obscure book of philosophy.

"It's great to meet you," I tell him. "I wish we had more time together, but—"

He holds up a hand. "Say no more. I've been with Brice, who's married to the theater, for decades. I know exactly how it gets right before a show opens. We just dropped in to surprise Jase and let you both know we've arrived."

"David!"

My jaw drops again as I hear what is unmistakably a squeal from my boyfriend. I had no idea his voice could reach that pitch, and I immediately make a mental note to see if I can get him to do that.

Jase throws himself at David for a hug and gets a squeeze.

"You guys! I was coming to pick you up at the airport." He pulls back and grins at them both, then grabs my hand and drags me to his side. "This is Dimi. Dimi, Brice and David." He points to each as he says their names. I love seeing him this animated and happy.

Brice looks me up and down and says, "So it wasn't just the photo," which throws me at first, but Jase turns red, and I realize he must have sent Brice a picture of me, which for some reason makes me blush too.

"It's good to finally meet you," I manage, holding out my hand. Brice gives it a derisive look, brushes it aside, and hugs me. He smells fantastic, and I'm just about to ask what cologne he wears when he whispers in my ear, "Hurt him and they'll never find all the pieces of you." Then he steps back and flashes a friendly smile.

"Great to meet you too, Dimi. We're so excited about the show tonight."

Oh my God, I love this guy. Screw one or two times a year, I'm going to make sure we see them once a month, no matter how hard it is to arrange. Jase needs his friends in his life.

"I was just telling David that I wished we had more time to spend with you," I say. "I have stuff to do in the theater, but Jase, why don't you show the guys around and get them settled at their hotel?" I can handle his to-do list at the theater this morning.

"Are you sure?" he asks, wavering between his sense of responsibility and his desire to spend time with his friends.

"Absolutely. I'll call if I have questions, but it should be fine."

His smile would be worth having to do a thousand hours' extra work.

"Wait, before you go," Brice says, "Jase said you know about the ex-who-shall-not-be-named?"

"We're naming him now," Jason informs him. "Names have power. He's no longer the bogeyman in the closet."

Brice's face lights up. "Right, so you know about Rick the dick. I'm really worried he's going to do something to fuck with Jase. It wasn't so much what he said, but the look on his face… I don't know."

"You need to meet Derek," I told him. Derek called me a couple days back, right after we told Trav about Rick, and swore he would make sure Rick never had a moment alone with Jason and that I could safely concentrate on work without worrying.

"Who's Derek?"

"You know Trav Jones, right?" Jase asks.

Brice nods. "Sure. I worked with him a couple times. Nice guy. Oh hey, he's here too, isn't he? I know I read that somewhere."

"He is, and living with Derek, who's one of the assistant directors for the company."

"Right, so this Derek guy is on Team Jason?"

"You and Derek are either going to get along great or kill each other," I tell him. "Whichever you decide, please make sure someone videos it for me."

David and Jase laugh, but Brice rolls his eyes.

"I'll call and see if Derek and Trav are home," Jason says. "We'll swing by and say hello."

I leave them to it and grab my stuff from my office. It's time to get back to work.

***

My first encounter with Rick the dick (I know it's obvious, but trust me when I say it suits him so well) is during the preshow VIP event. Jason and I are making only a flying appearance here, since the show looms before us and we want to ensure everything is going smoothly.

Control freak, you say? Guilty.

Anyway, Jase and I are doing a quick schmooze. I wanted to stick to his side the whole time, but he gave me a stern look and insisted we could get through the bigwigs in the crowd faster if we separated, so I reluctantly agreed to go right to his left. Fortunately, Derek winked at me and stepped up to join Jason within seconds. Given his position at JU and his relationship to Trav, it was entirely logical for him to do so and took a huge load off my chest.

I've just finished up with a theater critic from Atlanta—and left him smiling, I'll add—when someone taps me on the shoulder. I turn to see a nondescript middle-aged guy standing there. He looks like he reads *GQ* religiously but doesn't have the panache to pull off the style. I wrack my brains to think who he could be.

"Are you Dimitri Weston?" he asks, and his tone raises all my hackles. I don't let it show, smiling blandly as I pinpoint the location of a security guard from the corner of my eye. The fact that he's called me Dimitri concerns me; I made the decision when I took this job that all publicity would refer to me as Dimi. He would have had to dig to know my actual name.

"Dimi, please" is all I say. I don't offer a hand either, since he hasn't introduced himself yet.

He looks me up and down. "I guess I see it."

Yeah. Now I know who he is.

I don't give him the satisfaction of showing how much he's pissed me off just by being in the room.

"See what?" It sounds pleasant and vaguely bored. I deliberately let my gaze drift over his shoulder. Where's his lover, the critic who thought it was a clever idea to bring him along?

"You obviously don't know who I am."

Sighing, I drag my gaze back to his face. "Rick Henessy, right? Jason's ex? Was there something you wanted, because I have a lot of people to talk to in a very short time." That might be pushing my luck a bit. I mean, we already suspect this guy is here to cause trouble, and he does have the ear of a very influential critic.

He looks miffed, and I take the opportunity to examine him properly. Isn't he supposed to be some sort of shit-hot costume designer? I would have expected him to be dressed… better. Don't get me wrong, his clothes are top quality and everything matches beautifully, but there's nothing interesting about the outfit. He looks like a wealthy accountant. Where's the flair?

He recovers and sneers at me. "I just wanted to see what Jason has been doing lately. Don't get too comfortable." He spins on his heel and flounces away in a total diva move.

He's definitely planning something we won't like.

I don't have time to waste on him right now, but I look around for Brice and David as I make my way to the next group of VIPs. Brice is watching me, and from the look on his face, I know he saw the whole thing. I shake my head slightly, and he makes a face. He gets it, and he'll be on the lookout.

For now, I have a show to worry about.

***

I've never wanted to throw up so badly in my life.

Not the first time I produced a play for Joyville Amateur Theater.

Not when I decided to move home and applied for a job at Joy Universe.

Not my first day of college, when I was away from my family for the first time.

Not when I fumbled my way through asking Eric Gardner on a date when I was fifteen. Or when I fumbled through my first kiss on that same date.

Not even that time when I was eight and Sienna fell off her chair and hit her head because I poked her for stealing some of my waffle. There was blood everywhere, and Mom and Dad took her to the hospital, and for hours I thought she was dead and I'd killed her… over a waffle.

None of that compares to this moment. Although, it occurs to me that it might make me kind of heartless to be more concerned about a show than my sister's potential death.

Why am I even thinking about this? There is literally nothing I can do right now, in the silent moment between the house lights going down and the curtain going up. It's out of my hands.

The hands I'm wringing so hard, I fear water will start dripping from them. Or blood. I draw a deep breath and force myself to appear completely calm. I'm in the wings, and I don't want any of the performers to see me stressing and freak out themselves. There's a seat reserved for me in the VIP section, of course, but for these opening scenes, I didn't want to be out amongst the audience... just in case.

Yeah, you can say it. I'm a total coward.

Trav takes his place on the darkened stage.

This is it.

The curtain goes up.

The lights go on.

White noise fills my ears, and my vision blurs.

Breathe, Dimi!

I suck in a breath, and the world comes spinning back... in a cascade of laughter.

I focus on the stage, where the first scene is underway... and judging by the response from the audience, not a failure.

Yet, anyway.

Don't be negative.

I watch and slowly relax. Have I seen better performances? Honestly, yes. Trav is inarguably brilliant, and even with all our work, the others don't yet have his polish—or raw talent, to be blunt. But they *are* good, and if it continues like this, it will be a great performance.

It's near the first intermission when Jason finds me.

"I thought you'd be hovering somewhere," he whispers, and I shoot him a guilty glance. "Promise you'll go to your seat for the second act."

I've been planning on that anyway, so I cross my

heart with a finger. "I promise."

He kisses me quickly. "It's a success, Dimi. I can feel it, and I'm never wrong about these things." He disappears into the shadows, where I can just barely see Chloe and our stage manager waiting for him with tablets in hand.

It's probably foolish, but I'm more reassured by Jason's feeling than I could be by anything else.

***

The after-party is epic. I'm trying to keep my wits about me and not get too caught up in the high of a great show, because I'm working still, but it's hard. Everyone is happy. There's a lot of excitement, from the cast, the crew, the VIPs…. Opening night was a success and everyone knows it. We're still technically waiting for the reviews, but the smug little smirks and sparkling eyes of the critics who finally joined the party seem to be a good sign. My parents are here somewhere and managed not to embarrass me too much when they came to tell me I'm now their favorite son because they're at a party with Michael Douglas and Chris Evans. They're now in deep discussion with Mr. Douglas himself—about what, I'm not sure I want to know.

"Dimi."

I turn and immediately stand up straighter and pull

myself together. It's *them*. The bosses. Not the director of JU, who is nominally my boss but is so self-absorbed he possibly doesn't know who I am—although I did see him around earlier. No, these are *the bosses*, the CEO and CFO of Joy Incorporated, our parent company. The nephews of the founder, Edwin Joy.

The ones who cast the deciding vote to give me this job.

Suddenly, I doubt everything about my life, beginning with the suit I chose to wear tonight and ending with every decision I made for this show.

Seth Holder offers his hand. "Congratulations." He's smiling widely, and I shake his hand with a sense of relief.

Malcolm Joy claps me on the back. "Derek was right about you," he declares. "You've done a great job."

I'm almost dizzy with the compliments, but still manage to caution, "The reviews aren't in yet."

"Maybe not," Seth concedes, "but you still managed to sell out the first three weeks. And based on this evening, I don't think the reviews will be bad."

"Everyone's worked really hard," I boast, because they have, and they totally deserve the recognition. "Have you spoken to Jason yet?" I look around for him. We once again agreed to work the room separately, and I'm not ashamed to admit that I'll seize on any excuse to spend a few minutes with him.

I spot him across the room, pretty much cornered by

Rick the dick. Derek and Brice are there, and both have these shell-shocked looks on their faces. What the hell is going on?

"Good evening, gentlemen."

I force myself to smile at Mitch Craig, who's smiling expansively, and stop myself from demanding he take his lover in hand. Fortunately, he seems more interested in schmoozing with Seth and Malcolm than me, so I let them charm him while I try to look attentive and not like I'm glaring across the room.

"…and so I'm feeling quite smug," Mitch is saying, almost grinning, but Seth's smile seems to be a little set, and he's shooting glances toward me. Fuck, what did I miss? "Not only did I get to see the birth of what will be a wonderful theater company"—oooh, that's good!—"I got to reunite a couple who are so clearly meant to be together."

Wait.

What?

I open my mouth, then close it again, because what do I say? He might be talking about someone else. He probably is.

Malcolm clears his throat. "You seem to be in possession of insider information," he says, seemingly jovially. "The last I knew, Rick and Jason had separated some time ago and Rick was happily married."

Oh fuck me.

Mitch Craig shakes his head. "Oh no," he assured Malcolm, while Seth edges closer to me, and oh my

God, does this mean my bosses know Jase and I are together? The gossip has reached all the way to California? "Rick and I have been friends for years"—is that true? Wouldn't Jason have mentioned it?—"and when he left Reynolds because he realized he still loved Jason and moved back to town, I of course let him stay with me while he planned how to woo Jase back. This opportunity was just too perfect!"

I'm completely speechless.

Across the room, Jason is saying something to the dick. Brice has lost his stunned expression and looks like he's ready to beat something into dust. And Derek… looks taller than usual? And broader. Kind of threatening, really. He's not smiling. That's a big deal—Derek smiles a lot.

Mitch is still burbling on, although he seems to be talking about the show now. "…inexperienced cast, of course, but it's really only apparent because Trav Jones is there for contrast. They'll grow into their talent. I think it's very likely that some future big names will get their start here…"

"Excuse us," Seth murmurs as Malcolm nods along, "I see someone I want Dimi to talk to."

Mitch waves and smiles in acknowledgment as he continues talking, and Seth takes firm hold of my arm and draws me in the wrong direction. Can't he see I need to storm over and…

Cause a scene? At the after-party of our opening night?

Jase would kill me. And then, when I calmed down, I'd resurrect myself so I could kill myself.

"We're just going to wander around so it doesn't look like there's anything interesting going on," Seth tells me. Apparently the man is not only a brilliant CFO, but also a mind reader. "It looks like everything is under control anyway."

"We've been very careful not to let it interfere with work," I mumble, because... well, because it's that or start cursing Rick the dick.

"I think tonight is testament to that," Seth says drily. "Relax, Dimi. You've done a brilliant job, and as long as that continues, nobody cares that you and Jason are dating. Mal and I got in on the pool this time," he adds smugly, and I feel like my brain might just explode.

"Pool?" So it's not just gossip that's reached California. At least the betting couldn't have been very interesting. We went from just colleagues to together pretty much overnight. There was no flirting in the office.

He snickers. Snickers! Dignified older men who are CFOs of global corporations aren't supposed to snicker. It's just wrong somehow.

"You disappointed me," he admits. "I thought you'd move on him a lot sooner."

I.

What.

"Your endorsement of him on the short list you sent us was... enthusiastic. I got a feeling then. When I heard the rumor that Derek had a pool going"—I'm going to kill Derek, mentor or not—"I decided not to miss out this time."

I have to just leave that alone for now. There's too much else going on, especially the fact that Rick the dick is trying to steal my boyfriend in what should be my moment of triumph.

Every second it takes to casually wend our way across the room is torture.

CHAPTER FIFTEEN

Jason

YOU REMEMBER THE TIME when you were a kid eating an ice-cream cone and the ice cream fell off the cone? You had that glorious moment of pure joy and enjoyment, and then it was stolen from you.

That's how I feel right now.

Today was supposed to be the culmination of me rebuilding myself. A professional success to top off all my personal successes lately. And it was going so well. Despite the shadow that Rick's presence cast, I had a great wake-up this morning next to the love of my life, got to enjoy a couple hours with my best friends, and directed a wonderful performance this evening. This party was supposed to be about me and Dimi accepting accolades and building hype for future performances and seasons. I know Dimi's been stressed about his probation, but tonight should have put all those worries to rest. I've been looking forward to snatching a few private moments with him somewhere, then going home and fucking until we're both unconscious... and starting a new day tomorrow. With him. Here. Working together and *being* together in all aspects of our life.

Instead, I'm standing with Brice and Derek on either side like guards as Rick ruins the whole damn week for me.

"...know you feel the same. Us being apart was necessary so we could grow and realize how much we were meant to be together. Really, it catapulted us to the next phase of our relationship. I know you have commitments here, but that's fine. We can see out your contract. The quieter lifestyle will give us the chance to solidify our feelings before we go back to New York and pick up our lives."

Yep. The bastard who told me I was a drain on his being, who wished he'd never met me because I'd sucked the fun out of his life, who told me I was a person destined to go through life alone, but was lucky that my career success meant I would always be surrounded by people... that guy is declaring his love for me and planning our future together.

No, thanks.

I can sense that Brice's surprise is wearing off and that he'll soon have a few things to say. On my other side, Derek is... looming? I don't know, but he seems scary all of a sudden. Either of them is about to cause a scene, and the absolute last thing I want right now is to steal the spotlight of the evening from the Joy Village Theater Company and our brilliant opening night. Even if I have a bone-deep urge to punch Rick right in his stupid face and then loudly declare that I wouldn't even *look* at him if he and I were the last living organisms on the planet.

Instead, I say quietly, "I don't think this is the place to discuss this."

"I don't care who hears," he says with an earnestness that really doesn't fit him. "Everyone will know everything soon anyway. When Mitch agreed to help me win you back, I promised him an exclusive interview about our story."

Click.

Suddenly, this makes a lot more sense. Maybe Rick has fooled himself into thinking he actually gives a shit about me and that he wants a relationship, but the real reason he's here is to salvage his reputation. Being known far and wide as a cuckolded husband has to grate on his ego. A sympathetic article about his reunion with an ex-long-term-boyfriend, hinting that the marriage was over by his choice before that humiliating moment in the tabloids, would go a long way to fix things—in his mind, anyway.

"I didn't know Mitch wrote anything but critical reviews," I say casually. "But I'd still prefer to do this another time, somewhere quieter." Like never and nowhere. If I go out of my way to avoid him for the rest of the weekend, is he going to do something insane like make a public declaration in one of the parks and have it uploaded to YouTube? It wouldn't surprise me.

He looks like he's going to argue, maybe make a scene, and I'm calculating how fast security would be able to get him out when two men join us. One is Dimi, wearing a blandly pleasant expression that anyone who doesn't know him would think is genuine but, in reality, barely masks the rage boiling beneath. The other man is one of my ultimate bosses, Seth Holder. I've never actually met him in person, but we had a brief Skype meeting when I expressed serious interest in JU's offer. He and his cousin, the CEO, wanted me to understand how critical this venture is for them right now.

"Seth, Dimi," I say. "Have you met Rick Henessy? And Seth, this is a very good friend of mine, Brice Lang."

Seth's arrival seems to be the perfect distraction. Rick gives Dimi a disdainful glare, then turns his brightest, most charming smile on Seth. He's done work for Joy Inc. before—that was what initially put him in contact with Reynolds—but I'm not sure if he actually met anybody on the business side of things.

Seth finishes greeting Brice and turns to Rick. "I know you from somewhere, don't I?" he says, giving him a measuring look. "Have you worked for Joy Inc. before?"

Rick lights up, but I'm immediately suspicious. Seth might run—and own substantial shares in—one of the largest entertainment companies in the world, but he can't act for shit. If he were auditioning for me, he'd already be halfway home to cry in his beer.

While my ex-boyfriend and current pain in the ass reminds Seth about the movie he consulted on and waxes lyrical about how wonderful it was to work for Joy Inc., I raise an eyebrow at Dimi. Does he know what's going on? How could he? But why else would he be so angry? Has something else gone wrong? Surely we couldn't be that unlucky.

Oh hell, have some early reviews come in—bad ones?

I'm really starting to worry when Dimi shifts closer to me and subtly squeezes my arm. I meet his gaze, and he shakes his head ever so slightly.

Okay.

Whatever it is, he doesn't want me to worry about it.

I'm going to anyway, but maybe a little less. If it were something really devastating, he'd tell me.

I've tuned out the conversation going on beside me, so when Seth says, "You don't mind, do you, Jason?" it takes me a second to zone back in.

And I have no idea what he's asking.

The group has shifted a little, and Derek is standing beside and a little behind Rick, opposite me. He widens his eyes and nods emphatically.

"I don't mind at all." I try not to trip over my tongue in my haste to say the words. Dare I hope that Seth is going to get rid of Rick?

I think that must be it, because Rick looks torn. "I'd really love to, Seth, but Jason and I were in the middle of a really important conversation—"

"We can finish that later," I cut in hastily. "Tomorrow. When I can give you my full attention." *When I can hide and have security remove you without having a roomful of press look on.*

"This isn't an opportunity to pass up," Derek adds, clapping Rick firmly on the shoulder. Very firmly, I'd guess from the way Rick winces and shifts away. "How often do you get the opportunity to discuss future projects with Seth Holder?"

Oh. Seth really is saving the day. I mean, I don't think the CFO of Joy Inc. would usually discuss future projects with a costume designer. I give him a grateful smile. "That's definitely not something you can say no to, Rick, and I really should be working tonight anyway. There'll be plenty of time for us to talk." Or not.

With that vague sort-of promise from me, he lets his excitement take over and wanders off with Seth, who I now really need to get a gift for. Something amazing. I wonder if he needs a kidney?

As soon as they're out of earshot, I turn to Dimi. "We have a problem."

"You have no idea," he says grimly, and then tells me what Mitch Craig told him, Seth, and Malcolm. Because having the big bosses know that my life is a soap opera that could bring negative press to their company is just what I always wanted.

"Fuck." It's Derek who swears. "Seth's not going to be able to distract him for too long. He might be satisfied to wait for tonight, but what about tomorrow?"

Rubbing my temples, I mention my fears that Rick will make some kind of public scene if I try to ignore him.

Surprisingly, it's Brice who's the voice of reason. "Let's get through tonight before we worry about tomorrow. I'm sure between us we can find a way to have him running all over the complex looking for you until most of the opening night dignitaries have left. After that… well, he can still make a public spectacle of himself, but there'll be less chance of it being attached to the show and the company."

"That sounds like a plan," Dimi declares. "Jase? If we can hold him off until around four tomorrow, there should only be a few stragglers left. Then you can tell him to fuck off and it will be over." He freezes. "Ah… that is, if you want him to fuck off."

What? Where did that come from? Is he maybe having second thoughts about us? Is my life too dramatic for him?

No, that's bullshit. We're both letting Rick get to us, the asshole.

"I love you."

Er. I did not mean to blurt that out. Especially not in front of Brice, Derek, and some guy I've never met before who just walked over and is now watching us with unconcealed delight.

Dimi opens and closes his mouth.

Shit.

"I'm sorry, I…. You don't have to—"

"Thank Christ, because I love you too." He lunges toward me, but Derek grabs him almost before he begins the movement and yanks him back.

"Rick's facing this way," he hisses. "After everything we just went through to avoid a scene tonight, you cannot set him off by kissing Jason!"

"Sneak off and find a supply closet later," the stranger suggests, eyes dancing. "I'm Grant, by the way." He offers me his hand. "Congratulations—on the show and on being in love."

"Uh, thanks?" I shake his hand as Derek says, "Don't worry, Jase, Grant is one of the other ADs, and he's a good guy who knows when to keep his trap shut."

Grant grins. "Trap will officially be kept shut," he promises. "But first you have to spill all the secrets."

Brice starts to explain, and as all the attention focuses on him, I feel a hand close around my wrist. I glance at Dimi, and he tilts his head toward the door.

I grin.

Then we slip away to find that supply closet.

It's not that easy, of course, because we're in a hotel and all the supply closets are either in the staff areas or locked. You'd think this wouldn't be an issue, since we're both technically staff, but we don't have access to the staff areas of the hotels. Why would we?

We work in the Village.

From the way Dimi swears when his key card doesn't work, you'd think it was the end of the world. "I forgot they would have changed my clearance," he grumbles.

"You used to be able to go into the staff-only parts of the hotel?" I don't know why I'm asking. I mean, who cares?

"This is one of Derek's hotels. I used to have full access to anywhere in Derek's district." He pouts. "This new job had to have a downside, I guess."

I look around. "We're both intelligent men. There's got to be a solution."

Dimi looks to be deep in thought. "There is, but it would mean trading our privacy and integrity for a quickie."

"Just to be clear, you're referring to the quickie we"—I gesture to him and then me—"are going to have, not a quickie one or both of us would need to have with someone else?"

He rolls his eyes and grabs my hand. "Yes."

"I'm okay with that," I tell him as he tugs me along the hallway to the lobby.

We approach the concierge desk, and the woman there looks up with a warm smile. "Dimi! Hey, congratulations on the show tonight! I heard it was fantastic."

"Thanks, Tamara." He leans close. "I need a favor."

Her eyes widen and she leans in too.

"This is Jason, he's—"

"Your boyfriend," she cuts in, and I'm not sure how I feel about that. I love being Dimi's boyfriend, but I *do* work here in my own right. And hello, I directed the fantastic show she heard all about.

"Right," he says. "Anyway, Jase and I need somewhere private to… talk. Could you unlock one of the meeting rooms for us?"

Oh hell. He doesn't actually think that's going to work, does he? What was with that little pause? She's not going to believe we just want to talk.

Sure enough, she hesitates. "Dimi, we both know you're not going to talk, and letting you f—" She looks around for guests, then lowers her voice. "*Do that* in a meeting room is going to get me into trouble."

I knew she'd say no, but disappointment still sits heavy in my stomach.

"How about a trade," Dimi offers. "I'll tell you something about me and Jase that only Derek, Trav, and Grant Davis know—and they're busy socializing at the after-party. You could be the first one to share."

I'm speechless. Gossip as currency? This place….

Tamara bites her lip and thinks about it. When she finally shakes her head, I honestly believe she's on the verge of tears.

"I wish I could," she says, and yep, it sounds like she's about to start crying. "But the meeting rooms are guest spaces and they're available 24-7. Someone could wander past and hear you."

I guess that's it then. I have to respect her integrity, especially because Dimi and I just threw ours away.

But Dimi's not done yet.

"Compromise?" he suggests. "What about the janitor's storeroom outside the day spa? The spa is closed at this time so it's really unlikely anyone will be near there."

Her whole face lights up.

"I guess that would be okay. And you'll still tell me the secret?"

I don't think I've ever had to work this hard to have sex before.

"Of course," Dimi assures her. "In fact, I'll tell you right now. Jason and I just said 'I love you' to each other."

A hand covers her mouth. "Oh! That's so fabulous! I'm so happy for you guys."

Moments later, she's programmed a key card to give us access to the storeroom in question.

"We'll bring it back," Dimi promises, and she waves us off with a misty look in her eyes, even as she picks up her phone and begins texting.

Dimi leads me through a maze of corridors to the part of the hotel where the spa is. The lights here are dimmed.

"I feel like the spontaneity has been sucked out of this moment," I say as I wait for him to swipe the key card over the reader beside an unmarked door.

"That doesn't mean we can't still have fun." He opens

the door and gestures for me to precede him.

Inside, the "room" is really more of a closet, lined with shelves that hold cleaning and maintenance equipment. The overhead light is glaring florescent, and I honestly can't think of a less romantic place to have sex. Maybe a bathroom while someone is taking a shit in the next stall.

Don't judge me for the mistakes of my youth.

Dimi crowds in behind me, pulling the door closed and, at the same time, turning off the light. The tiny space plunges into darkness.

And suddenly, I'm in a dark room with Dimi pressed up against me.

Hello.

He kisses my neck, then runs his tongue up the side until he reaches my ear.

"I love you," he whispers. It seems romance is alive after all.

I turn in his arms, and our mouths meet, tongues tangling in a wet, impatient kiss. I yank his shirt free of his pants and get to work on his belt. It's taking too fucking long, and eventually I pull my mouth free so I can concentrate all my attention on the issue. Not being able to see *and* being distracted by how amazing he tastes makes it too hard.

No pun intended.

I finally get his pants open and sink to my knees, sliding down his body the whole way. Dimi groans, and a wicked little smirk tugs at my lips.

Going down on Dimi in the dark is amazing. I had no idea the lack of light would add so much to the experience. I've always liked sucking cock—there's such a huge power rush—but having to do it entirely without sight is…. Wow. There's the thickness of him stretching my mouth, his smell, his soft skin under my fingers. Nothing new, but yet all new, and so much more intense.

His hands are in my hair, holding my head, but he seems content to let me drive. Finally, though, he tugs me off. "Do you have a condom?" he gasps, and I shake my head in the cradle of his grip.

"I didn't think we'd need one tonight. Do we need one? I can just finish you like this." I hear a thud that could be his head falling back against the door.

"Sure," he says faintly. "If that's what you want, I guess I can make the sacrifice."

I grin in the darkness.

"You're such a giving guy." Lightly, I stroke my index finger over his balls, and his whole body shudders. "I'm sorry, was that uncomfortable?"

"It was awful," he says, voice strained. "Do it again."

So I do. And this time, I suck the head of his dick at the same time. The sound he makes has my already stiff cock going hard enough to pound nails.

It's not long before he's tugging on my hair again. "Jase, I'm gonna…."

He's so sweet to warn me, but I want everything

he has to give. Seconds later, he shouts something incomprehensible and comes.

I lick him clean, relishing his hissed-in breath—he's always sensitive after coming—then get to my feet and kiss him.

"I love you," I murmur finally, and I feel him smile against my lips.

"I love you. Your turn now."

***

We've been gone close to two hours before we rejoin the party, and we're both sex drunk and feeling amazing.

I don't even feel guilty that we left the party when we were supposed to be working the crowd.

Well, not very guilty.

At least, not until we get there to find that the *reviews are in*.

"We've been looking for you everywhere!" Trav exclaims, a tablet in one hand and a drink in the other. "Look!" He thrusts the tablet toward us and nearly overbalances. Derek, amused, steadies him.

Dimi takes the tablet and I crowd in beside him. We read Laurie Henderson's review. Then Mitch Craig's. Then the ones by the critics from Jacksonville and Atlanta. One from an LA entertainment site. A few more.

Finally, I lift my gaze to meet Dimi's. He has a crazy

grin on his face.

We did it.

***

It's past dawn before the party breaks up. To keep people's interest, Dimi and the events and marketing people packed all the VIPs up in buses and moved the party from the Village to one of JU's swanky themed hotels—one with a ballroom that opens onto a pool area overlooking the river (which is manmade, in case you're wondering. It runs through most of the complex and is really a canal, I guess). Most of the guests stick around to watch the sun rise over the river before the clever events people usher them away to take advantage of a buffet breakfast and be taken back to their hotels for a nap before heading home.

Dimi smiles tiredly at me and takes my hand. "You didn't want to go to the buffet, did you?"

"Hell no. Let's go home." These all-night parties were a lot easier thirty years ago. Heck, even twenty years ago.

We officially relieved our assistants of duty about five hours ago, but they hung around for the fun—plus I think they both appointed themselves our guardians, because they checked in a few times to make sure Rick hadn't caused any trouble. I see them now, talking to Derek and Trav, who somehow both manage to look as fresh as daisies. Trav should be in the throes of a hangover by now at the very least, but he's bright-eyed and looks ready to start the new day.

"I guess we should say goodbye," I concede, even though it's an extra forty-five-second delay to getting horizontal. Dimi chuckles and pulls me toward our friends.

Huh. "Our" friends. I like that.

Although speaking of friends... "Has anyone seen Brice and David?" It's been a couple of hours since Brice started a conga line around the pool. Yes, seriously.

"They're at the buffet," Chloe says with a grin. "Brice said he plans to eat until he feels sick, then sleep the day away. He did tell me to remind you that you're welcome to hide out in their room if you want?" She sounds a little confused by that, since we haven't had a chance to tell her about the plan for today. I'm too tired to recount the whole story now, so I just shrug and say, "Thanks, Chloe."

"Seth and Malcolm left a few hours back, but they said to tell you they want to meet tomorrow morning. They're going to hang around a few days, and I guess since your branch of the business is the reason they're here, you get the first meeting. Expect to get the formal request via the app sometime today," Derek informs us.

A few months—or even a few weeks—ago, I might have been nervous about that. But not today.

Dimi and I kicked ass, and I fully expect this meeting to be congratulatory, with maybe a side of "let's increase your budget." The gleam in Dimi's eyes tells me he's thinking the same thing.

We say our goodbyes and head back to my place, because it's closer by about ninety seconds, and fall asleep within minutes.

Only to be woken by the shrill ring of a phone.

I groan, because it's mine. Dimi pulls his pillow over his head as I roll toward the edge of the mattress and gracelessly clamber to my feet. By the time I get to where I dropped my pants earlier, the ringing has stopped. I'm tempted to just leave it and go back to bed, but—

BRRRRRIIIING!

Yep. What the hell possessed me to choose such an annoying and obtrusive ringtone?

I snatch up my pants and dig the phone out. I don't know the number on the screen, but since I blocked Rick's number, it wouldn't surprise me if he's just calling from another phone.

"Hello?" I mumble, swiping a hand over my face. I pull my phone away from my ear to check the time. We've slept nearly six hours, which is pretty good.

"…can't find you anywhere and none of the staff will give me your address," Rick is saying.

Fuck me, I would hope not. Is he nuts?

"None of the staff knows my address," I tell him, "and even if they did, they'd get into a lot of trouble for giving it out. Rick, I'm sleeping. It was a long night last night. Can this wait until I'm awake?"

I can practically *hear* him pouting. "Fine," he huffs. "When can we meet?"

In the bed, Dimi sits up, looking far more awake and alert than me. I roll my eyes at him.

"You're staying at the Chateau, right?" I'm pretty sure that's where we put the highest-profile VIPs. He makes a noise of agreement, so I say, "They have a small terrace lounge on the fifth floor—let's meet there at five. It's closed at that time, but I can get us in." That exclusiveness will appeal to him, but more importantly, it means we'll be private. No chance for a public scene that can be recorded by a tourist's iPhone and uploaded to the internet. Although depending on how long he draws it out, waiting until five might mean I'll have to hustle to get to the theater.

A thought occurs to me.

"What time is your flight?" No way do I want to delay his departure.

"Don't worry about that, this is more important," he says breezily.

Um. No.

"Don't throw money away." My dislike of wasting money even though I have plenty was one of the things he threw in my face when he left, and I figure reminding him of that right now can't hurt. Plus, I want him on that plane.

He hesitates, hopefully remembering how much he

apparently hated living with me, then admits, "It's at five thirty."

I instantly reassess, because he's getting on that plane if it kills me. "Why don't we meet in forty-five minutes?" There will still be some VIPs floating around, but if we stick to the terrace lounge, hopefully we can avoid them.

"That would be great. I can't wait to see you… I've missed you." He lowers his voice in that way I used to find so sexy, but it does nothing for me anymore.

"Yeah, see you soon." I end the call and sit down on the side of the bed. I'd really hoped to snooze a bit more, fool around with Dimi, have a long, hot shower and a decent meal while checking off my to-do list before going to the theater for tonight's show.

"I'll call the Chateau and warn them we're using the terrace lounge," Dimi says, crawling across the bed to kiss my shoulder. "Better to get it over with sooner and make sure he's on that plane."

"Yeah," I mutter. "Thanks." Wait. "You can't come with me."

He pauses while rummaging through his pants, presumably looking for his phone. "What?"

I shake my head. "I need to do this alone, Dimi. He… he made me feel like I wasn't good enough. I *let him* make me feel that way. It's taken me a long time to rebuild my self-worth, and I need to do this now without having backup there." It sounds faintly ridiculous, but it really means something to me, and I hope he gets that.

He studies me for a long time, then sighs. "Yeah, okay. I'm letting my ego get in the way here, but this isn't about me."

Have you ever given a small child something they really, really wanted and watch their whole being just light up? That's how I feel right now. Like I've lit up from the inside out.

"I love you."

We said it last night, many times after that first weird public declaration, but it bears repeating. It means something. Especially now. My man loves and respects me enough to push aside his own instinctive need to "protect" me.

His expression softens, and he drops his pants and comes back to the bed to kiss me.

A few minutes late won't hurt.

***

Rick's waiting when I get to the terrace lounge at the Chateau, and he's scowling. He doesn't like to be kept waiting. Fortunately, some accommodating staff member unlocked the door so he could wait inside—or outside, as the case may be.

"You're late," he snaps, and I try not to feel pissed about his tone. I *am* late, after all.

"I had to drive in from town," I remind him. "And I

was asleep when you called. I needed a shower and coffee." And some groping with my boyfriend. We thought about a quickie, but the fact is, I can't get it up multiple times a day anymore, especially after a big night like last night, so we decided to save it for later.

He doesn't look mollified. "I would have come to you if I'd known where you were."

I take a deep breath. "Rick, none of that matters. I'm here now."

His face changes. "You're right, of course." He comes forward, arms reaching to me, and I step back.

"Let's sit." I gesture to a pair of chairs and then plant myself in one. It's not a particularly roomy chair, but that's fine—it means there's definitely no way for Rick to join me in it. Not that that was something he ever used to do, but then, he never used to act like I was so eminently desirable, either. Not since that first year we were together.

A momentary fear seizes me. Is Dimi's interest going to wane after the first year, too? Will I become a pair of comfortable old socks, and then eventually a pair of threadbare socks that causes blisters, just like with Rick?

No. Even this early in our relationship, there are notable differences. And now is not the time to be worrying about something that may never happen.

Rick drops into the other chair and leans forward to take my hands. I draw them back, beginning to feel like I'm in some kind of farce. Shit, how to begin?

"There's been a lot of upheaval in both our lives over the past couple of years," I venture cautiously and watch as a repentant expression crosses his face. He's always been a good actor—not up to professional standard, but good enough to fool most people.

"We got too complacent in our relationship. We forgot how much we love each other and let ourselves get distracted by the world."

Ooookay. That's not quite how I remember it.

"You're right, we got complacent in our relationship. *I* got complacent. I was so comfortable in my life that I ignored all the signs that—" Nope, calling him a cheating dickbag is not going to help things. "—uh, that I wasn't really that happy anymore. I needed a change. This move has been great for me, and Rick, as wonderful as our life together was for so many years, we really just grew apart."

A flurry of emotions takes over his face. Anger, hurt, regret, fear... and that last is one I can understand. Starting over is hard, and in my own storm of bad memories, it's easy to forget that Rick was betrayed too. He's the bad guy in my story, but he has his own cheating ex... and his story was splashed across tabloids and gossip sites all over the country. It would be so easy for me to walk away and say he got what he deserved, but as much as he hurt me, aren't I in a better place now? My career is just as solid as ever, and I'm loving the challenges involved in this new venture. My real friends have rallied around me.

I've made new friends. And I have Dimi. Honestly, the last few years—maybe even as many as the last five—with Rick, I was just going through the motions. I told myself I loved him, but the truth is, I was just too comfortable in my life to realize that we'd both changed in different ways over the years.

I can be a better person here.

"Part of me is always going to love you," I say, because it's true. The memories I have of our early life together are good. Now that I no longer feel such vicious anger and bitterness toward him, I can look back on those times fondly. But it's a closed chapter for me. "You were a central part of my life for a long time. And I'm not going to lie, when—when we separated, it was really hard for me. I struggled to rediscover myself and what I wanted. Being single after being part of a couple for so long was a challenge I wasn't prepared for. But I found my feet, and I realized a few things about us. A relationship usually takes compromise and commitment, but neither party should feel like they have to sacrifice, like they have to live a life that doesn't suit them. We've both changed as we've gotten older, and even though we might have still loved each other, we didn't want the same things anymore. We wanted to live different lives. I didn't want to be as social anymore, and that meant that you were stuck with a party pooper every time we went out, or we stayed home—or you had to go out on your own. That's not fair for you." Or for me.

His jaw sets stubbornly. "I want to be with you."

Ugh. "Why?" I ask bluntly. Time to take off the kid gloves. "Because you don't want to be alone? Because you want a story to spin for the media so they'll forget about what Reynolds did? It doesn't work that way, Rick."

I may as well have punched him in the gut. He looks devastated. I soften my tone a little. "It's not easy to start again, but you're a strong person, Rick. You have friends. You have a solid career and a great professional reputation. You're good-looking. And now you're single. Take advantage of this great opportunity."

For a long moment, he stares at me, and I'm sure he's going to keep arguing.

Then he sighs and flops back in his chair. "It's just so fucking tough, you know?" He runs a hand through his hair, and now I'm looking at the real Rick, not the fake suitor who's been haunting me for the past week. "Everywhere I go lately, people look and me with sympathy, or they snigger and point."

"Someone's bound to do something newsworthy soon," I assure him. "Just ride it out until the next celebrity scandal, and then you can get back to your regular life."

He brightens. "True. I guess I've just never been the patient type." He looks around. "Are you really happy here, Jase? Because it's kind of cool, but in a short-term way."

I grin. "I'm happy," I assure him. "The slower pace

is perfect for me."

"Well, okay." He gets up, and I follow suit. "I'm gonna head to the airport. I'm glad things are good for you." For a long, awkward moment, we stare at each other, then he grabs me in a tight hug. "See you, Jase."

I stand there after he's gone, part of me sad. Mostly, though, I'm relieved and excited that I can move forward without anger and bitterness weighing me down.

CHAPTER SIXTEEN

$\mathcal{D}\textit{imi}$

JASON'S BEEN GONE LESS than half an hour when my mom calls. I'm ashamed to say I debate with myself for a second about whether to ignore it. I'm still tired from last night, distracted by thoughts of Jase meeting with his ex, and I have a pile of things to do before tonight's show.

But it's my mom, so I answer. "Hey, Mom."

"My sweet boy." I'm instantly on alert. She sounds like she's been crying.

"Mom, what's wrong? Is Gram okay?"

"She's fine, Dimi. I have something to tell you. Are you home?"

"Uh…" My mind races. What could it be? "I'm at Jason's. I'll come to you—ten minutes. Mom, are you alone? Is someone there with you?" Could she be sick?

"Your dad and gram are here," she assures me.

"I'm okay, baby. I just need to talk to you."

"Okay. I'm on my way."

Needless to say, I don't waste any time. I debate whether to text Jase and let him know I'm going but decide to wait. Depending on what Mom has to say, I might still be back before him.

I make it to my parents' house in record time and let myself in, calling, "Mom? Hello?"

"We're in here," Dad shouts back, and I follow the voices to the living room. Mom and Dad are sitting together on the couch, Gram in one of the armchairs. They all look solemn.

"What's going on?" I scan them all—nobody looks hurt or sick.

"Sit down, Dimi," Dad says, and he sounds sad. I'm not going to be able to rush them, so I sit in the other armchair and wait. "Your mom and I overheard something at the party last night," he begins. "It's something you really need to know."

I don't know why, but my mind immediately flashes to drugs. Is someone on the cast using? Or worse, dealing? JU has a pretty strict drug policy. This is not an ideal time to need to recast.

"Who is it?" I blurt. I know it can't be Trav, thank God, but there are some other key players we can't afford to lose right now.

Mom blinks, and Dad looks confused. Gram just sits there. "You mean you know?" Mom asks.

"No," I say honestly. "I had no idea. This is terrible.

Recasting right after opening night—a successful opening night—is going to cause gossip. The truth is going to get out, and the press will all be negative. Depending on how they spin it, this could cause issues for all of JU. I'm going to lose my job." Am I overreacting? I feel like maybe I'm overreacting.

My parents stare at me like I'm insane. Gram chuckles softly.

"Dimi," Dad says slowly, "what are you talking about?"

I sigh and lean back in the chair. "To be honest, I have no idea. You've freaked me out so much that I'm jumping to ridiculous conclusions. Just tell me straight out: did you hear something to make you think one of the cast has a drug problem?"

Dad laughs, and Mom's lips twitch. "No."

A load lifts from my chest. "Okay. Phew." I sit up straight. "So what is it, then?"

The humor disappears. "Dimi, we're so sorry," Dad says softly. "Last night we heard someone proposition Jason, and he made plans to meet up with him today."

Well, yeah.

It takes a second for the meaning behind their sorrowful faces and words to sink in, and then I laugh.

"Dimi?" Mom asks worriedly. "I think he's hysterical," she says to Dad and Gram.

"I'm not hysterical," I manage to say, sucking in a deep breath and trying to calm down. "Sorry. Just… I thought you were going to tell me something terrible."

"It's not terrible?" I've shocked Dad, but Mom looks… hopeful?

"It's not true."

Dad smiles sadly. "I'm so sorry, Dimi, but it is. I heard it myself."

"Yeah, but what you heard was Jason's ex being a pain in the ass and Jason trying to fob him off without causing a scene," I explain.

Mom shakes her head. "Maybe that's what Jason told you—"

"Mom, we'd been expecting the guy to cause trouble of some kind," I interrupt. "Not that, exactly, but something. The plan was to delay and distract until any scene caused wouldn't be attached to opening night. Jason's gone to meet him now to tell him to get lost."

"Are you sure?" Mom raises an eyebrow. "It sounds like Jason might be sneaking around."

"You're insane," I say flatly. "In fact, you both are. Derek was right there with Jason when Rick 'propositioned' him. Do you really think Jase is so stupid as to make an assignation in front of one of my friends—or that Derek would have stood there and let him?"

Dad blows out a huge breath and shakes his head ruefully, chuckling a little. "What a relief. Sorry, Dimi, I never saw them. I was facing the other way and didn't want to turn around in case I caught their attention," he says, then freezes.

We all look at Mom.

"Sascha? Did you see Derek there?" Dad sounds sad again, and I get why when Mom's face twists.

"Jason could still be sneaking around. He's convinced Dimi that this ex is here to cause problems—it's the perfect cover."

"Oh, Sascha." Gram gets up and goes to stand in front of Mom. "You need to let this go. Dimitri is in love with Jason. Jason loves Dimitri. They are good men who are good for each other. Why do you dislike him so?"

"That kind of age gap is just not right," Mom insists stubbornly, and my stomach sinks.

"Mom, we've talked about this."

"And I've been nice to him! But that doesn't mean I have to approve."

"You don't have to approve," I agree. "But respecting my choices also means not trying to break us up. Do you not care if I'm unhappy, as long as you get what you want?"

"That's a terrible thing to accuse me of. I'm your mother. The only thing I've ever wanted for you is that you're happy."

"It doesn't seem that way," I declare bluntly. "I'm happy now, with Jason, and yet you're going out of your way to cause problems."

"This is ridiculous, Dimi. I heard your boyfriend make plans to meet up with another man and I was not supposed to say anything to you?"

I level her with a look. "Context is important, Mom. The fact that one of my best friends was there is a pretty big indicator that nothing hinky was going on. And anyway, what did you hear exactly? What were these 'plans'?"

Mom clamps her mouth shut, and Dad sighs.

"There were no plans. Not really. Jason said something about discussing it somewhere else, another time. It was all very vague." He shakes his head. "I'm sorry, Dimi. I should have thought this through more clearly."

Yeah, he should've, but I can see why he didn't. Initially, even the suggestion that I was being cheated on would have raised his ire. And then when he calmed down and the critical thinking should have kicked in, he had Mom confusing the issue.

"This has to stop," I say firmly to Mom. "I mean it. The only reason I'm not walking away from you right now is because Jason isn't close to his family and he loves that I'm close to mine. I want to give him a close family, but if need be, I can live without that." I don't mention that my relationship with my siblings won't change, but that she'll be missing out. "I love you, Mom, but I love him too. And I'll choose him."

She looks utterly devastated, but I stand firm. She looked that way the last time we talked about this, and clearly it didn't stop her from trying to cause trouble. She needs to know I'm serious.

But fuck, how I wish we weren't having this conversation. My stomach hurts.

"There will be no choosing," Gram declares. "Go home, Dimi. Enjoy your Sunday afternoon. We will see you and Jason tomorrow night at dinner."

"But—" Mom begins, and I lose it.

"But what? There are no buts! Jesus, Mom, what's this really about? You don't like the age gap? Why? Why does it even matter?"

There's a moment of shocked silence. I keep my gaze firmly on Mom. I want answers. I want to know why she's so adamant about this and if it's going to keep coming back to haunt me.

Mom stares at me.

I stare back. I'm not going anywhere until she answers me.

Finally she sighs, leans back in her chair, and focuses on the ceiling.

"You have to understand, Dimi, as a parent, it kills me to watch my kids make mistakes when I know better."

Part of me wants to leap in and tell her she knows nothing, but I keep quiet.

"Most of the time, I make myself stand back and let things happen, but this… this is not something I can just let go."

I can't stop myself this time. "Why, Mom? Why is this the line?"

She sighs again and looks at me. "When I was in

college, I fell in love with one of my professors."

Well. That wasn't what I expected her to say.

"What?" Gram demands, eyes wide. I glance over at Dad and see surprise on his face too. Clearly this is something Mom's kept to herself all these years.

"I was eighteen," Mom says defensively. "I went to him for help with one of my assignments, and he was—I thought—charming and sophisticated and a real man, not like my classmates, who were more interested in getting drunk and high and telling fart jokes. I hadn't yet met the people I fit with, the ones who would be real friends, and I was a little lonely. So I kept making up things I needed help with and going to see him, and we talked a lot about all sorts of things. With the perspective of maturity, I can see how much he was humoring me, how condescending he actually was during those conversations, but at the time...." She shrugs. "One afternoon he invited me to go home with him and continue our discussion over dinner. Just a casual meal between friends, he called it, and I was so flattered that I went. It all developed from there."

I'm so completely off-balance that I can't think what to say. It's my *mom*. I mean, I know she has an identity beyond that, that she went to college in New York and lived there for a few years after, dated people, had friends, worked, met Dad... had a life outside of what I know for her, basically. But I can't quite compute that she was an innocent eighteen-year-old who was seduced by her professor.

"He was much older?" Dad asks quietly, and I force myself to pay attention.

"In his fifties." Mom smiles bitterly. "He actually had two children at that college. One of them was a classmate of mine. I never even knew until after."

Gram shakes her head. "Was he married?"

Mom nods. "I didn't know. At the time we were... his wife had gone home to New Hampshire to nurse her terminally ill mother. I found out he was married when she came home unexpectedly to surprise him one weekend."

We all wince. That must have been traumatic for her. I can't help but remember what Jase told me about Rick's alleged visits to his sick mother.

But....

"Mom, I'm so sorry that happened to you. And I can see why, after an experience like that—"

"Oh, I'm not done," Mom breaks in.

Sweet hell, there's more?

"When his wife came home and it came out that all his protestations of love and admiration were just a ploy to get a teenager into bed, he told me that there was no reason for us to stop seeing each other. When I made a dramatic declaration about never wanting to see him again, he threatened to tell the dean I'd cheated and then tried to bribe him to keep quiet by offering sex and have me thrown out of school."

Holy fuck.

"I was lucky. His wife, who had gone into the living

room to get some of her stuff before she stormed out, overheard him and told him if he dared to do any such thing, she'd tell the dean herself what had happened."

I wait. I don't think there's more, but just in case....

"So that's how I know it's a mistake to get involved with a man so much older."

Okay. She's done.

"It completely sucks that you had to go through that," I say carefully. "I really hope that he was punished in some way—maybe he died friendless and alone. We can hope, right?" I get why she didn't report him, especially back then. Things wouldn't have gone well for her.

She smiles weakly. "It's not nice to hope for someone else's misfortune," she chides. "But yes."

"But... there's no resemblance between what happened to you and my relationship with Jason."

She frowns. "Dimi—"

"No, Mom. Please listen. You were eighteen, living away from home for the first time, and you said it yourself, you were lonely. He was your professor, in a position of authority. He was also using you and didn't care about you at all or intend for the relationship to last. I'm an adult. I've been dating for a long time, have been looking after myself for over a decade. I have a lot of family and friends here—I'm not lonely at all. Jason is my colleague, but technically, I'm *his* boss. He's not married, not in a relationship with anyone else, and he genuinely loves me. I love him. This is not a fling, Mom—he and I are planning our future. You can't hate him just because he's older than me. I get why this flips a switch for you, but I also expect the logical, rational, mature part of you to step in and realize there's no similarity to what happened to you."

"I can't believe you can say that after—"

"Dimitri, go home."

There's no arguing with Gram when she uses that tone, so I get up, kiss her, hug Dad, and leave. Maybe it's a dick move not to kiss Mom too, but even though I do love her and my heart aches for what she went through, right now I kind of hate her too. We're dealing with enough this weekend without her adding to the pile.

***

By the time Jason gets home and recounts what happened with Rick, I've changed my mind about a dozen times about whether I should tell him about my visit to my parents. In the end, I figure he needs to know—it may come up at some stage. And anyway, I don't like the idea of keeping big secrets from him.

So now we're sitting on his couch, mentally and emotionally overloaded.

"Are you okay?" he asks finally. "I'm so sorry. I thought she'd... well, I don't think she'll ever like me, but I thought she'd gotten used to the idea of me. And it can't have been easy hearing about what happened to her."

I give a little shrug. "Same. I wish she felt different, and I hate that she had to go through that, but I guess it is what it is." I take his hand and squeeze. "I'm okay. What about you?"

He smiles and leans into me. "I wish your mom liked me, too. But I'm done trying to please other people. The only ones who matter are me and you."

Studying his face, I see something new there. He's always had an air of authority, of confidence, the kind that comes with decades of having people defer to you, but now it seems to radiate from him.

"You feel better now that you've talked to Rick." It's not a question, but he nods.

"Closure, I guess. A year ago, if someone had told me Rick would be in the position he was in today, dumped, humiliated, trying to weasel his way back into my life, I would have felt… triumphant. Vindicated. I had… I guess they were revenge fantasies, daydreams of me spurning him and walking away filled with satisfaction and pleasure that he was suffering what I'd suffered. I'm not proud of them," he adds, "especially not now. Because today I basically got to spurn him and walk away, and I felt sorry for him, for everything he's going through. I don't think I'll ever forgive him for the way he ended our relationship, but I'm glad now that it ended, and I don't want to waste more time or energy on hating him. I just want to let it go."

The tiny kernel of anxiety that's been doing

somersaults in my stomach since Rick called earlier finally dissipates. I lift a hand to Jason's face and cup his cheek.

"I love you."

He kisses me. "I love you too."

***

Jase and I meet with Seth Holder and Malcolm Joy at nine thirty on Monday morning. Outwardly, I'm confident that we're about to be praised, but there's a tiny inner voice that insists I be ready for anything.

So I am.

Jason had to drag me to bed at two in the morning, because I was determined to have all my i's dotted and t's crossed. There is nothing that could even remotely be considered a problem that I don't have an answer for—and just in case we *are* going to be praised, I'm ready with papers to support my bid for a bigger budget.

All bases covered.

So why am I still so nervous?

Malcolm grins at us. "Congratulations again on a fantastic opening weekend," he declares. "I hope you don't mind, but Seth and I had a look at the numbers this morning." As the CFO of Joy Inc., Seth has access to all financial records. Not that I would have denied him access to them—especially not when they look this good. After the reviews from opening night went live, marketing worked their mojo and did some clever email marketing to upcoming guests at JU. We're now sold out for six weeks, with limited availability for an additional two weeks after that.

"We don't mind at all," I say smoothly. "I had a look myself."

Seth laughs at that, and Jase elbows me.

"Were you dancing for *joy* while you looked?" Malcolm asks with a little twinkle in his eye, and it's my turn to laugh. "In all seriousness, the numbers are impressive. Given your record with the company and the references you were given for this job, we expected you to be successful, but this exceeds that. Well done, Dimi."

I push down the urge to jump up on the conference table and do a victory dance, and instead restrain myself to "Thank you. I know you took a risk on me, and I want you to know how much I've appreciated this opportunity. I can't take all the credit for our success—Jason and Trav and the team have all worked so hard."

"We know. You've all been a credit to the company," Seth says. "Jason, we never doubted that you could pull this off, even given the limitations that were imposed, but you, too, have surpassed our expectations. I know we're not even halfway through your contract, but we want to make it clear that we plan to extend it."

"Thank you," Jason says placidly. "I'd like to make it clear that I plan to accept the extension—as long as the terms are satisfactory."

It's my turn to elbow him, but Seth just smirks. "Speaking of satisfactory, can we assume that the situation from Saturday night has been resolved?"

"Of course." Jase doesn't add anything more, and neither do I. Our personal lives don't need any more stage time at work.

"Good. Now, we want to go through some details with you both, but first, I think we should discuss what Mal and I envision for the future."

Right. Crunch time.

I tell myself not to be stupid. Seth and Malcolm wouldn't have just spent ten minutes telling us how awesome we are if they planned to pull the rug out from under us.

Would they?

Jase must know what I'm thinking, because he pinches my leg.

"Dimi, I imagine you have a plan in place for growth, and it's probably an ambitious plan... am I right?"

"That depends on what you consider ambitious." I can't stop the smartass from peeking out. Malcolm snorts and tries to hide it with a cough.

"Well, ambitious or not, whatever plans you have are going to be limited by the practical fact that we only have a finite number of theaters and they're all booked for use through to the end of the year. The only reason we were able to get things moving so quickly for the Joy Village Theater Company was because of a cancellation for the show that was supposed to play late last year and early this year. The events department cleared the schedule, and that theater is now officially yours, but we can't get you another one until next year, no matter how well you do."

I mull that over. The average run of a show at JU is two to three months. Some have run a little longer, some less. When I began planning, I calculated each "season" to be on the longer side of JU's average at twelve weeks. If I managed to wrangle another theater, and if the timing lined up, production and rehearsals for our second show could have begun before the first show ended, and the third show could have opened while the second was still running. Having only one theater limits me—especially since we don't have any additional space. All auditions, rehearsals, and set construction take place in the theater. It would be difficult and impractical to begin production on another show while *Out of Line* is still running, which means the break between seasons is going to be longer than I wanted.

"That's fair enough," I concede, because what else am I going to do? Insist that they have events cancel one of the scheduled shows? I'd have to pay the contract penalties out of my budget, and that's not happening. "However, given our numbers so far, I think it's reasonable for me to ask that events put a temporary hold on one of the theaters for the first quarter of next year, pending the final numbers for our first run. If things continue as well as they have, at that stage they can allocate the theater to us for, let's say, six months, to be renegotiated depending on the outcomes of our next two shows. If for whatever reason the numbers tank by the end of this season, they'll still have about six months to find something for that theater."

Seth glances at Malcolm. "That sounds very reasonable. I have no problem okaying it."

I smile at him. "Great. I'd also like additional space to begin production for our second show so we can open as soon as possible after *Out of Line* closes."

Malcolm raises an eyebrow. "You don't ask for much, do you?"

"Believe me, if you saw his plan, you'd be marveling that he's restrained himself," Jason says drily. "But I have to second his request. Additional space may look like an expense right now, but it'll be less expensive than having the theater empty while we're in rehearsals between shows. The more nights we're selling tickets for, the better."

I mentally blow him a kiss.

"The issue with that is that we don't just have empty buildings lying around," Seth points out. "JU only constructs buildings for dedicated purposes. Let me talk to facilities and see if they have any ideas before I make promises."

"Sure," I immediately agree. I think I've pushed my luck enough for now, especially since we still need to go through all the JVTC books. Best not to antagonize them before that. We may be their pet project for now, but that could easily change.

All in all, I'm considering this meeting a win.

CHAPTER SEVENTEEN

Jason

I'M NERVOUS ABOUT DINNER tonight, more than I was for the meeting this morning. I know Dimi was freaked about the big bosses scrutinizing the company—last night I had to forcibly stop him from obsessing over reports we did not need—but given our success over the weekend, I was confident we would be getting the go-ahead to look at expansion.

Which we did.

But tonight….

I've mostly accepted that Dimi's mom will never like me. She might begin to accept me more over time, but it's unlikely she'll ever let go of her negative feelings. Especially now that they're tied to her family's disapproval. I don't blame Dimi and the others for telling her how they felt about her attitude, but to her, it had to feel like her loved ones were ganging up on her… and it was my fault. She'll never forget that, even if she is able to disassociate me from her bad memories.

Still, even though I've come to terms with not having a loving relationship with my future mother-in-law, I don't like it. And I'm nervous to face her tonight, so soon after her feelings were rubbed raw by Dimi… and her husband, and her mother.

Fun times.

So as Dimi and I approach the front door and he pulls out his keys, I brace myself for the worst.

Inside, everything is much like it always is for Monday night dinner. Dimi's dad and gram are in the kitchen, getting the food ready, and everyone else is lounging around in the living room. I do the greeting rounds, getting a real kick out of it when the kids call me Uncle Jason. I have nephews and nieces of my own, of course, pretty much grown up now, but I hardly ever saw them even when they were little. Maybe I should try reaching out to them now that they're older and don't have gatekeepers?

A thought for another day.

Dimi's family is made up of huggers and kissers, so when I reach Sascha, I'm not sure what to do. Previously, she's given me a small hug and an air kiss, but given what happened yesterday, should I come up with a workaround, make things easier for her?

I only have a split second to decide. Luckily for me, she takes control. The hug and kiss may look normal to an observer, but her smile is completely and utterly fake. It looks like she's just stretched her lips wide to show her teeth.

She moves away, and Dimi comes over and squeezes my hand. I squeeze back, because I might feel awkward right now, but this has to be killing him. It's his *mom*, and they've always been close.

"So are you going to tell us about Saturday?" Cait demands. "Come on, spill! Mom said Chris Evans was there."

We're easily distracted and happy to relive our moments of glory. I've had many successful opening nights before, but I can't lie, this one's a little sweeter than all the rest, because Dimi and I did it together.

I'm becoming sappy as I get older, apparently.

By the time we head in for dinner, I'm more relaxed. Sascha isn't obviously avoiding me, she isn't being obnoxious, and everyone else is their usual welcoming self, so I don't think I can really ask for more.

Or so I thought.

We're at coffee and dessert, and the kids have been excused to play or watch TV or plan total world domination—whatever they usually do when adults aren't around—when Sascha clears her throat.

"I wonder if I could have a moment, please," she says quietly, and yet it cuts through all conversation. Heads turn in her direction. From the corner of my eye, I spot Dimi and Patrick exchange a worried glance.

She hesitates, then says, "I originally planned to say

this privately, but it's played out in front of you all up until now, so I think it needs to continue that way. I've always prided myself on being an open-minded and accepting person, and especially on raising my kids to be the same. When you all were little, I encouraged you to call out bullying and prejudice and to draw your friends from wide circles, not just those who were 'like us.'" She hesitates again. "I am so proud of you all now. Because you're still drawing your friends from wide circles, and you're still calling out bullying and prejudice. Even when it's me doing it. It's hard for me to say that. To accept that I'm the one in the wrong here. I am, though, and Jason, I owe you an apology. I haven't been fair to you, and I'm sorry." She takes a deep breath. "Honestly, it does bother me that there is such a great disparity in age between you and Dimi, but that's my problem. It shouldn't have any bearing on how I act toward you, because the fact is, you're Dimi's choice and he's happy with you. That's all that matters. So I'm sorry for my behavior, and I'll do better in future. You're welcome in this family."

Tears sting my eyes. I want to take a moment to gather my composure before speaking, but I'm afraid that will be construed as hesitation, so my voice is a little shaky when I say, "Thank you, Sascha. I truly appreciate that."

She manages a smile.

"Thank you, Mom," Dimi adds, his voice husky, and her smile grows.

"Does anyone else feel like Tiny Tim should be here?" Sienna asks slyly, and laughter breaks the poignant moment.

"I am not Scrooge, thank you very much," Sascha snaps, but she's grinning.

I might not ever have a loving relationship with my mother-in-law, but I can have one based on respect and our mutual love for Dimi. Looking at him now, seeing his face lit up with happiness and relief, I'm completely okay with that.

EPILOGUE

Dimi

I'M NERVOUS. I SHOULDN'T be, because this is my fifth opening night in the past year—sixth if you count the Joyville Amateur Theater productions. But I've come to accept that opening night is going to mean nerves, no matter how many times I do it.

As usual, I'm hiding in the wings for the first act. Jason gave up on trying to get me to take my seat in the theater months ago—he and the rest of the crew have come to accept that I need to be in the wings until I see that everything is going well.

So far, things have—gone well, I mean. We've had four very successful shows on our hands, so successful that I've been assured we can have a third theater by the end of August. Entertainment has had to hire more performers twice since we opened to accommodate the additional numbers we need, and they'll have to hire more in the next few months—but according to them, we're now attracting attention from the drama schools. JU has always been a great first job for graduating performers, since it allows them to gain some experience, but now, with the opportunity to rotate into full-length productions also a factor, JU has become a great job, period.

My goal of only having one theater in the Village for touring shows, with all the others featuring JVTC productions, no longer seems like a dream. It's a very real possibility.

Does that mean work is perfect? Hell, no. I still want more budget, and Jason and I battle over all the details. We work really well together, but that doesn't mean we agree all the time. Or most of the time. In fact, for the whole month of October, we only communicated during working hours through our assistants. Then we'd go home at the end of the day and very carefully not talk about work before having energetic sex. Our rule about not bringing work problems home is still in force, so it made for an interesting month where we were simultaneously not speaking to each other and getting along fantastically at the same time. Kind of like the Schrödinger's cat of relationships.

On a purely personal level, things couldn't be better. As soon as the lease on Jason's apartment was up, he moved in with me, and we started looking for something a little bigger for the both of us. We found it about six weeks ago, and although we've technically been renting it for the past month, we won't move in for another two weeks. With the new show opening, we just didn't have time to pack, move, and unpack. For now, we're both committed to staying here in Joyville, but we've discussed it and decided that if something irresistible should come up elsewhere for either of us in the future, we're open to exploring options. To be honest, I think it will be harder for Jason to consider leaving than for me. He's gotten really attached to my family and the town over this past year.

Even my mom, I hear you ask. Short answer: yes. Long answer: they'll never be bosom besties, but they get along well. Mom actually really likes him as a person, but we can tell she occasionally still struggles with her memories and her automatic association between them and Jason. She's dealing with it well, though, and so, yeah, Jason's gotten attached to her. He joined the committee for the holiday party last year, and that was a real bonding experience for them both.

So, work, good, love life, good... what else? Friends? Enemies?

Things are good there too. Jase and I have managed two short jaunts up to New York to hang out with Brice and David, and they came down for a ten-day break last October, then again for the holidays. We spend a lot of our "spare" time at the community theater—although I've only produced one of the shows there since I started with JVTC, and I only did that one because the woman who was supposed to do it had to pull out halfway through and nobody else wanted to make the commitment at the last minute. But even when we can't volunteer much, we scrape out some time to spend with our community theater friends, and of course, there's Derek and Trav. Working with Trav as we do means we've gotten to know him really well, and Derek's just impossible to not get along with.

He and I try to have lunch, just us, once a month to give me a chance to pick his brain. He says I don't really need him to mentor me anymore, but I disagree. Last week, after I got the news about the third theater, I told him that I credited him for a lot of my success with JVTC, and he laughed in my face.

"Dimi, I may have taught you a few shortcuts, but you were going to get here on your own anyway. You're one of only three people I've ever given a personalized recommendation for in my entire career, and of those three, you're the best. I never had any doubt when I told Malcolm you were perfect for this job. I knew you'd succeed. You've just made me look good."

Yeah, that made me feel pretty awesome.

Which leaves enemies, I guess, although we really don't have any. Rick is the only person who might have qualified, but Jase left all enmity behind when he decided to forget Rick and move on. Last we heard, he's still doing his thing in New York. Good luck to him.

And so we're back to my nerves on this, Joy Village Theater Company's fifth opening night. I might have misled you earlier—there actually is a reason for me to be nervous tonight. You see, I *finally* got my way—after a whole lot of arguing, several pro and con lists, and a very detailed spreadsheet, Jason and Trav agreed that our fifth show could be *Walk of Life*. They both were (are) super excited to do this show, but they also had (have? Hell, I hope not) reservations about whether we're ready. With three successes under my belt and the fourth about to open, I decided I knew better, and the data seemed to support me... so I won.

Only now it doesn't feel like a win. It feels like maybe I set us up for our first failure.

I'm careful not to let my trepidation show. The last thing the cast needs is to think I doubt them. But as the house lights go down, the knots in my stomach tighten. The curtain goes up. So do the lights. Sam enters from stage right, opens his mouth, and—

I should never doubt myself.

***

The after-party is wall-to-wall VIPs. I wish I could say that's entirely due to our brilliance, but the truth is, the latest superhero movie is being filmed at the studio here at JU, so we had a lot of A-list stars literally on our doorstep who were encouraged to attend by Joy Inc. None of them seemed upset about it, though, and so far they've all been highly complimentary. I deserve a medal for not getting all starstruck.

I'm chatting with an actor who's such a big deal that I'm congratulating myself on actually being able to talk with any semblance of normality and trying not to notice that his abs are visible through his shirt—no padding needed in that costume!—when I sense someone come up behind me.

I smile involuntarily.

Mr. Eight-pack's gaze goes over my shoulder, and he grins. "I'll leave you to it, but don't forget to call me with the details of the amateur theater. I'd love to visit."

I agree, although I very much doubt we'll get any rehearsing done if he does, and then as he walks away, a hand touches my arm. I turn and look into a pair of warm sherry-brown eyes.

Warm tingles spread through me.

"Hi."

He leans in and kisses me. Around us, cast, friends, and VIPs alike hoot and holler, and we smile against each other's lips.

When he pulls back, those eyes I love so much are sparkling. "Congratulations, Dimi. You were right."

I pretend to shiver. "Oooh, baby, that sounds so good. Say it again," I tease, and he laughs.

"You were right. Play your cards right, and I'll say it again later." He winks, and it's my turn to laugh. I slide an arm around his waist and turn to survey the room, leaning into his side.

"Can you believe it's been nearly a year and a half since we started all this?"

"It's flown by," he admits. "My life before then seems like a distant dream."

"Mine too." It's weird. I was happy with my life before, but when I compare it to now—even to last October, the month of complicated communication—it seems pale and boring. Empty. Everything before that night at the community theater is colorless. Which reminds me….

"Hey, Jase?"

"Yeah?"

"You remember the night we met?"

He freezes. "Yes," he says cautiously.

"It was a night a lot like this one. On a smaller scale," I add as one of Hollywood's leading ladies walks past, talking animatedly to one of our cast members.

"Sure. I remember."

"We got off on the wrong foot that night."

He sighs.

"You know where I'm going with this, right?"

"Are you really going to make me say it?"

I can hear the pout in his voice. "Yes." I hesitate, then plunge onward. "Truthfully, Jase, it's bothered me. That first impression was… not you. I just don't get why you were such a…." I trail off. He gets it, and this way I don't have to call my live-in boyfriend a nasty name.

He huffs a disbelieving laugh. "Wait, you actually

want me to tell you because you don't know? I thought you just wanted me to say it—like when I said you were right."

I turn to face him, confused. "No. I… are you saying I should already know?" Am I being dense? From the incredulous looks on his face, I think I must be.

"I guess there's no reason why you should know, but hell, Dimi, I thought for sure you did."

This conversation is starting to really flummox me. "Well, I don't. Care to share?"

He laughs and kisses me again. "I was trying to hit on you, you idiot. I saw this incredibly good-looking, confident man with an amazing smile who seemed to get along with everyone, and I wanted you to be impressed by me. But it'd been a long time since I even thought about flirting, and I completely fucked it up."

I blink.

"You were hitting on me?"

"Badly, but yes."

A grin spreads across my face. "Wanna hear something funny?"

"Funny ha ha, or funny groan?"

"Well, it makes me want to laugh." My tone says it all, and he groans.

"Go on, then." He sounds resigned.

"I've had a celebrity crush on you for years. I was trying not to be impressed by you that night—right up until you opened your mouth and *insulted me*."

His jaw drops.

"Yeah. Just as well, though. It might have been awkward if we'd hooked up before we even started working together."

Jason shakes his head in disbelief. "I don't even know what to say," he admits.

"How about 'I love you,'" I prompt.

"I love you," he parrots, a smile creeping back onto his face.

"You could also say 'You were right, Dimi.'"

He chuckles. "You were right, Dimi."

"And 'Dimi, you can pick whatever show you want next.'"

"Dimi, you're dreaming if you think I'll say that," he says, mirroring my tone, and we both laugh.

I can't wait to spend the rest of my life laughing with him.

Arguing with him.

Loving him.

Just… with him.

***

See where it all started with the first book in the Joy Universe series, I've Got This.

Derek Bryer loves his life.

His job as an assistant director at Joy Universe, the second-largest theme park complex on the planet, makes him indirectly responsible for bringing joy (pun intended) to millions of people.

So what if none of his relationships are that close? Everyone he meets loves him.

Except Trav Jones.

For some reason, the visiting Broadway performer would rather Derek just go away. He appreciates Derek's work ethic, though, and after Trav steps up when Derek desperately needs someone to fill in for his sick staff, Derek seizes the chance to convince Trav he's not such a bad guy.

Falling in love while distracted by a murder at the park, food poisoning, and colleagues placing bets on their relationship won't be easy, but between the two of them and with the magic of Joy Universe, they've got this.

Get your copy now on Amazon!

ALSO BY LOUISA MASTERS

M/M

Met His Match
Charming Him
Offside Rules

Joy Universe
I've Got This
Follow My Lead

Novellas
Fake It 'Til You Make It
Out of the Office

M/F

An Irish Flirtation (Emerald Isle Enchantment)
An Irish Attraction (Emerald Isle Enchantment)
Trials & Tribulations of Online Dating

Writing as Olivia Ventura
Miss Fix-It
Catch a Shooting Star

ABOUT THE AUTHOR

LOUISA MASTERS STARTED reading romance much earlier than her mother thought she should. While other teenagers were sneaking out of the house, Louisa was sneaking romance novels in and working out how to read them without being discovered. She's spent most of her life feeling sorry for people who don't read, convinced that books are the solution to every problem. As an adult, she feeds her addiction in every spare second, only occasionally tearing herself away to do things like answer the phone and pay bills. She spent years trying to build a "sensible" career, working in bookstores, recruitment, resource management, administration, and as a travel agent, before finally conceding defeat and devoting herself to the world of romance novels.

Louisa has a long list of places first discovered in books that she wants to visit, and every so often she overcomes her loathing of jet lag and takes a trip that charges her imagination. She lives in Melbourne, Australia, where she whines about the weather for most of the year while secretly admitting she'll probably never move.

Connect with Louisa

WWW.LOUISAMASTERS.COM
www.facebook.com/LouisaMastersAuthor
www.facebook.com/groups/seymourbookswithmasterfulmen
Twitter: @AuthorLouisaM
Instagram: @AuthorLouisaM
Subscribe for a free novella! https://bit.ly/subscribeLouisaM

Printed in the USA
CPSIA information can be obtained
at www.ICGtesting.com
CBHW030959040524
8055CB00024B/177